HILLARY AVIS

A Cop and a Coop

Clucks and Clues Cozy Mysteries Book One

Contents

Chapter 1

I'd be darned if I was going to ask anyone for help.

I wiped the sweat off my forehead using the shoulder of my T-shirt and jammed the narrow trenching shovel into the ground again. This dirt was mine now, and if it had any sense, it would yield to me. I jumped on the shovel, hoping the few extra pounds I'd put on since the divorce would be an asset for once. But the tool just clanked against something, tipping me over into the prickly, dry grass.

"Dug up anything interesting?" a drawling, gravelly voice behind me asked.

I scrambled to my feet, annoyance crawling up my back. I hate it when people sneak up on me when I'm in the middle of something. In this case it was my ancient neighbor, Walt Sutherland, who was leaning on a post that held up the barbed-wire fence that separated my land from his U-pick blueberry orchard. The whole point of buying a farm out here was to get away from prying eyes, but somehow prying eyes had a way of finding me.

"Just dirt."

He tipped his white cowboy hat back and squinted at me like Clint Eastwood at a gunslinger. "That didn't sound like any dirt I've dug in my years. You hit a rock?"

I used the shovel to scrape at the spot where the shovel had hit something, revealing the glint of amber-brown glass. "Beer bottle," I said. I levered it out of the ground and tossed it on the growing pile of flattened cans, bottles, hubcaps, and plastic lighters that I'd uncovered so far.

"I'm guessing you'll find a few more. Amos didn't mind if the local kids had their bonfire nights on his place. Said he'd rather have them under his watch than out in the woods somewhere doing who knows what." He meant Amos Chapman, the former owner of the property.

I stuck the shovel in the hole where the bottle had been exhumed and tried again. The shovel sank in all the way, much to my satisfaction. When I'd dug that short section of trench, I moved down the line toward the next stake I'd put out to mark the foundation of my dream chicken coop, trying to ignore Walt's continued scrutiny from the fence post.

This time the shovel unearthed an old work boot, the kind that Popeye might reel in on a Saturday morning cartoon. I'd caught myself a whopper. Size twelve, at least. I cursed at it and threw it onto the trash pile, where it landed with a rattle.

"That'd be faster with a power trencher," Walt remarked.

I pursed my lips and rolled my eyes. "If I had one, I'd be using it."

"Pretty sure Mike Spence's got one."

I ignored him and dug another foot of trench, grunting and sweating like a music video backup dancer.

Walt didn't take the hint. "I'd bet a bushel of berries that he'd bring it over if you gave him a call."

"No thanks," I said between gritted teeth. The last thing I needed was another man doing me the favor of bossing me around. "Anyway, I'm about done."

Walt eyed the stakes that remained—more than three-quarters of the sixteen I'd hammered into the ground yesterday to mark the coop's future foundation. Then he looked at me and back to the ten feet of trench I'd already dug. Then back to me. I braced myself for a smart remark.

"What're you building?" he asked mildly.

I paused with my foot on the shovel. "Chicken coop."

Not just any chicken coop. My *dream* chicken coop. Most people wouldn't bother with a concrete foundation for a coop and run, but I wasn't most people.

"The Chapmans kept their chickens in the barn," Walt said, nodding toward the ancient building to my left that backed up to the railroad tracks behind my place. Its posts and beams were sound—I'd made sure of it before I put in my offer—but the dark, rough-hewn siding was suffering, rotting from the bottom up. It wasn't secure enough to keep poultry safe from a determined predator. Anyway, I had another use for the barn that Walt didn't need to know anything about.

"Well, mine are going to live in a coop. Keeping chickens in a barn is like keeping cookies in a jar, as far as a raccoon is concerned."

He chuckled. "Fair enough. I don't want you to run afoul of disclosure laws should you sell the place, so I won't trouble you. 'A fowl,' get it?" He laughed at his own joke. "Do let me know if you uncover anything notable."

He patted the fence post and moseyed back down a row of blueberry bushes toward the bright white farmhouse he shared with his much-younger wife, Anne, whistling a tuneless melody as he went.

I shook my head and got back to work. It wasn't until I'd pulled a tuna can and a crumbling Styrofoam cup out of the ground that I realized I'd been finding things all morning, and Walt had seen the pile of junk that was accumulating nearby. When he said he wanted to know if I found anything interesting, he didn't mean the trash I'd uncovered thus far. Clearly, he had a more specific idea of what might be buried here.

Just my luck, I was going to hit some pipes or underground electrical lines that he knew about and I didn't. Time to call out the utility company to mark the lines before I did anything stupid. Oh well, a glass of lemonade didn't sound like a bad idea, anyway.

I left the shovel in the half-dug trench and headed back to the house. I still couldn't believe the little yellow clapboard cottage was mine, let alone the generous orchard of apple trees older than I was that surrounded it. Sure, a few years of neglect while the place stood empty meant that there were a million little things that needed attention, from roof leaks to pruning. The apples were wormy and small because the orchard hadn't been tended. But a year from now, when my pullets were laying and the first real orchard harvest was in, I'd be swimming in eggs and apples.

Self-sufficient for the first time in my life.

I mounted the steps to the wrap-around porch and caught a glimpse of myself in the glass on the front door. Good lord, I was a mess. My blonde-and-gray ponytail had frizzed into a lion's mane, and you couldn't even see my freckles, I had so much dirt on my face. One sleeve of my shirt was rolled up and the other one had fallen down, and you could see my dingy old bra strap hanging out of the one that was still rolled up. Walt Sutherland must think I was a crazy person.

Well, good. I was done giving two toots what men thought

of my appearance. I'd borne enough of that for two lifetimes, living in Beverly Hills for the last thirty years. I blew a kiss to my dirty-girl reflection and went inside.

With a glass of cold lemonade dripping on the kitchen table, I phoned the utility people and scheduled them to come out and mark all the lines for my own peace of mind. Two days, the shrill woman on the phone said. That's when they'd come out and place flags on my electrical lines.

Ugh. Two days of sitting in the house and counting the minutes wasted. I pulled out my planning notebook and scanned the detailed schedule I'd prepared. I thought I'd have the perimeter foundation poured and all the posts set in concrete by the end of the day today, but that wasn't going to happen.

Thankfully, I had the foresight to write the schedule in pencil. I carefully erased the dates for chicken coop construction and changed them by two days. Then I paused, my pencil still pressing a dent in the paper.

The utility company would only flag buried power lines. They wouldn't be marking sewer pipes, because the farm had a septic tank. And they wouldn't be marking water, either—the property was on a well. The pump house was on the other side of the main house, so I knew the water pipes ran that direction, not way over by the fence.

Maybe I didn't have to wait for the utility folks. I scraped back my chair and looked out the kitchen window. Sure enough, the house had a service wire from a pole along the fence line that serviced my house and the Sutherlands. There weren't any buried power lines.

Triumphantly, I chugged my glass of lemonade while I scrubbed out the new dates and replaced them with the old ones. Whatever was buried in my yard, it wasn't going to zap me to the moon if I hit it with a shovel. I could dig my little heart out without fear of being electrocuted. I marched back outside and, refreshed by the prospects of keeping to my schedule as much as the lemonade, laid into digging.

Right away, my shovel hit something about eighteen inches down. A rock or another beer bottle, probably. I kneeled in the grass and used a hand trowel to excavate it. I quickly realized it wasn't glass, though…it was something softer, organic. A root left from an old apple tree? I jammed my trowel under the object and levered it out. When I realized what it was, I laughed aloud.

It was the left boot that matched the right one I'd already dug up. I tossed it onto the pile of trash behind me and heard it rattle as it landed. It wasn't the soft sound of earth and pebbles. It was more of a clatter.

There was something inside it.

At first I ignored it and kept my attention on the growing trench, eager to finish it. But curiosity gnawed at me, so finally I set down my shovel, dusted my hands, and went to investigate. I picked up the boot and poured the contents into my hand, nearly choking on my own tongue when I saw what had been inside.

Bones.

The boot was full of bones.

Instinctively, I dropped them. The bones scattered on the half-green, late-summer grass, and I crouched to stare at them. They were small bones, but they didn't belong to a chicken or a deer. They were clearly the bones of a human foot. They were inside a boot, for heaven's sake—nobody would stuff a dead cat into a shoe for burial.

I dumped out the second boot—or rather, the first one I'd found. It, too, was full of bones.

Two feet in two boots.

I couldn't deny it any longer. There was a dead guy buried in my front yard.

Chapter 2

I tipped back onto the grass, pondering what I should do.
The right thing would be to call the sheriff, but I found
myself hesitant to do so. What would come of it, anyway?
A big, expensive hole in my yard, a delay building my coop, and
for what? An official rubber stamp that the guy in my yard was
Old Leonard So-and-so, buried by his loving grandchildren
in the family plot? I didn't need an official stamp—I could just
ask around town and find out who was buried here.

Luckily I knew just the person to ask: Ruth Chapman. Not
only was she the realtor who sold me the property, she was
the granddaughter of the former owners and had spent a good
part of her childhood here, back when we were classmates in
school. If anyone knew the ins and outs of this farm, it was
her. I found her number in my cell phone and placed the call.

"Do or Dye!" she answered. Do or Dye was Ruth's side
business, or maybe real estate was her side business and the
salon was her main gig. In Honeytree, Oregon, there weren't
enough acres to sell or hairs on people's heads to make a full-
time living at either one on its own, so Ruth did both.

"It's Leona," I said. "Do you have a minute?"

"For you I do. Since you came back to town, I've been
dying to get my hands on that head of yours—pun intended.

8

Hairdresser humor, sorry." Her loud, brassy laugh echoed in the receiver and I held the phone away from my ear, grinning, until the sound died down.

"This isn't about hair. It's about the farm."

"Shoot," she said, her voice still good-humored. "I guessed wrong. Hold on a minute, hon, I'll be right with you." The phone clattered. "Tambra, can you get Grace started? She needs a shampoo and then I'll do her cut and set. OK, Leona, go ahead."

Hot flash. I blew air up to cool my forehead and took a deep breath before continuing my question. "I was wondering if you knew of anything buried on the farm?"

"What, like what, pirate gold? We're a little too far inland for that kind of thing, although if you have a hot tip on buried treasure, I'll help you dig as long as I get a cut. A cut, get it? Because I cut hair?"

I was too flustered to laugh at her joke. "No, not buried treasure. A person. Or people. Did you Chapmans have a family plot?"

"Not that I know of. Could be an older one on the property, though—my grandparents bought the place in the Fifties, but the house was built probably sixty years before that. Why, do you think there might be one?"

I stared at the bones in the grass, considering whether to tell her what I'd found. "I'm not sure. I dug up some boots when I was working on my chicken coop and got worried. I thought you might have an idea what it's all about since you know the property so well."

"Hm. Where are you putting the coop? Near the house or up by the road?"

"That spot in front of the barn between the driveway and

9

the fence, across from the house."

"I can't think of anything over there off the top of my head. We had a fire pit there for a while, and once my grandpa got a wild hair to put a duck pond in that spot, but he changed his mind. Walt Sutherland might know about something I don't, though. He's had his place since before my grandparents bought our farm. Your farm, now," she corrected. "You could ask him."

I sighed. I already knew he wasn't going to tell me anything, if his smug questions this morning were any indication. "Sorry, I've sworn off being patronized."

Ruth giggled, but then her voice turned serious. "Come down here and you can look through the county property records on my computer. Maybe that'll shed some light on your underground surprise."

Relief washed over me. "Thanks. I'll owe you one."

"Oh, I know. And I know just how you can repay me. I aim to get you in my chair so I can work my magic. You'll be amazed what a cut and color can do for your whole vibe—you'll have a new husband before you know it."

"Not interested." Not even a little bit. Peterson Davis had been enough husband for nine lifetimes.

"We'll see," Ruth sing-songed.

I hung up on her, grabbed my purse and keys from inside the house, and headed back out to the driveway. I almost locked the front door out of habit—I'd locked the door even when I was *home* in Beverly Hills—but I forced myself not to. That was my old life: keep people out, keep *things* in. Any thieves who stopped in here would be sorely disappointed by my selection of second-hand furniture and outdated appliances. Anyway, in Honeytree, someone stopping by was probably bringing over a note, a bunch of wildflowers, or a hot casserole. Not a thief, but a friend or neighbor. Someone you wanted to come through the door.

I started up the crotchety Suburban I'd picked up when I bought the farm. Though it was twenty years old if it was a day, I chose it because it could haul chicken feed and straw bales in any weather and because it was the type of rig people drove around here. I didn't want to stand out any more than I already did. In fact, I'd prefer that nobody noticed me at all.

I pulled out onto the long, straight stretch of highway that fronted my place and Walt's considerably larger property. The Flats, the locals called it, a favorite place for late-night drag racing. Past the Flats were the Curves, a winding section along the river, infamous for the many car accidents that ended with a vehicle nose-down in the rushing water.

I eased off the gas when I approached the Curves; the years away from Honeytree meant I hadn't yet regained a feel for the tight turns. I took them well under the speed limit, and by the time I reached the railroad crossing that marked the city limits, a half-dozen cars had piled up politely behind me and tailed me through town like an informal parade. So much for not drawing attention. By the end of the day, word would be out that a newcomer in town was holding up traffic. Not that there was any such thing as traffic, here. Honeytree traffic just meant "more than one car on the road."

When I was a child, the joke was that Honeytree was a one-stoplight town. It wasn't even that, though—the light had been a blinking red, meaning that most people took it as sort of optional. But in the intervening decades, the blinking light had been removed, replaced with a couple of stop signs. It felt downright civilized to make a full stop at the main intersection instead of just coasting through. I turned off the highway onto Main Street and parked right smack in front of the Do or Dye.

The salon was across the street from the brick building that operated as the fire station, the sheriff's office, and City Hall. In fact, the three-block Main Street held half the businesses in town: in addition to the city building and the salon, there was a bank, a lawyer, an accountant, an insurance agent, a pharmacy with a tiny restaurant attached to it called the Rx Café, and the post office. The short street dead-ended at a dusty old building that had a bowling alley downstairs and a VFW hall upstairs that could be considered the social center of the community, at least for those over a certain age...an age I had not yet achieved, I hoped.

Bells jangled as I pushed open the door into Ruth's shop. The interior of the Do or Dye was low-ceilinged and might have felt cramped if it weren't for Ruth's unique decorating style that involved a lot of white twinkle lights webbed across the ceiling and vibrant tapestries hung on the walls. Somehow, she made it feel charmingly eclectic and bohemian rather than like college-dorm chic.

Two barber chairs faced a couple of sinks and hood dryers, and the manicurist's station up front doubled as the reception desk, a rainbow of nail polish arranged in an artful mandala on one side. I spotted Ruth in the back, her back bowed over a client at the sink. She was really getting into the head massage, and her whole body was jiggling with the effort.

"No tipping, no touching." The red-haired woman seated at the desk winked at me. If I didn't know better, I'd say she was making a joke about the size of Ruth's bosoms, as though I'd walked into a strip joint and not a hair salon. They were ample, it was true, like the rest of her. Big hair, big laugh, big boobs. Ruth's spirit was as generous as everything else.

"I'm Tambra." The redheaded receptionist held out her hand across the desk to shake mine. She was one of those put-together, ageless women who could be twenty-five or forty-five underneath all her makeup, where I suspected a crop of freckles much like mine lurked in secret. I couldn't help noticing her long, almond-shaped nails that were painted a frosty, glittering pink. The ring finger of each hand was a slightly darker shade and had a crystal flower glued to the tip. She had to be the manicurist as well as the receptionist, but I had no idea how she managed to do anything with nails like those, whether that was shampooing clients for Ruth or wiping her own—

"Leona!" Ruth had finally spotted me. She wrapped a towel around her client's head and ushered her to the barber chair, pumping the chair's hydraulics with her foot as she motioned me over. "It's so good to see you in town!"

"Yeah. It's going to be awesome having everyone witness my fall from grace. Here I am, home with my tail between my legs."

"Your loss, our gain!" Ruth's eyes snapped mischievously as she looked me up and down, taking in my grubby T-shirt and baggy overalls. "You've really taken this chicken lady thing to heart. Last time I saw you, you were wearing a cashmere twin set and some pearl earrings."

She meant the day I'd closed on the farm. It was only a month ago and it already felt like years, like another life. I wasn't even sure where that cardigan was. I'd been too busy packing and moving and unpacking to make the rounds and say hello to everyone in town. If I was being honest, I'd been hiding.

13

"Nothing wrong with a little dirt," I said defensively. "I'm a farmer now; you can't farm with nails like those." I nodded across the room at Tambra and her frosty fingers and curled my hands into fists so my own grubby nails, broken from my digging misadventures, wouldn't show.

"No one's suggesting you try and measure up to Miss Oregon 2003," Ruth said wryly, combing out her client's wet hair with gentle, efficient strokes. "Even Beverly Hills can't match her sparkle."

"I can hear you talking about me!" Tambra scurried over, and I noticed her pink plaid shirt had snaps decorated with the same rhinestone flowers as her nails. She grabbed my hand to examine my fingers and clicked her tongue disapprovingly. "There's nothing wrong with a little sparkle in the country. Trust me…I work on plenty of farm girls. They all want a little glamor."

"Well, I don't." I pulled my hand out of Tambra's grasp and stuck it in the back pocket of my overalls. I wondered if I had never left Honeytree, never gone away to school, never married a high-powered plastic surgeon in the most plastic place on earth, would I be more susceptible to Tambra's brand of glamor? Would I have yearned for glitter if I'd never had it? Maybe. But now I knew what I was missing, and I didn't miss it. "Been there, done that, have the tennis bracelet to prove it. Give me chicken turds over diamonds any day."

"I don't think you're going to have any shortage of those!" Ruth chuckled. She twisted her client's hair into sections and began trimming the lowest one with careful snips of her scissors, her bottom lip caught in her teeth as she concentrated on her work.

I certainly hadn't been a fan of chicken turds when I'd left

Honeytree as fast as I could at age eighteen, and I'd have laughed in the face of anyone who said my life's dream would be to own an egg farm like my dad's. I had bigger dreams then, and everyone in town knew it. They were all going to have a good laugh at my expense when they learned I was single and broke now that I'd spent my whole divorce settlement on the farm. That's why I'd been such a hermit since I moved back—I didn't want to be a joke.

"It's going to be a few minutes while I catch up with Cheryl here." Her client's eyes brightened at the prospect of an update from Ruth, who, between hairdressing and house-hunting, knew everyone's business in town. In particular, she knew my business. "Why don't you let Tambra work on you while you wait? I promise I'll get those records pulled up for you as soon as I'm done."

I sighed. Who was I kidding? With Ruth Chapman as my realtor, everyone in town already knew I bought her grandparents' place. Word travels quickly from a hairdresser's chair, so there was no point in trying to hide. People were going to be looking, anyway. Might as well have pretty nails.

"Fine," I said to Tambra. "Just to pass the time while Ruth finishes up."

Tambra clapped her hands, her armful of silver bracelets jangling. "Go ahead and pick out your polish while I get set up."

She pulled an array of tools out of a sanitizing bath and arranged them on her station as I scanned the rack of nail polish looking for a color that didn't remind me of my old life. No sedate nudes, no classy mauves. Nothing that would match the pink marble master bathroom that the son of a peach, Peterson, was now sharing with an aspiring actress younger than our daughter.

That gave me an idea. I handed Tambra a dark peach bottle and she raised a perfectly plucked eyebrow. "I didn't expect orange. It's a little early for pumpkin spice."

"I think of it more as the color of a good laying hen," I said, obediently splaying my fingers for Tambra's ministrations.

"You're getting *chicken fingers*?!" Ruth hooted with laughter from across the salon. "You want some fries with that?"

My stomach growled in response to her question. "Actually—yeah."

Ruth deftly untwisted another section of her client's hair and combed it out as she glanced at the clock on the wall. "Well, listen. Cheryl'll be set and under the dryer in fifteen minutes, and then we'll get lunch and see what we can rustle up in the property records. My treat."

Chapter 3

I relaxed into my seat. Tambra, who'd already managed to clean all the dirt from my nails and file them smooth, trimmed my ragged cuticles and began applying polish in thin, even strokes.

"What kind of chickens do you keep?"

I knew she was asking to be polite, the chitchat every manicurist makes. I don't know if they train them to do that or if it's just the kind of person that the profession attracts. *What does your husband do? How old are your kids?* This was the country version. "None just yet. I ordered a batch of chicks from the hatchery that are coming in soon. Hopefully I'll be done building the coop by the time they're off the heat lamp."

"Mm. You're doing the work yourself?"

I nodded and she twitched—I'd inadvertently jogged the hand she was working on. "Sorry."

"Don't worry about it." She flashed me a smile. "You know, if you wear the right gloves to work, your nails will last longer. The pillow-top ones are made especially to protect your nails. They have them at the feed store. I have some in purple." She sat up and replaced the polish brush back in the bottle. "I gave you an extra-strong topcoat so you don't destroy my work immediately."

"I can't make any promises," I said, thinking of the trench I intended to dig as soon as I solved my pesky skeleton problem, and the accompanying beer bottles I'd have to pry out of the ground.

She gave me a mock glare and clicked her nails menacingly on the tabletop. "I will hunt you down for touchups. Don't think I won't."

"She's not lying. Tambra is a pitbull. Once she sinks her teeth in, she doesn't let go." Ruth clipped a final row of curlers into Cheryl's hair and led her over to one of the dryer chairs. She settled the hood over her head and handed her a magazine before looking over at me. "Ready to eat?"

I checked with Princess Pitbull, who gave my hands a quick once-over before nodding her permission. Ruth gave Tambra quick instructions for freeing Cheryl from her roaring plastic prison when the timer went off and grabbed her laptop with the "Chapman Realty" sticker on it from the back room. Then we headed down the street to the Rx Café.

"Wanna sit outside?" Ruth asked, pausing at the café door and look up at the sky where the morning clouds had burned off, leaving a clear blue expanse. A lone table for two was parked in front of the window, like it was waiting for us.

"Sure." The plastic chair skidded on the concrete as I pulled it out and sat down to admire my shiny orange fingertips. While it hadn't been the two-hour spa experience I'd experienced in Beverly Hills, it was a first-class manicure. "Tambra does good work."

"She has high standards—for herself and everyone else. That's what makes her a good business partner. You know me...I'd let the dust accumulate a little. I'd let the polish chip. I'd be a mess without her." Ruth waved her hand and I saw that her nails were a deep, iridescent teal that flashed magenta in the sunlight like a peacock feather. Tambra's work, for sure. Ruth opened her laptop and stared intently at the screen as she clicked the trackpad. "Let's see what we've got in the files."

"You ladies want the salad special?" A short woman with her hair in two unnaturally red braids squinted at us. "It's five bucks, drink included."

"Sounds good to me." Ruth was back to staring at her screen.

"Me too," I told the waitress, a little stunned by the low price tag.

"Iced tea?" she asked.

Ruth nodded absentmindedly, and I shrugged in acquiescence. Why not let the waitress choose? No need to make decisions for yourself when your hometown could do it for you.

Red-braids dimpled at me. "You're Leona Landers."

I nodded. Of course she knew who I was. "Davis, now."

"Well, we're glad to have you back under any name." She patted my hand before darting back inside to put in our order, leaving me a bit bewildered. Surely, she was related to someone I knew, but I had no idea who that might be or why anyone in Honeytree would be glad to have me back.

"It's true." Ruth looked up from her screen, fixing me in her dark blue gaze.

"What is?" I craned my neck to look at her screen. What had she uncovered in the old records?

She held the laptop screen away from me. "We're glad you're here. *I'm* glad you're here. I missed you. I knew you'd return to Honeytree eventually, but I didn't know when. It's been a long wait."

I couldn't help smiling. This was the reason Ruth was the

19

only person I'd kept in touch with all these years—she knew me better than I knew myself. I never would have guessed that I'd find myself right back where I started, both literally and figuratively, but she did. "I missed me, too."

"Orange looks good on you. Full of life. Your aura is popping. I'm glad you got our farm." Her smile stretched thin across her teeth and it looked like she was trying not to cry. She shook her head. "It was hard to let it go—Rusty dragged his feet, but I convinced him you were the right person, and I can tell that was a good decision just by your energy shift."

Rusty was Ruth's older brother. He'd been held back a year, so the three of us had been in the same classes with the same teachers. As a result, Ruth and Rusty were often mistaken for twins when we were growing up, but even though they had the same wild, curly hair and mesmerizing blue eyes, they couldn't be more different in temperament. Where Ruth was free-spirited and loud, Rusty was conservative and quiet, a rugged athlete who always stood in the back row of team photos. After graduation, when Ruth was juggling beauty school, art classes at the community college, and a part-time assistant job at the real estate office in Duma, Rusty joined the Air Force. I was gone to LA before he came back.

"How's he doing? Married? Kids?" The waitress returned and set down two glasses of iced tea with lemon wedges. I sipped my straw and waited for Ruth's answer.

"Nope and nope. Living in a trailer behind my house, feeling sorry for himself. He's been a little lost since Grandpa passed." Ruth wrinkled her nose sympathetically. "He was pretty much running the orchard by then, and now he doesn't know what to do. He better figure it out, though. Ah, here we go."

She turned the laptop around and pushed it toward me.

It showed a line drawing of my farm and some numerical notations along the property lines. I scrolled down the document she had pulled up. It listed the dimensions and details of the farm and then had a list of known defects. Lead paint, a fireplace that didn't meet burn efficiency requirements but was grandfathered in, a well with untreated water, a roof with only a few years left, an easement where the Sutherlands' driveway cut across the northeast corner of the property. There was no mention of any family graveyard or anything else buried in the yard other than the aging septic tank.

"I don't see a family graveyard."

She nodded and sipped her own glass of tea, grimacing when the cold liquid hit the roof of her mouth. "Doesn't mean there isn't one, though. A permit wasn't required before 1946."

The waitress returned, sliding two heavy china plates onto the table in front of us. She stood back and looped her thumbs into the waistband of her apron, surveying the spread. "Need anything else?"

I stared at my so-called salad plate. This was not the microgreens-and-shaved-fennel salad that the ladies who lunched in LA so often ate. No—on one side of the plate, a single piece of white bread held an ice cream scoop of egg salad. On the other side, a ruffly lettuce leaf cradled an identical blob of potato salad. Each scoop was topped with a single olive, which made the plate look like it held a pair of lumpy, mayonnaise-y boobs. I bit my lip to keep from laughing.

"You don't have to eat the bread," the waitress said, noticing my expression. "But if you want, you can turn it into a sandwich."

"Looks good," I choked out, not daring to look her in the face. In my peripheral vision, I saw Ruth's shoulders shaking as she suppressed her own laughter until the waitress went back inside the café. Our eyes met over our plates and we giggled like naughty schoolgirls.

"What do you think? C-cup?" I asked her, nudging my right mayo boob with my fork. The olive nipple rolled off its potato salad mountain and bounced off my plate, coming to a stop somewhere near Ruth's iced tea. "Or maybe a D?"

Ruth snorted and speared the olive, gently placed it back in its original proud position.

"Careful!" I warned her. "It's very sensitive."

At that, she threw her head back, tears streaming down her cheeks as she gave in to the laughter, her whole body jiggling. By the time we both recovered, my stomach muscles ached.

Ruth shook her head as she surveyed her plate and crossed her arms, cupping her own chest protectively in her hands. "I don't think I can eat. I feel like I'd be disturbing some female deity if I destroyed this perfect pair."

"The mayo salad goddess won't mind." I grinned at her. "Anyway, you'll feel better about it tomorrow, when the special is going to be a bratwurst and two boiled eggs."

Ruth dissolved into giggles again, shaking her head and rocking back and forth. "I can't...I can't."

"There's only one solution." My fork hovered over the egg salad boob. "On three. One, two..."

We smashed our forks down simultaneously, flattening the egg salad onto our respective slices of bread. I popped the olive into my mouth, and suddenly the plates were just ordinary.

"By the skin of our teeth," Ruth said solemnly. "I feel like Indiana Jones, destroying an idol."

"The egg salad idol is no more." I folded the bread over and took a bite. The egg salad was perfect—creamy, garlicky, salty, with the just right hint of mustard and dill. And the bread, which I'd assumed was regular white sandwich bread, was a delightfully tangy sourdough. "Hey, this isn't bad. Better than I was expecting."

Ruth nodded around her own mouthful of sandwich. She chipmunked her bite and mumbled, "They're known for it. The Rx goes through a lot of eggs. Maybe when you're up and running, you can supply them."

Hm, an interesting possibility. I'd only thought of selling eggs to individuals, but now I wondered if there were any more restaurants in town that might like a local supplier. I wouldn't have thought of that on my own, but that's why Ruth was such a good entrepreneur: she was always looking for the angle, the niche where she could nestle. "Good idea, thanks!"

"I want a cut. A per-egg royalty." She winked at me. "I'm just kidding. I am an expert in many things, but the chicken business isn't one of them. Oh, shoot!" she said, as a chunk of egg salad fell onto her laptop. She wiped it off with a napkin and moved the computer under the table.

I set down my sandwich on the plate. "So what do you think about the boots I found? Am I going to dig up the rest of a dead guy or what?"

Ruth laughed. "They're just boots, not bones."

"Well…" I winced, and her mouth dropped open again.

"You did find bones?!"

"Inside the boots. Just a few…and I'm not one hundred percent sure they're human." Only ninety-nine percent sure, I didn't say.

"You need to stop digging right now." Ruth was serious, all business as she ate the olive off her potato salad. "If the county finds out you disturbed a potential archaeological site and

23

slaps you with a fine and a cease work order, it's going to cost you a lot of time and money."

"I don't have much of either of those," I said, thinking of the newborn chicks that were already in transit, packed peeping in a box as they traveled a few hundred miles via USPS from the hatchery to Honeytree. All my divorce settlement money was in the property, and the coop needed to be done in six weeks, when the chicks were half-grown and didn't need the heat lamp anymore. "What do you think I should do?"

"My advice? And this is as your friend, not as your realtor—if there are more bones in the ground, leave them for someone else to find. You don't want the hassle. Bury those boots. Move the coop somewhere else. It'll save you a lot of grief."

I sighed. Ruth was right—I couldn't afford to keep digging. But I couldn't afford not to, either. Without the chicken coop, I couldn't earn a living. "Another thing to worry about."

"The only thing you need to worry about is keeping whatever's buried there a secret from yourself. Once you know about it, you have a legal obligation to disclose when you sell the property, and historical graveyards aren't good for property value. Hypothetical graveyards? Those can't hurt you. Stop digging." Ruth glared at me. "That's an order."

Irritation prickled my spine. Turns out, I hate being ordered around even more than I hate surprises. And I wanted my chicken coop *there*. The only other place for it, the only other part of the property that wasn't rows of gnarled apple trees, was in the back corner of the lot, up against the railroad tracks. Freight trains thundering by five feet away from the nesting boxes would be very bad for egg production. I needed the barn between the coop and the tracks for insulation.

"Maybe it's not a graveyard."

"It is." She stopped mid-bite and pointed her fork at me. "It's not *definitely* a graveyard—you don't want it to be definite—but it's definitely a graveyard."

Chapter 4

"What if I just move any bones I find to a new grave?" I mused aloud. "You know—respectfully? I'm only digging a narrow trench, so I'm probably not going to run into more than one dead guy."

"Leona! I can't believe you're even considering it. I'm pretty sure that's illegal!" But before Ruth could scold me any further, the waitress brought the check.

"Thanks for lunch, no thanks for the advice," I said as Ruth rummaged in her huge purple tapestry purse for her wallet.

She stuck out her tongue at me. "Then it's your turn to buy next time."

After she paid the bill and walked me back to my truck, Ruth hooked me into a warm hug, enveloping me in the cucumber-melon scent of her wild hair. It was nice. Really nice. I didn't know why I was getting choked up about it until I remembered that I hadn't had a real hug since the last time I saw my daughter and her husband in Chicago, months ago. "Thanks, Ruth. For everything. I mean it," I said into the side of her head.

"Oh hush. I didn't do anything." She pulled back. "Now that I think about it, maybe you should talk to Rusty. He worked that farm like it was his own for so long. I'm sure he'd know for sure if there was an old family plot in that part of the yard. Stop off at my place on the way home and ask him."

"He still lives with you?"

"It's temporary. Like, been three years kind of temporary." She sighed. "He could run his own farm if he just set his mind to it, like you're doing. He just can't get it together since Grandpa died."

I swallowed. I didn't exactly have it together. Some days, my broken heart felt like a cannonball chained to my leg, dragging me down. It's not that I missed my husband. I didn't even *like* Peterson by the end of our marriage. But my heart was broken because I'd wasted thirty years building something that could just vanish in an instant. I'd built a castle in the air and now it was gone, poof.

Well, now I was going to build a motherclucking henhouse. Something real. And nobody would be able to take that from me.

"See you around, Ruth."

She gave a quick nod and disappeared through the door of the Do or Dye. In the truck, I made the turn back onto the highway and headed out of town. As soon as the in-town speed zone ended, I hit the gas. The turn to Ruth's place flashed by in my peripheral vision, but I didn't slow down. I didn't need Rusty's permission to dig in my own darn yard.

I settled into my seat and took the Curves like a Grand Prix driver, pushing the old Suburban to its limits, and when the Flats appeared around the last bend, I crammed the gas pedal all the way to the floor. The truck leaped forward and the engine roared so loud that I almost missed the sound of the police siren behind me.

A glance in the rearview told me I wasn't imagining things.

A sheriff's car was riding my tail. Great.

I stomped the brake and pulled over not a hundred yards from the end of my driveway. I glared at my mailbox, so close but so far, as I cranked down the window.

"Le-o-na Landers." The officer leaned in the window and whipped off his mirrored sunglasses. "I heard you were back in town."

I groaned internally. He was literally the last person I wanted to see in my current state— my high school boyfriend, Eli Ramirez. The last time he saw me, I was a petite blonde, headed for USC on a cheerleading scholarship. Now, I was twice the woman I used to be—literally—and I had all the lumps, bumps, and wrinkles you'd expect on a woman heading toward sixty. Not to mention the thin film of dried sweat and farm dust that surely made it look like I'd visited a DIY spray-tan booth.

He, on the other hand, was twice the man he used to be, but in a good way. The boy had been to the gym a few times since graduation, and I swear to God, the few more lines in his face just threw his chiseled features into greater relief, like a comic book superhero. His biceps bulged as he shifted to get a better look at me, and I desperately tried to keep my eyes trained on the steering wheel.

"Just write me the ticket, Eli."

He bit his lip, chuckling. "No 'hi'? No 'how's it going'? You're supposed to butter me up, buttercup."

I bristled at the familiar nickname. "I'm not a wildflower, Deputy. I'm just in a hurry. Write the darn ticket."

"Captain." He tapped the nametag on his shirt. Sure enough, it read Capt. Ramirez. He'd been promoted a few times since the last I'd heard, it seemed. "You *were* going pretty fast back there."

He said it like it was an afterthought, and I didn't appreciate the condescension. "Obviously. That's why you stopped me, isn't it, *Captain*?"

He stood up suddenly, cracking his head on the top of the window frame. He rubbed the back of his skull ruefully. "Confession time. I was waiting for you. I happened to see you head into town earlier, so I figured you'd be back this way later. I just got lucky that you still have a lead foot. Remember that Z28 you drove back in the day? We really burned some rubber in that thing."

Heat rose in my face as I remembered the miles we'd put on the back seat, too. And judging by the sappy grin on his face, he was thinking the same thing. My embarrassment vanished, replaced with anger. "You pulled me over to reminisce about swapping spit?!"

He dropped his hand to his side. "Aw, come on, Leona. Don't be like that. I thought—"

"What? That I'd bend over backward to entertain your pervy little detour down Memory Lane to avoid paying a fine? Fat chance. Write me the ticket." I handed him my license and then trained my eyes on the mailbox, gripping the steering wheel so tight that my knuckles turned white.

"Naw." He tried to hand my ID back to me, but I refused to take it. "Sheesh. I wanted to talk to you because I thought maybe you could use some help around your place. It's a lot of farm for one little girl. So I was going to ask if I could lend a hand. The siren and everything—that was just for a little fun." He winked at me, and I thought my eyeballs were going to explode with rage. *A lot of farm for one little girl?!*

I clenched my jaw and spoke through my teeth to avoid

punching him in the face through the open window. "It's just the right amount of farm, and I'm just the right amount of woman. I was speeding. Now, the ticket, *please*."

His face fell as my words finally penetrated his thick, country-boy skull. Avoiding my face, he gave a curt nod and quickly scribbled a ticket, then handed it and my license to me through the window. "Leona, I mean it. You need—"

I cranked the window up as fast as I could, cutting him off. I didn't need help from him or anyone, thanks very much. I just needed to get back to work. It wasn't until a few minutes later, after I bumped down the gravel driveway and parked next to the cottage, that I looked at the ticket. All the fields were blank.

Call me when you change your mind was scrawled across the top in blue ballpoint, and then his stupid cell phone number. I groaned, crumpled up the ticket, and tossed it to the floor on the passenger side. What was it with men thinking they knew what I needed—what I *wanted*? They didn't. This little girl could manage the farm just fine.

Whatever problems came my way, I could solve—*by myself*, I thought as I drummed on the steering wheel. Dig up a pair of boots with feet in them? I could just pretend I didn't find them and build my coop right on top. But I had dozens more feet of trench to dig; I was likely to hit more bones if I kept digging.

A better plan—and a more respectful one—was to simply unearth Mr. Bones and rebury him on another part of the property. Nobody knew the guy was there, and nobody needed to know. He could rest in peace over in the back corner of the yard by the train tracks and no one would be the wiser. As far as anyone was concerned, he didn't exist.

The more I thought about it, the better the idea seemed. The thought of moving a body, even in skeleton form, was distasteful, but I had to admit it was less distasteful than calling Eli Ramirez to oversee a more official exhumation. It was just a dead guy, right? Guys die all the time. It's the circle of life, and if I was going to be a farmer, I'd better get used to the idea.

I went straight from the truck to where the pair of boots lay in the grass and flipped them over, examining them. Right away I saw that whoever this guy was—and it was a guy, judging by the large shoe size—he wasn't an archaeological find. The boots' leather was partly rotted, but their rubber soles and nylon laces were intact; they were modern boots, the kind you could buy at Bi-Mart tomorrow if you wanted a pair. In other words—they weren't antique.

Ugh. That was a bad thing. A really bad thing.

While it's true that I was better off if a family plot on the farm had no historical value, Ruth's county records search had turned up empty. That meant that it wasn't a permitted burial. And Mr. Bones wasn't laid to rest in a proper grave, either. The lack of even a simple pine box attested to that, plus his feet were way too close to the surface. Nobody buries their beloved Grandpa eighteen inches deep. A shallow burial is a hasty burial, and a hasty burial is…well, let's just say not something I wanted in my front yard.

See what I mean about those boots being a bad thing? Now I had to make a phone call I *really* didn't want to make. I cursed under my breath as I searched the floor of the front seat for the crumpled-up ticket with Eli's phone number and gritted my teeth while I dialed.

"I wasn't expecting to hear your voice so soon," he said when he picked up, his tone amused. "You didn't seem too happy to see me. It's a pleasant surprise."

I snorted. "No surprise is pleasant, trust me. This isn't a personal call. I require a law enforcement presence at my farm. I don't care if it's you or someone else. I just figured you were closest."

"I'll be there in just a few," he said cheerfully. Way too cheerfully, if you asked me.

Chapter 5

A few minutes later, I heard the crackle of tires on my gravel driveway. I looked up, expecting to see a sheriff's vehicle. But instead it was a bright red dualie pickup that I didn't recognize, a few years old but as shiny as new. Someone had installed spotlights on top and an after-market brush guard on the front bumper, giveaway signs of someone who liked to hunt. As it drew closer I saw who was behind the wheel—Rusty Chapman. I'd know that shock of dark bushy hair anywhere. It was shot with gray now, unlike when we were kids, but it still stood straight up like Frankenstein's bride.

He tumbled out of the driver's seat as soon as he parked the truck next to mine and speed-walked toward me. But for all the urgency in his movements, his out-of-breath words were casual. "Hey, Leona. Looks like you're all moved in."

"Getting there." My eyes couldn't help darting toward the boot on the grass, and Rusty's gaze followed mine. I scooted so he was looking at me instead of the small pile of bones. "What brings you by?"

"Ruth called me and said you might need my help," he said, awkwardly sticking his hands in the pockets of his jean jacket and craning his neck to see around me. "You had questions about the place?"

I shook my head and waved away his concern. "Oh, no. I got it figured out." As in, I figured out exactly *what* was buried in my yard, and now I needed the cops to figure out *who*. What I *didn't* need was the whole town showing up when I was trying to stealthily rid my yard of a skeleton. I was pretty sure the rumor mill was already churning out stories about me and why I was back in town. I didn't need people speculating that the skeleton was my ex-husband or something like that.

Not that he didn't *deserve* to be six feet under.

"Well, good." He stood there awkwardly a minute, shifting his weight from one foot to the other as he scanned the yard. It didn't seem like he was planning to leave any time soon.

"Anything else?"

He shook his head, and looked down at his boots, rubbing one toe in the dirt. Though his face was tan from working outside all summer, the color still rose in his cheeks. "I just miss the place. I'm glad you got it—someone we trust—instead of a stranger."

"Oh, I'm pretty strange, Rusty Chapman." I grinned at him, and he returned the smile. Just then, the sound of another set of tires on the driveway caught my ear, and both our heads swiveled toward the road. This time, I recognized the car. It was a sheriff's SUV and I had a good inkling who was inside.

"Maybe I should go," Rusty said, shooting me an apologetic look. But Eli pulled his SUV up behind Rusty's truck, parking him in. Rusty shrugged. "Then again, maybe not."

"Did I break any laws this time, Eli?" I called as soon as he exited the car. He adjusted his gun belt as he walked toward us, checking to make sure his shirt was tucked in.

"Ha ha, very funny," he said.

"He literally just wrote me a speeding ticket an hour ago," I explained to Rusty.

"No, I didn't." Eli grinned wickedly at me, his arms crossed smugly across his chest, and I glared at him.

"He's a liar, too," I said. He *had* written the ticket, even if it was filled in with his phone number instead of a fine. Frankly, I didn't know which was worse.

Rusty put up his hands and started walking backward toward his truck. "I'm not getting involved in a lovers' quarrel. I'll wait in my truck until you're done with—well, whatever this is. Then I can give you a hand around the place, Leona."

Eli jogged after him. "I'll move my rig so you don't have to wait on us. I'm going to stick around and help Leona out."

I wanted to screech with frustration. I didn't appreciate surprise visitors, I didn't have a lover, and I didn't need every person in the county with a Y-chromosome "helping" me, either. I just needed this dumb pile of bones taken out of my yard.

Eli swung into the driver's seat and then deftly maneuvered his SUV out of the way of Rusty's cherry-red pickup, parking behind my truck instead. I watched as Rusty turned around and eased down the driveway, avoiding the hardened ruts left from last spring's mud, then pulled out onto the highway and headed back toward Honeytree.

"What was he after? A date with the new girl?"

I bristled. "One, I'm not a girl. And two, I'm not new, either."

"So, you're saying you're an old woman?"

I whacked him on the shoulder with the back of my hand. He caught my arm and his dimples deepened. "Ma'am, I'm going to have to ask you to keep your hands to yourself. I could charge you with assault on an officer."

35

I narrowed my eyes and jerked my arm away. "Write. Me. The. Ticket."

"Lost my number already, huh?" He pulled out his ticket pad, scribbled something on the top sheet, and handed it to me.

I took the ticket automatically but then, annoyed by the whole exchange, crumpled it up and tossed it to the ground. The wad of paper bounced and rolled, landing right next to the upturned boot. Right next to the bones. Eli's expression changed as he stared at the grass. His eyes lost their amusement and his whole body tensed like a cougar ready to spring.

"What did you find there?" he asked, his voice carefully neutral.

I matched his tone. "Looks like a pair of work boots."

He nodded, crouching close to the grass to get a better look at the bones. "Looks to me like you found the guy who was wearing them, too."

Chapter 6

I swallowed, my earlier blithe bravery crumbling a bit now that Eli had said it out loud—there really was a dead guy in my yard. What had I been thinking when I considered digging up a skeleton by myself? I felt the muscles in my legs start to tremble and I shook them out individually, the way I used to before cheerleading competitions to get rid of the nerves. Despite my best efforts, I felt a little bit woozy.

Eli stood up and, with a concerned look in my direction, shepherded me to the front porch. "Sit here on the steps while I call it in, OK? I'm going to get somebody out here to take a look and tell us what we've got here."

He returned to his SUV and I could hear the crackle and buzz of the radio as he talked to someone at dispatch. I rubbed my clammy hands on the knees of my overalls as I studied his profile in the driver's seat and wondered who was waiting at home for him. Who'd be picking a fight when the word got out that Eli was flirting determinedly with me? Because word *would* get out—if Rusty knew, then Ruth would know, and if Ruth knew, everybody knew.

People would be talking about me and Eli getting married if I didn't nip this in the bud. He returned to the front steps and sat down beside me, surveying the row of stakes I'd laid out to mark the remaining post holes. "They're sending a team out from Roseburg. I hate to say it, but they're probably going to make a mess of your yard. We'll get it squared away, though. I can help you level the dirt when they're done." He patted my knee.

"I don't need help!" I snapped, scooting away.

"But I want to. Really."

"I think I'll wait inside." I stood up and he nodded, his expression a little injured, and I headed for the door. I paused, halfway inside, when a question occurred to me. "Eli?"

He jerked his head up.

"You don't think it's…" My voice caught, and I could barely finish the question. "You know. Murder?"

He shook his head *no*. "The Chapmans are a good family. There aren't any missing persons reports on my desk, either. If a murder occurred in Honeytree, I'd know about it."

"I only trenched down eighteen inches," I said. "That's a shallow grave."

The lines in his face grew deeper, but he shook his head stubbornly. "I'm sure there's a reasonable explanation. The water table rose and pushed up the bones, maybe. Or Amos did some landscaping and moved some dirt around."

I nodded and, my discomfort eased by his rationale, went in and puttered around unpacking kitchen boxes while I waited for the county crew to show up. My new kitchen was a whole lot smaller than my old one. That one, I'd renovated in a French country theme, with hand-distressed cabinetry and tumbled marble floor tiles. But despite my slavish commitment to authenticity, it'd always felt like it was someone else's…maybe because it was. Our full-time housekeeper, Gloria, always shooed me out of it, insisting that I should sit and rest while she whipped me up something from her seemingly bottomless supply of gourmet recipes. She didn't believe me that I liked cooking—that was her job. My job was to endure being served.

This kitchen, tiny and worn though it was, was all mine. I intended to shoo everyone else out of it for the rest of my life. The cabinetry was hand-distressed, too, many colorful layers of paint showing through the chips, and the slate floors had foot-sized scoops worn into them where a generation or two of cooks had stood at the sink and stove. I could sense the envy of my Beverly Hills interior decorator from eight-hundred miles away.

I heard the crackle of a vehicle pulling up to the house and peeked out the window. To my surprise, it wasn't a sheriff's car or a coroner's van—it was a four-wheeler. Anne Sutherland, Walt's wife, was astride it, balancing a covered dish in her lap. Though she was my age, mid-fifties, she looked older. Her hair, pulled back into a tight, low ponytail, looked more gray than its true mousey brown, and though her pale forehead was unlined, her eyes were tired. My mother, rest her soul, always said that being married to an older man made her age faster. My father was ten years her senior, and they died within weeks of each other, so maybe she was on to something. Anne's husband was twenty years older so perhaps that aged her twice as fast.

I dropped the curtain so she wouldn't see me staring as she mounted the porch steps, and then counted to three after she knocked before opening the door. She held the dish up.

"Walt wanted me to bring you this. He saw the sheriff over here and said you might need it. Plus he wanted me to warn you about the chicken. It's a cobbler," she added. "I didn't have time to roll a pie crust this morning."

I took it from her, puzzled at the chicken comment. "Thanks. Do you want to come in for a minute and have a bite of this with me?"

Anne looked back over her shoulder in the direction of her white farmhouse and then back at me. "Maybe just a bite."

I offered her a seat in my kitchen at the small vintage table that I bought for a song at the junk shop in Deer Valley, then dug a couple of my grandmother's jadeite dessert plates out of the half-empty packing box on the floor. I opened up the cobbler dish to admire the perfectly browned biscuit topping. The scent of sweet blueberries hit my nostrils and made my mouth water. "Wow, this smells heavenly."

Anne smiled tightly, carefully avoiding my gaze. "I put vanilla in the dough. Most people don't, but I think it adds a little something."

I scooped two generous helpings onto the plates, rejoicing silently that I could eat mayonnaise and dessert in one day without a cutting comment from anybody, and slid one across the table to Anne. I hoped it'd help her relax. I knew she had interests—her pies won prizes at the fair, according to Ruth when she showed me the farm—but she had a nervous temperament, the kind like a rabbit, quiet and quivering. Hard to get to know without spooking her.

"Walt wanted me to tell you to keep your birds on your side of the fence," she said abruptly.

Well, that's one way to start a conversation. "You can tell Walt not to worry—I don't have any chickens. Not yet, anyway."

She stared at me with her cool gray eyes. "That's a lie. One's been pooping on our porch, and Walt hates a messy porch."

I shrugged. "Well, it's not my chicken. I have an order in at the hatchery, but it hasn't been delivered yet. Maybe it's someone else's bird."

Anne shook her head. "Nobody's kept hens in the Flats for ten years. It's only since you've been here that I've had to hose off the porch every day."

"Wild turkeys, maybe?"

"I think I know the difference between turkey trots and chicken crap."

Wow, she was a ball of fun. Sometimes when you finally get to know people, you find out that you never should have bothered to begin with. I was saved from further scintillating conversation by a second knock at the door. "Excuse me," I said, grateful for the excuse to leave the table.

Whoever I'd been expecting—Eli or some other county official—I was wrong. Ruth stood on the porch, her hair even wilder than usual, clutching her purple purse and staring at me, her eyes large and concerned.

"Are you OK?" She brushed past me into the house. "Oh, hi Anne. Did you bake? I guess I came at the right time."

I shut the door and turned around. "Of course I'm OK. Why wouldn't I be?"

Ruth went to the counter and, unaware of the plates in the packing box beside her, sniffed an empty coffee mug to determine whether it was clean and then scooped a serving of cobbler into it. "Well, the dead body. The more I thought about it, the more I got freaked out and I figured you might be freaked out, too. Listen"—she set down the mug and dug around in her purse, then pulled out a bundle of sticks triumphantly—"I brought sage! So we can clear out the bad juju."

41

Anne gasped, her spoon clattering on the green enamel tabletop. "A body?! Is that why the sheriff is here?"

"No—yes. I mean, it's a skeleton, not a body." I shook my head. "Eli said the county guys will take care of it. He said not to worry—it's probably not a murder."

At the word "murder," Anne's face turned as gray as her hair and she looked like she was about to lose her blueberry cobbler all over my kitchen table. I decided not to mention the part about how I'd been planning to move the skeleton to a new grave myself before I caught the heebie-jeebies.

"Emergency saging time!" Ruth yanked open drawers in the kitchen until she found what she was looking for, a box of matches, and quickly lit the end of her sage bundle. She waved it around the room, flipping her wrist so the smoke trailed behind her in little loops, humming to herself. She paid special attention to the door and window frames, and gave Anne's back an extra swirl, too, her face sympathetic. She stubbed out the still-smoldering bundle in the sink.

"I'll do the whole house later," she said, recovering her coffee mug full of cobbler and poking a spoon into it. "But don't you feel better already?"

I waved away the smoke that smelled a whole lot like the time our Christmas tree caught on fire when my mother decided to use birthday candles instead of twinkle lights. "Sure. I love cobbler with a side of coughing."

Ruth rolled her eyes at me and then, noticing Anne's silence, slid into the chair next to her and patted her on the arm. "Hey. Don't be upset. The old pioneer families are buried all over the valley. Leona probably just hit a family plot. Nothing creepy."

Anne nodded, but she pushed her half-eaten cobbler away

and stood up from the table. "I ought to get back. Walt's missing me. We're gleaning the bushes now that U-pick season is over, so there's a lot to be done. Don't worry about the dish—you can drop it by any time."

I nodded and followed her out, watching as she bunched up her flowered skirt to straddle the four-wheeler and peeled out past where Eli was marking off a rectangle on my grass using spray paint, the studded tiles kicking up the gravel. On her way down the driveway, she veered into the orchard to pass a caravan of vehicles coming in: a sheriff's cruiser with its sirens off but its lights flashing, a white van, and a yellow county utility truck. A mint-green Prius brought up the rear.

"That's Tambra," Ruth said from behind me, where she was standing on tiptoe to peer over my shoulder. She settled back down onto her heels when I turned to look at her. "She'd have been here earlier, but she was finishing up a client."

I could only assume Ruth meant the Prius. I spotted two heads inside as it parked under the apple tree to the right of the porch, which meant Tambra had brought company. "How'd she find out?"

Ruth explained around a mouthful of blueberry cobbler. "We overheard it on the police scanner when Eli called it in to county. When she heard I was going to drive over, she wanted to come for moral support."

"She's probably afraid I chipped my new manicure digging the guy up." I gave my nails a quick once-over before Tambra reached the front door. Luckily, they were all in pretty good shape even though I hadn't picked up those cushioned gloves she mentioned.

"I brought flowers," Tambra announced, thrusting a bouquet of pink Gerbera daisies in my face. She stepped aside so I could see the woman behind her. "And Yelena. I was just finishing up a deep conditioning treatment and figured why wait—I can rinse her out in your sink."

Yelena, an elderly woman with deeply tanned skin and beautiful, crinkling laugh lines, beamed at me from underneath a plastic-wrap turban. She produced a large glass bottle from a tote bag on her arm and held it up. "And I brought vodka! Death requires a stiff drink...get it?" she joked in a thick Russian accent.

Ruth grinned as she showed Tambra and Yelena to the kitchen. I found an empty yogurt container in the recycling to put the flowers in, my good vases all left behind in Los Angeles. "Well, I guess we have the essentials," she said. "Dessert, liquor, flowers, and friends."

"And sage, apparently," Tambra added, sniffing the air and then nodding at the slightly damp bundle in the sink. "Good. I'm not normally one for that stuff, but it can't hurt." She didn't sit down at the table, but instead peered out the window over the sink at where Eli and the folks from county were setting up across the driveway from the house. I reached around her to add water to the flower-filled yogurt tub.

"Sit, both of you," Yelena ordered, patting the table on either side of her as Ruth, having discovered my box of plates, dished out the first round of cobbler for them and a second round for us. Ruth set four flowered teacups on the table and poured an inch of vodka in them, then rattled around the top shelf of my ancient refrigerator and plunked an ice cube in each cup. Well, if ever there was a day for a second helping of dessert and a shot of vodka, it was the day you dug up a boot full of foot.

I put the pink daisies in the center of the table and sat, but

Tambra stayed at the window, absentmindedly accepting her plate of cobbler and setting it on the counter to the side of the sink, next to her car keys. Ruth took one of the teacups and raised it. Yelena and I followed suit. "Cheers, ladies."

"What's happening out there?" I asked after I recovered from my sip of alcohol. Yelena didn't mess around—the vodka was crisp like a punch in the face.

"They taped off a big area and now a guy is digging," Tambra reported from the window. "He's making a mess of his jumpsuit—whose idea was it to wear white for digging in the dirt? Oh, he's pulling something out!"

We all sat forward in our chairs, half eager for and half dreading the gruesome details.

"It's"—Tambra leaned forward and squinted—"I think it's a guitar case." She gasped and turned toward us, her eyes wide and shiny and her lower lip quivering. "Oh, God. It *is* him. It has to be."

My heart stilled. "What do you mean? Do you know who it is?"

Ruth scooted the fourth teacup in Tambra's direction, but Tambra shook her head. "Maybe I'm wrong. I don't know. I have to go." She snatched her keys from the counter and hurried out the front door. We all stayed frozen at the table until a few seconds later when we heard Tambra's car crunch on the gravel driveway, the sound fading from earshot as we sat.

Ruth and I shared a concerned look. "What's that all about?" I asked her.

"I wish I knew. She must be really upset. It's not like Tambra to leave a client." She nodded to Yelena. "Don't worry, I'll rinse you out. And I'll have a talk with her tomorrow." She stood up and began carefully unwrapping the plastic from Yelena's head, revealing a head of long, silver hair coiled up like frosting on a cupcake. "Let's move you to the sink. Can you grab me a towel, Leona?"

I looked around frantically for my box of linens and, locating it just outside the kitchen, found her a couple of hand towels. She draped one over Yelena's shoulders and the other over her own arm.

"Don't worry about it, I understand." Yelena grabbed the bottle of vodka and refilled her teacup, tossing it back like an old pro, before standing up and following Ruth. "She has demons buried in her past, it seems. I guess we all do. It's just that usually, they stay buried. This one is coming to the surface."

Chapter 7

While Ruth worked her hairdresser magic in my kitchen sink, I went out to see what—or who—the crew had unearthed. After all, a guitar case wasn't exactly an identifying possession. Lots of people had guitar cases. Maybe Tambra was upset over nothing.

Eli intercepted me in the driveway before I could get too close. "I'm glad you have company up there," he said, nodding toward the house. "It's good to have moral support. I'm here for you, too."

"In a professional capacity," I reminded him. "Do you know who it is? The skeleton, I mean?"

"We found some stuff near him—garbage, mostly. Old garbage. We found a Josta can on top of him, and I don't think that stuff's been for sale for twenty years. Don't know if it belongs to the deceased, though. And no wallet, not yet anyway. It's slow going. We'll probably be here late. Shift ends at midnight. Will you be up then?"

I nodded.

"Good. I'll let you know if we find anything else."

Back in the kitchen, Ruth was combing out Yelena's hair, which, now that it was stretched to its full length, I saw reached well past her waist. "Do they know who it is yet?" Ruth asked when she saw me.

I shook my head. "No ID. Just a guitar case and some twenty-year-old junk that might not even be his."

"I was hoping to put Tambra's mind at ease. She seemed pretty shaken. You don't have a hair dryer, do you?" She eyed Yelena's long, dripping locks.

I shook my head. "They don't agree with my curls."

"I'm just going to braid it. Is that OK?" Ruth asked Yelena.

"Yes, I like braids." Yelena folded her hands in her lap, her back strong and straight. I couldn't guess her age if I tried. She might be in her seventies, like Walt, or she could be older. "They remind me of my childhood in Russia. My mother braided my hair every day and wrapped it around my head like a crown. Can you do it like that?" She craned her neck around to meet Ruth's eye, who nodded enthusiastically.

"I love a good braid crown! That's very trendy these days, you know. Tuck a few flowers in it, and you could be an Instagrammer." Ruth grinned and began parting and sectioning Yelena's hair. I sat down and watched her meditative movements.

Yelena chuckled. "I don't even know what that is."

"Trust me, you don't want to know," I said. I felt the same way about Instagram as about the skeleton in the yard. One could be curious about it and also know enough to stay away. I couldn't resist standing on tiptoe to catch a peek out the window at the activity in the yard. As I watched, a guy set up large spotlights and began connecting them to a generator. Eli hadn't been exaggerating—the forensics team intended to work past sunset. They were taking this as seriously as if it were a murder scene. And who knows, maybe it was. I shivered.

"Do you think Tambra really recognized that guitar case?" I asked over my shoulder.

Ruth paused in mid-braid. "She must. I've never seen her rattled like that. Usually she's so poised. I remember once, a bat flew into the salon, and she didn't even blink. The rest of us were shrieking and laying on the floor, and she used a tipping cap—you know, the bonnets for highlights—to catch it and put it outside. People don't guess it because she's so girly and sparkly, but Tambra's not a wimp."

Yelena chuckled. "I'm not surprised. Beauty queens have nerves of steel. How else can they stand up on stage in a bathing suit?"

Ruth grinned, but I couldn't even smile past the lump in my throat. "What if it was murder?" I asked quietly, turning away from the window. Ruth's smile faded, and the amused crinkles around Yelena's eyes disappeared, too. "What if Tambra knew the victim?"

"It's not a murder," Ruth declared staunchly, her fingers deftly weaving Yelena's silver hair. "That kind of thing doesn't happen around here. Don't get worked up about it. Tambra probably just got spooked."

She sounded so sure that my shoulders relaxed a little. "Yeah, so. Eli said the dead guy's been there a while, maybe a couple decades. Tambra would be too young to know him. She was a teenager twenty years ago, right? Just a kid."

Ruth dropped her comb. She held the braid tight with one hand as she stooped to pick it up again, and I saw an expression briefly flash across her face—she remembered something.

"What? Tell me," I demanded.

Ruth kept her eyes on Yelena's growing gray-and-black crown. "I don't want to start any rumors."

I snorted. The Do or Dye was the nexus of Honeytree gossip. Ruth was like the vending machine of local rumors. Maybe she was more comfortable passing them along than she was creating them, though.

"We're among friends," Yelena said mildly. "If you speak hypothetically, we won't hold it against you."

Ruth shook her head, her fingers swiftly weaving the intricate braid. "It's probably nothing. It's just when you said Tambra was a teenager twenty years ago, I remembered that she hung around here a lot back then. So did a lot of kids. My grandpa had a soft spot for people down on their luck, especially young people, and the farm was a place they could come hang out when things weren't so great at home."

"The bonfires?" I asked. "Walt said something about them. When he saw all the beer bottles I'd dug up, he told me teenagers used to party here."

"That's right." Ruth nodded. "I rarely came to the bonfires. I'd just bought the Do or Dye from the previous owner and between that and selling real estate, I was working eighteen-hour days—I was way too busy to party. But I remember the bonfires were a big thing for a while. And they weren't just for kids—plenty of adults shared a beer by Grandpa Amos's fire, from what I heard. He liked building a community and filling it with friends, kind of like I do at the salon."

"I was never invited," Yelena said, indignation creeping into her tone. "I considered Amos a good friend, too."

"I think he stopped having the bonfires before you moved here," Ruth said. "Fifteen, twenty years ago?"

Yelena nodded. "I moved here when I retired. Fifteen years ago—no, sixteen."

"Yeah, Grandpa Amos quit having them about that time."

That caught my attention. Fifteen or twenty years was about how long Eli estimated my skeleton friend had been in the ground. If the bonfires ended around the same time, maybe they were connected. "Why'd he stop?"

Ruth frowned and held up the end of Yelena's completed braid. "Do you have a rubber band or a piece of ribbon? Even string would work." I grabbed a hair elastic from the jar by the door and brought it to her. She carefully fastened it around the braid and then tucked the end into the complete crown. She gave the hairdo a pat and then circled the chair, examining her handiwork from all sides.

"I don't know why," she finally said, when she seemed to be satisfied with her braid crown. She nudged Yelena toward the bathroom. "Go look in the mirror and see what you think."

I waited until Yelena was out of the room before I pressed Ruth further. "You never asked?"

"I never thought about it, since I didn't go to them. I didn't even really notice when they ended. They just…did. Maybe Grandpa just got tired of picking up beer bottles. Maybe the fire danger was too high one year and people forgot about it. Maybe his back pain was making him crabby. Who knows. The whole point is that it wouldn't be crazy if Tambra knew something—or someone—connected to the dead guy buried here. Bunch of drunk people, late at night…an accident could have happened."

I nodded as I thought about all the bottles and cans still in the ground. I doubted whether Amos Chapman ever picked any of them up. Maybe he'd just gathered them up and thrown them into a pit; it wasn't such an uncommon thing when I was growing up for people to dig a trash pit instead of hauling stuff to the county dump. People would throw all kinds of stuff into their mini landfills, and when they were full, they'd just cover them up and dig a new one.

My blood chilled. What better way to bury a body than in a trash pit, covered with bottles and cans? Nobody would blink twice if you filled it in and dug a new one. And few people would dig past the layer of trash on top, as I did, so the body was unlikely to be discovered, even decades in the future.

I watched as Yelena returned from the bathroom and Ruth touched up some tendrils that had escaped from the back of her hair. Had Amos Chapman killed someone and buried the body here on the farm? If he had, Ruth didn't know about it—her face was smooth and unconcerned as she chatted and smiled with Yelena.

Tambra certainly hadn't been so relaxed when she left. She was worried—and in a hurry to go. Perhaps her haste in leaving was because she didn't want Ruth to hear that her grandfather was a murderer...a murderer who'd slept in my little bedroom. I settled into a chair and tried to shake off the uneasy feeling that my little cottage had once housed a killer.

Chapter 8

"We're done for the night," Eli said, shifting his weight to the other foot as he stood on my porch fiddling with his sunglasses like an idiot. It was almost midnight, so it wasn't like he was going to wear them. Behind him, I could see the forensics team in their jumpsuits setting up a tent over the trench they'd dug to exhume the skeleton to protect it from any possible rain.

Or maybe to protect it from prying eyes like mine.

"I take it that means you'll all be back tomorrow."

He nodded. "I really don't think you should be alone tonight, though." He glanced toward where Ruth's car had been parked next to mine. She'd driven Yelena home hours ago, leaving me alone with the bottle of vodka and remains of Anne's extraordinary cobbler. I didn't know if it was the alcohol, the sugar, or the gravity of the exhumation going on in my front yard, but I didn't feel so good.

"I'll be fine," I slurred. "Everything's fine."

"At least let me check around your place to make certain it's safe?"

I guffawed. "Safe? Why wouldn't it be?"

"Well. We found the victim's skull. And unfortunately—"

"The victim?" I swallowed hard. "What do you mean? He

didn't die of natural causes?"

Eli shook his head. "Not unless getting your head bashed in is a natural cause."

Suddenly my peaceful little farm felt like it was tilting on an axis, shifting from a safe place to rebuild my life to a gruesome murder scene. I felt the blood drain from my face, and my knees went wobbly. "Someone was murdered...here?"

"Whoa, whoa!" Eli caught my elbow before I could collapse to the floor. "Don't worry, it happened a long time ago. At least twenty years ago, judging by the soda cans that were around him."

"So what you're saying is you didn't catch a murderer for decades. He's still out there. That isn't a very reassuring testimonial for your investigative skills." I shivered and opened the door wide. "Well, if you think a murderer's been hiding in my closet for twenty years, please, feel free to evict him."

He ducked his head sheepishly and made a beeline past me to the coat closet, and then proceeded to check under and behind every piece of furniture before heading upstairs.

"You're all clear. No bad guys here," Eli said when he came back down a minute later. He eyed the cobbler on the counter behind me hungrily. I waited for him to ask, but he didn't. I sighed and made a plate for him anyway, since there was only one serving left, give or take, and if I ate it, I'd sorely regret it. He gave me a goofy grin when I handed him a fork.

"I just don't feel like trying to Tetris the cobbler leftovers into the fridge. You can sit." I pulled out a chair for him and sat down in the seat across from it. "But only 'til you're done eating. Then you have to go sleep in your own bed." I blushed, realizing that I'd implied he'd be sleeping in my bed if he stayed here.

Thankfully, he didn't make the joke. He was too busy devouring the cobbler to notice my wording. When he finally looked up from the plate, he grinned at me. A crumb clung to the side of his mouth and I resisted the itch to brush it away. "You're a good baker," he said admiringly.

"You're just hungry from all the digging. Anyway, I didn't bake it—Anne Sutherland brought it over earlier on the four-wheeler, remember? When she and Walt saw you over here, they figured a sheriff means trouble, I guess."

"They're not wrong." He winked mischievously and pushed his empty plate away. "I'm going to try and get out of your hair as quick as I can, though."

I thought about my coop-building schedule, which was already completely thrown off by today's delay. "How quick is that?"

He licked his bottom lip, a habit I recognized from sitting next to him during high school algebra class. He was doing mental math. "Um. A week, minimum? Could be three or four weeks, though, easy."

My stomach sank. "You're kidding. A month? How long does it take to dig up one skeleton? I already did the feet for you."

"Oh, we got him all dug up this evening. He's off to Roseburg so the ME can do an autopsy. We'll circulate impressions of his teeth to all the dentists in the county and see if anybody has a record of him so we can figure out who this guy is. Dental records take forever."

"Surely I can build my coop even if he hasn't been identified," I said, frowning as I did my own mental calculations and rejiggered my schedule by a week. I hoped the rain wouldn't start until after I got the concrete poured for my foundation.

"Well, the forensics team wants to bring in some heavy equipment and excavate a bigger area to sift for potential evidence. You're going to have a nice size hole in the yard, I'm sorry to say. Don't worry," he rushed to finish. "I'll help you fill it in. I've got a little tractor with a loader that I can haul over on a trailer; it'll be a piece of cake."

"I have my own tractor," I said sharply. I did—it was in the barn. Of course, it wasn't exactly working, but I was sure I could fix it. Pretty sure.

He pushed his chair back from the table and stood up. "Well. We'll try and keep the crime scene small so you can go about business as usual, but the equipment might need to block the driveway now and then."

I nodded, my eyes trained on the jar of pink Gerberas in the center of the table to avoid meeting his eyes—I knew I was running hot and cold, and he didn't deserve it. Sure, it was late and I was tired, but that was no excuse. I was the one who offered him dessert and a seat. My mother taught me better than to make a guest feel uncomfortable in my house.

Eli didn't seem too put out, though. "As soon as we identify the victim, I'll let you know. Don't hold your breath, though. Like I said, sometimes it takes dentists weeks to get back to us, and even then, they might not have his records."

"You should talk to Tambra." The words were out of my mouth before I could stop them.

Eli arched one eyebrow. "Oh yeah?"

I nodded, feeling slightly guilty. I didn't know why—it's not like I thought Tambra killed the guy. But I felt bad sending cops her way without telling her first, even if it *was* just Eli, after she'd come all the way out here on my behalf and brought flowers to boot, no pun intended. "She said something when she was here earlier, when you unearthed the guitar case? It seemed like she might have recognized it. She left in a hurry, so I didn't get a chance to ask, but maybe she could give you some leads."

"I'll swing by the salon and talk to her tomorrow. Thanks. For everything. I mean it." He paused halfway out the front door, then leaned closer to me and put his arm around my shoulders. "I can stay here tonight if it'll make you feel safer."

I was suddenly conscious of the county crew's eyes on us and the blood came rushing back to my face. I scooted out from under his side-hug. "If you stay here overnight, everyone will be talking. They probably already are talking."

"So?" Eli straightened and glanced over his shoulder at the forensics team. They quickly got back to loading up their van and pretended they hadn't been staring up at the porch. "I don't care what anyone says."

"Your girlfriend might care. Or fiancée or wife or whoever."

"Considering she left me for a Portland Trailblazer a few years back, I'm guessing she won't." He grinned ruefully. "She traded up."

I knew how that felt. My face must have shown my sympathy, because he quickly added, "Don't feel bad for me; I deserved it. I can sleep in my truck instead of the couch if it suits your sense of propriety better."

I almost took him up on it. Almost. But a nagging voice in the back of my head said I didn't need him or his assumptions about my sense of propriety. I didn't need a man watching over me just because things were getting a little spooky. This was exactly the kind of situation I should deal with on my own, now that I was single. I couldn't call a man every time a scary spider crossed my path, not anymore. Plus, I didn't need the gossip buzzards circling me any more than they already were.

"I'll be fine."

He frowned at me. "'Fine' is a pretty low bar."

"Not for me." It was meant as a joke, but the truth in it stung. I hadn't been fine for a while now. Tambra wasn't the only one with demons buried in her past. When mine came to the surface, they destroyed my life. I hoped hers wouldn't do the same.

"I'll keep you updated," Eli said, his eyes full of concern. "In the meantime—lock your doors, Leona. And thanks for everything."

Irritation at being told what to do prickled my skin, but I knew he wouldn't give that kind of advice unless he was truly worried. Nobody locked their doors in Honeytree. They might lock their shed or their gun cabinet, but not their house. If he thought I needed to do that, he was more worried about a potential murderer on the loose than he let on.

I nodded and closed the door behind him, grudgingly locking the deadbolt as he'd instructed. Then I cleared his dishes from the kitchen table and sat there for a minute, flustered for no reason. *Thanks for everything?* What in the world had I done for him besides act like a pain in the rear? Here I was trying to keep him out, and he was grateful for some unfathomable reason. I swear, fifty-six years old and I still could never understand men.

Chapter 9

A rooster's crow, nature's alarm clock, woke me before my phone alarm went off. Anne was wrong—someone in the Flats definitely had chickens. I peeked out the seersucker curtains of my attic bedroom and saw Eli's SUV was parked next to my Suburban. Eli was standing in the driveway, staring at the person-size hole the forensic team dug yesterday and the pile of loose dirt next to it. Either he'd risen early or he'd never left. I suspected the latter, given the way the hair was sticking up on the back of his head, silhouetted by the rising sun.

I found a pair of polka-dot PJ pants on top of the laundry pile, tugged them on, and headed down the narrow stairs for the front door. I grabbed a hair tie from the jar by the door and wrestled my unruly curls into something resembling a ponytail on my way out.

Eli turned toward the house when he heard the door hinges creak. I leaned out over the porch railing and called across the driveway to him. "You want coffee?"

He shook his head *no*. "Don't worry about it. The crew is bringing me breakfast." He turned back to the dirt pile. I guessed my efforts yesterday to reduce his attentions had worked. The message had been received: Leona's not interested. That's what I wanted, so why did I feel a little disappointed that he didn't accept my offer?

Probably just my pesky ego, I thought, as I went back inside and put the coffee on. On some level, I'd enjoyed that a man found me attractive for the first time in what—fifteen years?—even when I'd eaten three plates of dessert and was wearing dirty overalls. But that didn't mean I had to cling to Eli to get that kind of attention. The standards of beauty were different here than in LA and it was going to take me a while to get used to it.

While the coffee brewed, I took a long, hot shower and got dressed—in clean jeans, this time, and a red T-shirt with a chicken on it that said "Hens Before Mens." Then I sipped my coffee and kept an eye out the window over the sink until the white van returned.

Sure enough, they'd brought a huge Dutch Brothers cup for Eli and a box of doughnuts that they propped open on the hood of the van. The group clustered around the box, and I watched as he chose a chocolate-glazed doughnut and took a bite. My stomach rumbled and I wished I hadn't given away that last piece of cobbler.

One of the forensic techs reached out and rumpled Eli's hair where it was sticking up in the back, and the whole group rocked with laughter. They were probably ribbing him about sleeping here overnight. That meant the word was already out and it was only—I glanced at the clock—eight a.m.

Damage control time. I needed to spend the day as far away from Eli as possible so that people didn't start assuming we were a couple.

I pulled a plaid flannel on over my T-shirt. Far from being unseasonably warm, it acted as a light jacket during these cool, late-summer mornings. When the clouds burned off by noon and the temperatures rose, I'd tie it around my waist, but for now, it was the perfect outer layer. I located Anne's squeaky-clean casserole dish and, tucking it under my arm, got into my car and headed for the Sutherlands' house.

As I drove by, I saw the forensic team had finished their sugar-bomb breakfast and were starting to work, half of them digging and half of them sifting through the dirt they'd piled up yesterday. Every time they came across something bigger than a pebble, they bagged and tagged it. They were going to be bagging and tagging for a long time, given the trash-to-dirt ratio that I'd observed while working on my foundation trench.

Just a hundred yards down the highway, the Sutherlands' driveway was smoother than mine. Walt must have paid special attention to it for blueberry season so the U-pickers didn't have trouble coming and going, and the extra grading and graveling he'd done really paid off. I'd have to do the same on my driveway, or pretty soon I'd be risking my axles. One more line on the to-do list.

I rolled up to the house and spotted Anne hanging laundry on the clothesline stretching from the porch to the blueberry shed. I got out and waved to her. "Just bringing back your dish!"

"Set it on the porch there." She jerked her head toward the house, her hands full of the wet bedsheets she was pinning to the line.

Their porch was as tidy as their driveway, swept clean and empty of any of the usual porch clutter—yard tools, boots, empty flowerpots, seasonal decorations past their expiration date, faded furniture. None of that. Instead, a cheerful pot of well-watered geraniums sat near the steps where it'd get some sun, and a single wrought-iron chair was pulled up to a small telescope on a tripod.

I set the casserole dish on the chair before I registered that the telescope was pointed straight at my house. I didn't know how I felt about that. I leaned over to look through the eyepiece and saw the crime scene techs milling around. I could see them better through the telescope than I could through my kitchen window. I turned and narrowed my eyes at Anne's back.

"You've sure got a good view," I said, loudly enough for her to hear.

She flung a towel over the line and fastened it with a clothespin before turning around to see what I was talking about. "Oh, that. It's Walt's," she said, and went back to hanging clothes. Socks, now, clipped in pairs.

How long had Walt been surveilling my place? Was his interest in the law enforcement activity, or had he been watching my trench digging, too? Likely both. That's probably why he came over to investigate my project in the first place. Spying wasn't very neighborly, but people didn't move out to the country because they had good social skills. "Does he spend a lot of time doing Neighborhood Watch?" I asked.

Anne joined me on the porch and swooped up the empty baking dish from the chair, setting it inside the empty laundry basket balanced on her hip before answering me. "He's had a telescope on that porch since before I married him," she said. It didn't answer my question, but on the other hand, it did.

"Well, if he sees any murderers…"

Anne's eyebrows jumped so high they nearly hit her hairline. "What?!"

62

"I'm joking. Sort of. Eli says the guy buried in my yard didn't die of natural causes, that's all. I thought you and Walt should know, since you're right next door. I didn't want you hearing it from someone else."

Anne gave a brisk nod, apparently recovered from the initial news. "Well, nobody else will hear it from us. We'll keep an eye on your place and you do the same for ours. Oh, speaking of"—she set down the laundry basket, hurried back down the steps and into the blueberry shed, and then came back out with a cardboard box and shoved it into my hands—"I believe this is yours."

I pulled back a flap of the box to look inside. Two beady eyes under a dashingly floppy comb stared back at me...this morning's alarm clock, no question. "Oh! He's not mine! I don't have a rooster." I held the box back out to her, but she picked up the laundry basket and turned away.

"Neither do we. Someone probably dumped him when they heard you had a chicken operation out here. Happens all the time. You pet a dog in town and say you've been thinking about getting a puppy, and you've got a box of squirming little spuds at the end of your driveway the next morning. He's yours now. Do keep him off our porch, please. Walt's very fussy about birds because of the berries." She gave me a little half-smile and went in the house.

I frowned at the alarm clock in a box, who pecked hopefully at a speck on the cardboard flap as I closed it over his head. A hollow *thunk-thunk* emanated from the box as he searched for his breakfast in vain inside. I didn't need a rooster—a rooster wasn't part of my plan. Eggs, yes. Hens, yes. But roosters... that was a hard no.

The feed store had a colony for unwanted roosters, I

remembered. I could drop him off there and be done with it. I put him in the back of the Suburban and headed for Honeytree. While I was there, I could warn Tambra that Eli would be coming to question her and kill two birds with one stone.

Chapter 10

Tambra's Prius was parked on the street in front of the grocery store in the spot unofficially reserved for people who were just grabbing a few things, so I spotted it easily. I pulled in behind her and caught her just as she was leaving the store, a cantaloupe cradled in each arm.

"Nice melons," I said.

Ruth would have laughed at my joke, but Tambra just raised her perfectly plucked eyebrows, her expression cool. "They're for the back-to-school picnic. What brings you to town?"

"You, actually."

"Oh?" She popped the hatchback open and rolled the cantaloupes into a mesh compartment so they wouldn't roll around while she was driving.

"You left so quickly last night—I wanted to make sure you were OK. You looked like you'd seen a ghost."

Tambra shut the back of her car and passed a hand over her face. Her nails were lavender with mint-green stripes today and matched her sporty yoga pants. "I guess I did. Being at the Chapman place brought back a lot of memories. I haven't been over there since I was a kid, and I'd rather forget those years. They were tough ones."

"Well, steel yourself. I think Eli's going to come talk to you.

I told him what you said—you know, about knowing who the victim was."

"The victim," she repeated, her expression dazed.

I waited a beat, and then when she didn't continue, prompted, "The skeleton in my yard. You recognized his guitar case."

"He was murdered?" Her eyes welled up, her lavender-frosted lower lip trembling.

"Eli thinks so. If you have any information about the guy, it'll be useful to the police. Do you know who it is?"

Tambra scanned the sidewalk and then looked across the street at the few people who were going shopping or heading to work—it was rush hour in Honeytree, after all, and I could tell she didn't want anyone to overhear our conversation. She grabbed my hand, inspected my orange nails, then said, "You chipped your polish already. I'll touch you up."

I cracked a window for the rooster in my back seat and then followed her on foot the half-block to the salon, where she nervously unlocked the door and then closed the blinds so nobody walking by could see inside. She sat down behind her station and patted the table. "Sit, sit. Show me your paws."

I sat and submitted to her ministrations in silence until I couldn't stand it anymore. "Well?"

"There was a guy," Tambra began, never taking her eyes from my fingernails. "He worked for Mr. Chapman the summer I was seventeen, so it was twenty years ago. He was a train-hopper, you know? From Canada. We called him Toronto Joe to his face and Hobo Joe behind his back. I got to know him at the bonfire nights—he'd sing and play his guitar. When I saw the guitar case …"

"You thought it might be him," I finished. "You thought the

skeleton might be Toronto Joe."

Tambra's shoulders sank and she nodded. "He disappeared one day with no warning. Just...gone. I wanted to file a missing persons report, but everyone said he probably just hopped another train and headed back to Canada, so I didn't. I should have trusted my gut and filed a report." Her lower lip trembled. "I didn't even know his last name, though. So..." She gave a small, sad shrug.

"You were just a kid." I watched as she slicked a topcoat on over my repaired nail. "You can do something now, though. I bet your information will be really helpful to the investigation. They'll at least have a first name. I can go with you to the sheriff's office for moral support, if you want."

Tambra gave me a wobbly smile and shook her head *no*. "I'm sure someone else in town already came up with the name. Joe had a ton of friends; everyone liked him."

"Not everyone," I said quietly. "Someone wanted him dead. Can you think of anybody he didn't get along with back then? That might be helpful to the police, too."

She shook her head again, but her brow was furrowed.

"What is it?" I pressed. I could tell she was holding something back.

"I just—I remember the last time I saw Joe was at a bonfire night. We were sitting on a hay bale chatting, and then Rusty interrupted us. He seemed upset about something, and Joe went to talk with him. I could tell they were arguing, but I couldn't hear what they were saying because the fire was roaring. I'm sure it was nothing, though. I don't know why I even mentioned it."

She looked so pale and worried that I reached across the table to pat her hand. "This is great, Tambra. This is exactly the kind of thing that will help catch whoever killed Joe."

She pushed back her chair and stood up. "I don't want to get Rusty in trouble! Please don't tell anyone what I said about their argument, OK? You know how it is around here...rumors stick, even when they aren't true."

I knew, but I also knew that Eli had nothing to go on for the investigation, and that meant that the Douglas County Sheriff's Department was going to be sifting through my yard for the next three years unless they figured this thing out another way. "You have to tell Eli. Let's just walk across the street together and you can make a report. It could be really important!"

"Or it could be nothing. Maybe I'm not even remembering it right—it's been a long time. I'm not going to tangle my friends up in police business without a good reason." She pressed her lips together tightly.

"What if Rusty knows something, and that leads to the killer?" I pleaded.

"Well, ask him. If he knows something, he can tell Eli himself. I'm sorry, Leona—I have to make melon balls." She flashed me an apologetic smile. "Now, go get yourself some of those gloves I was talking about!"

I swallowed and nodded. "Thanks for fixing my nails. How much do I owe you?"

"Not a dime." She held the door open for me, her face a mask of tight politeness.

I could tell I had already overstayed my welcome, so I hurried back to my car, my mind swirling. I felt responsible for Toronto Joe, somehow—maybe because I unearthed him—and I wanted to know what happened to him. It was more than simple curiosity, and Tambra's reluctance to share what she knew didn't dampen my interest; it only increased it. What had Joe and Rusty argued about that night?

I needed to find out. I put the Suburban into gear and flipped a U-turn right in front of the grocery store; Eli was still busy out at my place, so there were no cops around to write me a ticket, anyway. I drove on the street parallel to the railroad tracks until the road turned to gravel. When the road crossed under the tracks, I knew I was getting close. Ruth's place—and Rusty's—was only a quarter mile further.

I pulled up to the house and heard a thumping in the back of my car. At first I thought maybe I'd scraped the muffler with a rock on the bumpy dirt road, but when the thumping turned into scratching and squawking, I remembered the bird in the box. Alarm Clock was clearly trying to make his escape.

"Chill out!" I reprimanded the back seat as I turned off the car. The scuffle stopped immediately at the sound of my voice. "I'll just be a minute."

Ruth's car wasn't in the driveway, so I bypassed her turquoise-painted front door and walked around the exuberant dahlia bed to the brown-and-white single-wide trailer behind the house. It was no wonder Ruth had planted tall flowers in front of Rusty's place. Unlike her tidy, charming vintage home, Rusty's was aging badly. Green algae grew on the aluminum siding, and a layer of fir needles covered the concrete pavers that led to the door. The wood porch looked ready to capsize, and the windows hadn't been washed in months—if not years. I could hear the faint noise of a television game show through the trailer's thin walls.

I knocked and stood back from the door. Nobody answered, so I knocked again, louder. This time, Rusty appeared in his tighty-whitey underwear, his hair sticking up even more than usual. He yelped when he saw me and slammed the door in my face.

"I thought you were Ruth!" he howled from inside.

"I'm not! Put your pants on, I need to talk." I leaned against the porch railing to wait, but it started to give, so I quickly stood up again. When the door reopened, he was in a much more presentable jeans-and-Coors-Light-sweatshirt ensemble. "Even your sister didn't need to see that."

He flushed and avoided eye contact. "What do you want? Ruth's running errands, I think. She won't be back until after work."

"I came to see you, actually. I dug up a skeleton over at my place, and Eli is pretty sure he was murdered." His eyes bulged, and I nodded. "You heard me right. I'm pretty sure it's Toronto Joe. Remember him?"

Rusty clearly did. He took a step back from me, his mouth hanging open. "You dug up Hobo Joe?"

I bulldozed on. "I heard you had a fight with him the night he disappeared."

"I never did!" Rusty blurted out, running his fingers through his hair. "I swear, I never threw a punch."

"An argument," I amended. "At the bonfire."

"Oh—that. Yeah, we had some words." Rusty looked back over his shoulder. "You want some coffee? It's already made."

I nodded. "Sure, if you're having some. Milk, no sugar."

He brought out two mugs and, slipping on a pair of flipflops from the porch, led me over to Ruth's back patio and set the mugs down on a mosaic-tile table.

"Pretty," I said as I sat down, running my hand admiringly over the colorful tilework after I took a seat on one of the bright patio chairs.

"Ruth made it," Rusty said, plopping down in the chair across from me.

I figured. Ruth was always applying her artistic talents to new mediums, whether that was pottery, jewelry, or hairdressing. When we were kids, she was the one with the cool sneakers decorated with Sharpies and stick-on gems when the rest of us just had plain white Keds. I picked up my mug and took a sip. "Good coffee," I lied. "So tell me about Joe. I hear he was a friendly guy…what was your problem with him?"

Rusty sighed. "*He* had a problem, not me. I found out that he stole something from Walt Sutherland. I was trying to convince him to return it, but he didn't have it anymore. I told him that unless he admitted what he did and paid Walt back, I was going to tell my granddad that he was a thief. Granddad liked to help people out, but he had a low tolerance for sticky fingers."

"He would have fired Joe if he found out?"

"Yup. And Joe knew it—he'd been at the farm long enough to see how things worked. Some farmers will look the other way to keep good help during the harvest, figuring it's the cost of doing business, but not Amos Chapman. He found out you were stealing? Didn't matter if you were friend, foe, or family—he'd fire your rear end so fast, your pants would smoke."

"So did you tell your grandfather?"

"I did, actually. The next morning, I told Granddad first thing. We went out to the barn to confront Joe together—that's where he stayed, in the hayloft—but he was gone. We figured he'd hopped a freight train out of town. Maybe he went back to Canada or something."

I swallowed, thinking of Rusty and Amos walking around the farm looking for Joe, when he was right under their feet. "But he didn't leave. He was there. You didn't notice the ground was disturbed?"

To my surprise, Rusty laughed. "Of course the ground was disturbed! Granddad was putting in a duck pond, of all things. I think it was just an excuse for him to hire Joe, to be honest, because as soon as Joe left, he had me fill it in. I spent a good week shoveling dirt into that hole. Boy, I was glad to see the end of that job. I think I cursed Joe the whole time I was doing it. Freakin' Canadian!" His face shifted and grew more serious, and I could tell he was thinking about how he'd shoveled all that dirt on top of Joe's body without knowing it. "I liked the man, honestly. He was a hard worker. We broke our backs on whatever harebrained scheme my granddad came up with that summer. I'd call him a friend—I think everybody did."

I nodded sympathetically. "He must have ticked someone off, though. Otherwise he wouldn't have had his skull smashed in."

Rusty winced at my poor choice of words.

"Sorry."

"It's OK. It's just a lot to take in, Joe being dead. I thought he was up in Canada all these years, married to a moose and having maple-flavored babies. I can't think of a single person who disliked Joe." Rusty paused, his face thoughtful. "Well..."

I raised my eyebrows and scooted to the edge of my seat. "What? What are you thinking?"

He shook his head, the movement so slight it was barely perceptible. "I don't want to point fingers."

"It didn't come from you," I assured him.

"Well..." he repeated, pausing uneasily. "Walt was missing

his porch telescope, right? He came over and asked if I'd seen it. I *may* have said I'd ask Joe about it. I knew Joe'd been working over there a lot, so it was a natural assumption. I'm just afraid that Walt..." He trailed off, letting the words sit between us for a minute.

"That Walt took it into his own hands," I said, trying to phrase it as gently as I could.

Rusty shrugged. "Maybe. Walt's got a bad temper."

I nodded as I thought about the implications of what Rusty was saying. I couldn't deny it: Walt was very concerned about what I might have found when I was digging the foundation trenches for the coop. Maybe his question was more than simple curiosity. Maybe it was self-interest. I had a mind to ask him about it—I just had one little stop to make first.

Chapter 11

"The rooster colony's full. Overfull, actually," Sherman Dice drawled, snapping his nicotine gum. Sherman kept a coop behind the feed store like a take-a-penny, leave-a-penny dish for roosters. If you had an extra, he'd take it, and if you needed a new one, you could have your pick. Roosters didn't usually like their own company, but if you kept the hens away, they could get along. "Spring chicks are starting to crow and everyone's looking to unload their cockerels. The young ones are poor flock-tenders, though. Hens get tired of their antics real quick."

He waggled his eyebrows at me and I shifted the box to my other hip so I could open a flap and give him a peek inside at Alarm Clock.

"This one isn't a cockerel." I said. "He's mature—and very well behaved, actually. Isn't he a beauty? He's been riding around in the car with me all morning and he's been a champ. Calm, friendly, quiet. He could probably teach the young ones a thing or two if you could make room for him."

Sherman grunted. "Then you should keep 'im. Breed him with your girls. Temperament comes from the father, they say."

Of course, that was nonsense. Anyone with an eighth-grade

science education knows that genes don't work that way. I had a feeling Sherman gave more weight to superstition than science, though. All these old farmers were that way, which was why they consulted the *Farmer's Almanac* instead of the darn weather report. I didn't want to be on the bad side of the feed store guy, though—I had a feeling I'd be here a lot once my egg business was booming.

"I don't have a need for a rooster," I said politely. "I'm getting hatchery chicks and they're all layers. I doubt they'll ever go broody, so I don't want fertilized eggs anyway."

Sherman grinned at me so widely I could see his wad of gum clenched between his molars. "A good cock does a whole lot more than spread his seed."

I rolled my eyes, hard. "I'm not feeding an animal if it doesn't give me something in return. You have to earn your keep in my coop, and last time I checked, roosters don't lay eggs."

He whistled in surprise. "Shoot, they do a lot more! They keep order in the flock. If a flock doesn't have a rooster, one of the hens takes on the job, and let me tell you—hens make terrible leaders. Mean as heck. They'll eat the feathers right off each other. Why do you think the commercial egg farms keep 'em all in cages?"

I snorted. "That is *not* why. Anyway, lots of operations raise cage-free eggs."

"You ever see their birds? *Bald*." Sherman opened his eyes wide, daring me to believe him, but then his face cracked into another wide grin. "Just joshing you. But really. A good rooster is worth his weight in gold. He keeps his ladies in line, plus he'll sound the alarm when predators are near and fight 'em to the death if necessary. It can save you a bundle if you don't lose your layers to a red-tailed hawk or raccoon what-have-you." He nodded at my box. "Give this mister some sisters and you'll see."

I looked at Alarm Clock through the gap in the flaps and he turned one beady, hopeful eye on me. I closed the flap before I fell for it. "No. Nope. A rooster is not in the plans."

Sherman shrugged and reached across the counter, motioning for me to give him the box. "Fine. I'll take him, but his name'll be Stewie Dumpling, if you catch my drift."

I sighed. The poor thing didn't intend to wander onto my property—or more accurately, the Sutherlands'. Why did he deserve to die just because Walt was a stickler for a clean porch? The skeleton in my yard was enough death on my farm for one week. "Never mind, I'll keep him until you've got room in the colony. I don't want this guy to end up as supper."

"You some kind of vegetarian?" Sherman raised his eyebrows and looked me up and down, smirking. "I heard a lot of folks down in California only eat vegetables. You one of those? I sell rabbit pellets if you want some. They're organic."

I giggled and patted my hip with my free hand. "This rear end didn't get extra padding because I ate too much lettuce. But while I'm here, I'll take some all-flock and some chick starter."

"Chick starter? This time of year?"

I nodded. "That way they'll be laying as soon as the spring sunshine shows its face."

"Makes sense. I think I have some from earlier in the season that's still within dates. Pull around back and I'll load it for you."

"How much do I owe you?" I shifted the box again as I struggled to access my purse.

He waved his hand. "Don't worry about it. I'll start you a

tab. I know you're good for it."

Now this was the reason I moved back home. For all the parts I dreaded—the rumor mill, the old-fashioned attitudes toward women, the judgment—there were good parts, too. People knew me—the real me. They remembered my parents and the kind of people they were. They trusted that my heart didn't change when my ZIP code changed to 90210.

I put Alarm Clock's box back in the car and pulled around by the loading area near the rooster pen. Sherman hadn't been exaggerating—the pen bustled with strutting young cockerels who were just sprouting their first crop of tail feathers. When I got out to open up the back of the Suburban, several of them hurried to the wire nearest me, hoping for a snack. One in particular could have been Alarm Clock's little brother, with a ruddy orange head and long, beetle-green tailfeathers. He looked like he walked straight off a box of Corn Flakes.

I pointed to him. "What breed is that guy?"

"Welsummer, same as yours. Good birds." Sherman scooped a handful of dried mealworms from a bin near the rear door of the shop and tossed them into the coop. A frenzied swarm of roosters descended on the crispy critters, snatching them and then running away to avoid having the treats stolen right out of their beaks by their compatriots. The Welsummer kept his head low to the ground, pecking up as many as he could, his large comb flopping over his eye with every bite. "See? Good forager, cool-headed, and pretty hardy."

He grasped the corners of a feed bag and swung it into the back of my car, and then went and got a second one. "That one's your starter. When are your chicks coming in?"

"Tomorrow, maybe." I pulled my phone out and opened my email. Sure enough, the tracking number had arrived in my inbox. "Yep, tomorrow. Phew, I've got some work to do."

"Good luck with 'em."

I nodded. "Thanks, Sherman."

On the way home, I couldn't help updating Alarm Clock on the current situation, even though I knew he couldn't understand me. "OK, big guy, listen up. I'm giving you a stay of execution, but you're just a temporary guest at my place, so don't get comfortable. As soon as I find another farm for you, off you go. Understand?"

Silence from the box. If only the other men in my life were so good at holding their tongues. A siren wailed behind me as soon as I hit the Flats, and I groaned. Of course, Eli was waiting for me *again.* I pulled over, rolled my window down a crack, and braced myself for a lecture, but he just leaned on the door and flashed me a cheeky grin through the one-inch gap.

"Going pretty fast, there. Couldn't wait to get home and see me, huh?"

"For your information, I wasn't even going home. I was going to the Sutherlands' place," I said primly.

"Oh yeah? Why's that?"

I squirmed in my seat, regretting my own smart mouth. I *had* to pop off on Eli so he didn't think I had a thing for him, and now here I was, stuck between lying to a cop or accusing my neighbor of murder. Shame on me. I chose the coward's way out, a lie of omission. "I just wanted to ask Walt a few things."

"About?"

I flushed. "About the farm."

"Well, perfect. I have some questions for him, too. I'll come with you." Eli patted the window frame, walked briskly around to the passenger side, and slid into the seat. When I stared at him, wondering why he wasn't taking his own vehicle, he just smirked at me. "What, you want me to drive? We can switch." He motioned between us.

I snorted and cranked the Suburban. It took a couple of tries, but the engine finally turned over and I eased along the shoulder to Walt and Anne's mailbox, then made the turn without pulling out onto the highway. The car crawled up the gravel drive as I babied the gas pedal. I was trying to prove something to Eli by driving as slowly as I could—that I wasn't reckless, that I wasn't up to something behind his back, who knows. He didn't say a word, just hopped out when we reached the house.

Walt, who'd been sitting in the lone porch chair and peering through his telescope, jumped up in surprise when he saw Eli mounting the porch steps. He opened and closed his mouth a few times, looking every bit like an ancient goldfish gasping for air. For once, know-it-all Walt Sutherland was at a loss to explain why he was spying on a murder investigation.

I checked on ol' Alarm Clock, but he seemed settled in his box, preening his tail feathers, so I left him in the car and joined Eli on the porch.

"I'm just curious about the goings on," Walt was saying gruffly. "I like to keep an eye on the neighborhood. There's nothing wrong with that."

Eli nodded, casually took a seat on the chair Walt had vacated, and looked through the telescope's eyepiece. He sat back, his expression troubled. "You've got quite a view," he said quietly. "Good thing you have curtains up, Leona."

Walt, to his credit, turned beet red, but before he could make any excuses for why he was looking in my windows, Anne pushed open the screen door.

"Everything all right?" she asked, tucking a strand of her colorless hair behind her ear and touching the silver, heart-shaped locket around her neck out of habit. For all their plainness, her simple blouse and skirt had their own pleasant harmony, as though she could be a farmer's wife from any era. Seeing her next to Walt reminded me of the famous "American Gothic" painting of a farmer and his daughter. Of course, Anne was Walt's wife, not his daughter, but she could have been, given her age. Then her gray eyes settled on me, and she didn't look happy. "I'm surprised you're back so soon."

Walt and Eli looked at me, too, so I shrugged and went for it. "I was wondering how you knew somebody was buried in my yard, Walt."

Chapter 12

Walt stood there frozen for a moment, then said, "Anne, why are you being so rude to our guests? Offer these folks something to eat."

"That's not necessary," Eli began, but Walt held up his hand.

"I insist." He nodded to Anne, who had her gaze trained on the freshly painted floorboards of the porch.

"Can I offer you some pie and coffee?" she mumbled.

"No—" I started, but upon seeing Walt's furious expression directed at Anne, I revised what I'd been about to say. "No coffee for me, but I'd never turn down Anne's baking."

"Coffee for me," Eli said, catching my eye. "I'd love a slice of pie, too, if you've got some, Anne."

She slipped away and Walt forced a smile. "Now, where were we? Oh yes, the business on the Chapman farm. I had no idea anything was buried there, I'm sorry to say. I'm as curious to know who it could be as anyone."

I put my hands on my hips and gave Walt my best mother-who's-disappointed-in-you stare. "You were *real* curious when I started digging in that spot, so don't play dumb with me. I'm pretty sure you remember Toronto Joe, the guy who stole your telescope. That's him over in that yard, and I think you knew that."

Eli's head jerked toward me and I knew he was dying to ask how I'd found out the skeleton's name. But he just waited as Walt worked his lips over his teeth and squinted at me, deciding whether or not to take me seriously, and then rose smoothly from his seat. "I'd like to know the answer to that, too. Why'd you get interested when Leona started digging. What did you know?"

Walt's expression turned sour. "I didn't know. Not for sure. I just saw something over there a while back—"

"Like twenty years back?" I interrupted, raising an eyebrow.

He nodded slowly. "I saw someone filling in Amos's dadgum duck pond at five o'clock in the morning. I figured something interesting was at the bottom of that hole. 'Course I didn't know what. I thought it might be a cash deposit in the Bank of Redneck, but nobody ever made a withdrawal. Been wondering what was down there since, so when I saw you digging, I figured I'd ask."

"You witnessed the burial through your telescope?" Eli asked gesturing to the telescope next to him, but Walt shook his head.

"Nope. My telescope was stolen, like *she* said. This here I got to replace it. I don't know who took the old one, unless it was that hobo hanging around Amos's place. Can't think who else would have swiped it but him."

"Joe," I reminded him.

"Joe," Eli echoed, pulling a notepad out of his uniform pocket. "You have a last name?"

"No," Walt and I said simultaneously.

"Who had the shovel that morning?" Eli's voice was level but I could sense the excitement jittering under his skin as he asked the question.

Walt bristled. "Didn't I just tell you my telescope was gone?

I couldn't get a new one until the next blueberry harvest paid out. All I could see was that it was a person. Shoveling dirt. Nothing more."

"A man? A woman?" Eli took a step toward him.

"A human. With two legs and two arms. That's all I know." Walt crossed his arms just as Anne re-emerged from the house with a tray that held three pieces of pie and two cups of coffee.

"Sorry it took so long. I had to brew a fresh pot," she said nervously.

"Cream and sugar!" Walt barked. Anne shoved the tray into my hands and scurried back inside. He sneered at the screen door as it banged shut. "I swear, as if women weren't useless enough…"

If I hadn't had my hands full, I might have socked him in the mouth. Eli looked dismayed, too.

"Is that kind of talk really necessary, Walt?" Eli's tone was gently chiding. He took the tray from my hands and set it on the seat of the chair, then handed me a plate of pie and a fork. He blew on his mug of coffee before slugging it and setting his mug on the porch rail, then dug into his own plate of pie. "Good lord, you eat this well every day and you call your wife useless?"

"I don't ask much. Sugar in my coffee, clean sheets, loyalty…" Walt squinted across the blueberry field toward my house and ignored the tray completely, even though presumably the remaining pie and coffee were for him. He hadn't asked for them, but after I'd seen how he treated Anne, I imagined that she would hedge her bets and risk wasting a piece of pie before she'd risk angering him by asking—or worse, by not bringing him anything. "That's not setting too high a standard, is it? And yet…"

Anne returned and set a cut-glass bowl of sugar cubes and a tiny pitcher of cream on the tray. "Is the pie all right?" she asked.

"Perfection," I said thickly around a mouthful of the jewel-like berries and tender, golden crust. The pie was even better than the cobbler, if that were possible.

Eli nodded and poured a heavy dollop of cream into his coffee even though he'd been happily drinking it black a moment before. "You've outdone yourself. Your husband is a lucky man."

Anne's pale cheeks flushed pink and Walt glowered at her; perhaps Eli's praise felt like criticism to a husband with an inflated ego and thin skin. I suspected Eli had meant it that way, judging by his smug expression. Anne's hand went to her neck and she nervously adjusted her heavy silver locket again.

"Pretty necklace," I said, trying to ease the tension between them. "Is it antique? There must be a story behind it."

Anne blanched at the attention. "It's a family piece." She spoke so quietly that her voice was almost a whisper. "If you'll excuse me, I should get back to my chores. Just leave your dishes on the tray and I'll get them later."

"Thanks for the refreshments," Eli said cheerfully. He pinched the last crumb of piecrust from his plate and popped it into his mouth before setting his plate on the tray. "What a treat."

She smiled tightly. "Walt's very hospitable." At her words, the tension in Walt's shoulders visibly eased; she clearly knew the best way to defuse his anger was to give him the credit. Disgust balled in my stomach on her behalf. She shouldn't have to debase herself every day of her life to soothe some old man's narcissism. Nobody should. She should stand up to him, and if she wouldn't, then I would!

I slid my own empty plate on top of Eli's and opened my mouth to lay into Walt when Eli caught my eye and gave a subtle shake of his head, as though he were the one driving this conversation. Mister, you rode here in the passenger seat!

"For someone who spends their time spying on other people's business, you sure don't see your own too clearly," I snapped. Walt jerked his head toward me, and Anne didn't wait to hear his response. She grabbed the tray of dishes and nearly bolted back through the door into the house.

"I don't think I like what you're saying."

"I don't think you really hear me." I leaned toward Walt and punctuated my words with my finger. "You knew a dead man was buried in my yard. You've had your telescope trained on the spot for the last twenty years. You were the only one I've heard who had a grudge against the guy. And all you have to say for yourself is that your wife isn't up to your standards because she forgot the creamer? I hope she waits until you're old and then leaves you in a puddle of your own—"

"Leona!" Eli said, and then, maybe seeing the rising tide of fury spreading across my face at being cut off, added, "Is right." He looked back at Walt. "You likely saw the murderer that morning. It does no one any good to avoid that simple truth. I need you to tell me every little detail you recall so I can write it up properly. We can do it here or we can do it down at my office, whichever you prefer."

"What I'd *prefer*," Walt said stiffly, his wattles bobbing, "is a little more *privacy* while we chat."

He meant me. He probably thought a man would be more friendly to his ornery old misogyny, but I guess he didn't know Eli very well if he thought that. Eli'd grown up in a house with seven older sisters who made sure to educate him about how to treat women. He was the only guy I knew in high school who carried Tampax in his backpack in case his female friends needed one. I wished I could stick around to see Walt get his comeuppance, but I had a cock in a box in the back of my Suburban who really needed to doodle-doo on down the road.

"It's fine. I've got better things to do, anyway," I said. I gave Eli a half-wave, half-salute. Let him sort out Walt Sutherland.

"Don't worry about me; I can walk back to the road," Eli called after me.

I grinned at him over my shoulder. "Oh, I wasn't worried."

Chapter 13

I left Alarm Clock in the car and tried to ignore the sounds of the forensics team at work while I set up a pen for the rooster in the barn. The barn had one of those antique sliding doors that was so rusted up that it took all my strength to get it open. I had to put my back into it, literally, and it squealed and protested the whole way. When I finally wrestled it open, sunlight pierced the dim interior, illuminating the dust that swirled in the air, and I breathed in the scent of a century of farming: machine oil, hay, animal, earth. The faint odor of apples was there, too, residue from previous years' harvest.

The left side of the barn was outfitted with stables, a work bench stretched along the back wall, and the rest of the space was open. Well, not *open*—the right side was crammed with junk that Amos Chapman had stored there, whatever wasn't valuable enough for Ruth and Rusty to sell off or keep after he died: rolls of fencing wire, rusty old tools, empty buckets, half-full paint cans, the tractor that wouldn't start.

Taking up the center of the barn, directly inside the doors, was my prize possession, a flaming-red convertible Porsche. My fiftieth birthday present to myself. I bought it after I unwrapped Peterson's present to me—a gift certificate for liposuction at his plastic surgery practice. Needless to say,

I felt I deserved the car. Though a convertible was almost pointless to own in rainy Oregon, I just couldn't give it up, not even when I left every other scrap of my LA lifestyle behind. But the poor car had been sitting here in the barn since I moved in—I hadn't worked up the guts to drive it anywhere and draw the attention it was sure to bring.

I'd lied to Walt about why I didn't want chickens in the barn. Sure, I was worried about predators, but the main reason was that I wasn't keen on chicken poop messing up my paint job. I rummaged in the pile of junk and found a grayed canvas tarp and spread it over the car. That'd keep Alarm Clock from using my side mirrors as a roost until I could finish the coop and move him outside.

One stubborn corner of the tarp kept curling up, though. I needed to weigh it down with something. My eyes lit on a bucket laying on its side nearby and I reached for the handle without really thinking about it. But before I could move the bucket to secure the tarp, something inside it bit me!

I yanked my hand back, instinctively sucking the wound, then inspected my finger for damage. A nice little chunk had been taken out of my right index finger. Whatever critter had taken up residence in there meant business. I picked up a pitchfork and, bracing myself for the worst, stooped to get a better look at my enemy.

Inside the bucket crouched not a snarling raccoon or feral barn cat, but a puffed-up, hissing speckled hen. She flattened herself over her makeshift nest and glared at me with one beady eye, as broody as they come.

Apparently Anne Sutherland had been right—if possession was nine tenths of the law, I *did* own a chicken who probably *had* pooped on her porch. Two of them, now. Not for long, though. A broody, barnyard-mix hen fit into my well-laid plans about as neatly as a stray rooster. That is, not at all. She needed to find a new place to live.

"Honey, you aren't going to hatch anything out of those golf balls you probably have under there," I said to her, chuckling. I reached out to evict her from my bucket, and she lashed out at my hand again, quick as a cobra. This time I had more warning and avoided another brutal peck. She ruffled her feathers, puffing up to completely fill the round opening, and clucked at me indignantly, as though the very *thought* of disturbing her was a mortal sin. She wasn't about to give up her clutch—not without drawing blood.

I sighed. "OK, little dinosaur. I won't steal your egg babies. But as soon you quit the nest, you're going to the auction house along with Alarm Clock."

I set up a station for food and water under the workbench and went to retrieve the rooster from the car. Eli pulled up as I slid Alarm Clock's box out of the back of the Suburban.

"Aw, did you get me a present?" he asked as he walked toward me.

"Why, yes I did." I smiled innocently and handed him the box. His face lit up and he eagerly pulled open the flaps. Alarm Clock launched out of the box, squawking and beating Eli's face with his wings until Eli stumbled backward and the rooster landed on the ground, loose feathers swirling around him. The rooster immediately began scratching and pecking in the driveway dust; the morning spent crammed inside a cardboard box had left him hungry.

"Gee, thanks." Eli frowned at me. I didn't know why—his question hadn't been serious, and neither was my answer. Anyway, how was I supposed to know that Alarm Clock would fly out like that?

"You said this farm was a lot for one little girl, so I figured I'd bring in a Y-chromosome to help me out," I said sweetly. I shooed Alarm Clock toward the barn so I could introduce him to the broody hen. As I headed back inside, I hoped she wouldn't peck the crud out of him the way she had my finger.

"You know I didn't mean it like that!" Eli trotted after us, and I rolled my eyes.

"What *did* you mean, then? Because it sure sounded like you think I can't handle my business, and I assure you that I can."

He caught up to me just as I entered the barn and cleared his throat awkwardly. "When I said this was a lot of farm for one woman, I just meant that I wanted to help you with whatever you need. You know, because I'm happy you're back. You might not have the same nostalgia for our high school days as I do, but honestly, Leona—Honeytree hasn't been the same without you. I'm sorry if my smart remarks came off wrong, because I know you can do whatever you put your mind to. I mean, look at the life you've led!"

Heat rose in my cheeks and then spread down to my collarbones. I didn't really want to look at my life. Eli could only see it from the outside: the glamor of my former address, the jewelry and European vacations, the TV-ready family. He didn't know how miserable all of that had made me, and bursting his bubble would be admitting my own failure. I wasn't ready for that, but Eli's hangdog expression made me realize I couldn't keep berating him for extending friendship to me, either. Nobody deserved that kind of treatment.

Nobody deserved this hot flash, either.

I fanned myself, then stripped off my plaid flannel and tied it around my waist. "That's just it—it wasn't *my* life. It was my husband's and that was my mistake—listening when he told me how to live my life instead of making my own decisions. I won't make that mistake again. I know that makes me seem prickly, but maybe I just *am* prickly now."

"A rose with thorns." Eli grinned.

I snorted. "I'm a bleeping cactus."

"Don't sweat it. You're great." Eli stepped toward me and reached out a hand. "Truce? I'll keep offering to help, and you can keep saying no for as long as you want. I won't hold it against you—as long as you don't hold it against me for offering."

I nodded and took his hand. "Truce."

His eyes lingered on my face as he searched it for something. Whatever he was looking for, he didn't seem to find it. Then his expression changed to one of curiosity as he looked past me into the barn and dropped my hand. "What've you got under here?"

My stomach sank. "Nothing!" But it was too late; he'd already sidestepped me and pulled aside the canvas tarp, revealing my little red convertible.

Eli gave a low whistle as he circled the car. "Nice ride! Have you taken this out on the Flats and put the pedal to the metal yet?"

"Not yet. Every time I try and get a little speed out there, the cops pull me over." I grinned sheepishly at him.

"I'll let you in on a little secret. You didn't hear it from me, but the way we're scheduled, there's nobody on highway patrol from two to four a.m." He winked.

"Duly noted. Now where's Alarm Clock?" I looked around my feet for the rooster and then, when I didn't find him, took in the rest of the barn's interior. I could hear him clucking softly, so I knew he was close by.

"Look." Eli nodded toward the other side of the car. I stepped around to get a better view and saw Alarm Clock scratching and dragging his wings in the dust in front of the bucket where the broody hen was still squatting. "I think he's made a lady friend."

"Aw, he's tidbitting. He's trying to impress her by bringing her a treat. He must have found a bug." I watched him dance and sing for a moment, my affection for Alarm Clock growing by the minute. One less bug in the barn was fine by me. "What a good boy."

Eli grinned wickedly at me. I knew he was about to make a joke about how he and the rooster being on the same mission to impress a lady, and I held up my hand to stop him. "Don't start, Elias Ramirez! What are you doing hanging around my barn, anyway? Don't you have work to do? File Walt's statement or something, since I know you're not doing the digging."

"What do you mean? I dig! Look at these blisters from yesterday." He held out his hands and I could see where painful-looking blisters were raised on top of his already-calloused palms. "The forensics team has it under control. I emailed Walt Sutherland's witness statement from my phone. And I'm here on business, anyway. I need to know how you found out the victim's name."

"Joe." I nodded. "He was a hobo from Toronto."

He gaped at me. "How in the world did you figure that out so quickly?"

"I told you last night—Tambra recognized the guitar case. I saw her in town and just asked her." I shrugged. "Is that all? If so, I need to get back to work."

"Yep, all done. Now I am at your service. Let me help you with whatever you've got going on."

My first instinct was to send him out. I could get the barn ready for two stray chickens and my upcoming shipment of hatchery chicks on my own. But on the other hand, I had a hundred pounds of chicken feed sitting in the back of my Suburban. "Be careful what you wish for. I got a couple of feed sacks in the car—you can haul them in here if you want and then dump 'em in there." I nodded at two shiny metal trash cans I'd bought specifically to keep pests and moisture out of the food.

"You got it." Eli saluted and pretend-marched out toward the parking area, lifting his knees high. He didn't seem to care that half the sheriff's department was out there watching him act like a goofball. I couldn't help smiling at his back.

I heard a flapping behind me and turned to see Alarm Clock perched on the leather-covered steering wheel of my Porsche, preening his majestic tail feathers.

"Don't you crap on my dash!" I rushed toward him and waved my arms until he decided he was better off preening somewhere else. He dove from my steering wheel to the top of his lady friend's bucket. Of course, that made the bucket wobble, turning her into an angry puffball of doom. *Someone* was messing with her nest, and she decided that someone was me.

She rocketed out of the bucket, screeching, with a murderous glint in her eye. She went straight for my knees and went at them like they'd personally insulted her. I booted her softly to get her away from me. Clucking, she stormed back to her nest, but Alarm Clock took up the cause, squawking indignantly as he lowered his wings and charged at me. At the last second, he jumped and tried to nail me with his spurs, but I turned so he only grazed the back of my thighs.

I grabbed him while he was still near me and tucked him firmly under my arm. "Nice try, mister. I appreciate that you love your lady already, but I'm the boss around here. Anyway, it was your fault for landing on her bucket, not mine."

With my free hand, I pulled the cover back over my car so it wouldn't become his favorite roost. Eli returned with a feed sack on each shoulder, his biceps bulging—I have to admit, I didn't mind the gun show—and slung them down by the trash cans. He grinned at the rooster under my arm. "Farm girl looks good on you. Those jeans look good on you, too."

"Don't get fresh," I said, self-consciously smoothing my hair in case the chicken kerfuffle had loosened my ponytail and let my obstreperous curls escape. "This guy tried to spur me, and this is the best way to teach him a lesson. I'm going to haul him around until he's sufficiently humiliated, like he's a chihuahua in a purse."

Eli nodded as he pulled the strings that opened the top of the feed bags. "There's nothing more humiliating than being a lapdog." With a smirk, he hoisted the first bag of feed and poured it into the trash can, then did the same with the second. The lids clanged shut and he dusted his hands before looking at me expectantly. "What's next?"

I raised my eyebrows. "Speaking of lapdogs..."

The look on his face—it was like someone pulled the slot machine lever, emotions whirling past as he decided whether to be amused or offended.

"I'm kidding," I added, and he relaxed. "I think I've got it from here. I just need to clean out this place a little to make room for my chicks until I can get the coop finished."

He glanced around the barn, taking in the dusty piles of junk that surrounded my Porsche. "Well, if you change your mind…"

"I have your number," I said, crossing my fingers behind my back to negate the lie. It wasn't really a lie. I mean, the crumpled ticket with his scribbled cell number was probably still on the floorboards of the Suburban.

"Well. Goodbye, then." He looked embarrassed as he left. Maybe he realized that his goon squad was going to tease him mercilessly about his earlier caper to the car. I didn't dwell on it; what did I care what Eli was thinking? I wasn't like Anne Sutherland, scurrying away at the merest hint of a man's displeasure. I was the boss of this place.

Chapter 14

Under my arm, Alarm Clock clucked softly. As an experiment, I set him down, and he went straight to work, scratching in the dust on the floor, not a hint of aggression toward me. "That's more like it."

I scooped a handful of all-flock from the can and filled the food dish under the work bench for him and the hen. She really needed a name, now that I thought about it. I squatted down so I could see into her bucket and get a better look at her beautiful speckled feathers. She puffed up, ready to take a beakful out of me, if necessary, and tucked one of her eggs more securely underneath her breast. Broody hens had such a split personality, tender with their babies and evil with everyone else.

"More Dr. Jekyll, please, and less Mr. Hyde." The instant the words were out of my mouth, I snapped my fingers. "That's it. We're calling you Dr. Speckle."

The hen muttered unappreciatively and huddled over her eggs, so I let her be and stood to assess the space. The barn had electricity, thankfully, though the outlets were few and far between. I needed one for the brooder plate that would keep my chicks warm until they grew enough feathers to self-regulate their temperature. I located a good outlet in a back corner and set to work moving the true junk—it *was* mostly junk that I'd inherited from Amos—out behind the barn. I'd haul it off to the dump when I had the time.

Most of the stuff was old building materials, stuff left over from completed projects, or maybe projects that were never started. Folks that grew up during the Depression stockpiled everything useful, from rolls of used baling twine to empty feed sacks, and Amos Chapman was no exception. He'd stashed about twenty coffee cans full of washers, screws, and nails, too. I decided to keep those—it was a supply to last a lifetime.

I moved them over to the shelves above the work bench. The pile of two-by-four offcuts went into the wheelbarrow until I could decide what to do with them, and the forgotten tools crammed into the corner—a blunted old shovel and a metal rake—I decided to hang on the wall. I tapped in a couple of nails from the hoard into a post and rested the shovel between them.

It was only then, once the shovel was hanging on the wall, that I noticed the handle was stained with something dark. It looked as though the substance had dripped from the shovel's rusted blade down onto the wooden shaft where it had soaked in, leaving black streaks. I swallowed hard.

Could it be...blood?

My ears started to ring. I backed out of the barn as quickly as I could and crashed directly into a brick wall.

Or at least, it felt like it.

"I think your gears got stuck in reverse." Eli chuckled as he extended a hand to help me up off the ground. I ignored it and scrambled to my feet, my face on fire.

"Sorry I ran into you. I got a little spooked." I brushed my hand over my face and regretted it instantly as I felt the grit of barn dirt smudge across my forehead.

"What's wrong?"

"I found something you should see." I led him into the barn and pointed at the shovel hanging on the post. "Tell me that's not a bloodstain."

Eli leaned close and examined the ominously dark drips from all possible angles. "Well…I can't say it isn't. Now, is it human blood, is it Joe's blood? I can't say that, either. But I have a guy." He winked at me, but then his expression grew serious as he studied my face. He reached out to touch my shoulder. "Hey, are you OK?"

I shrugged off his hand and shook my head, trying to quash the willies crawling all over my skin. Was my cute little barn a murder scene? "Fine. I'll be fine. Just…take the shovel, please."

He gave a brisk nod. "Don't touch it. I'll be right back."

"I already touched…" I began, but he was already outside, calling to someone named Blake. I felt something brush against my leg and nearly jumped out of my skin, but it was just Alarm Clock staring up at me. He clucked and stretched his neck up, turning his head to the side to get a better look at my hands, hoping for a treat. His cute expression reminded me that I had better things to do then quail at the sight of old yard tools. I had a flock to tend. "You ate all your food already? Did you save any for your friend?"

I glanced over at Dr. Speckle and saw she was dozing in her bucket, her beak dipping down toward the straw where she'd made her nest. I hoped she'd give up on the eggs soon. Broody hens didn't eat or drink much and only left the nest once a day, usually, and the whole experience was as hard on their bodies as pregnancy is on a human. I'd even heard of broody hens dying because they refused to give up the nest long after the eggs should have hatched. I might have to take the eggs away from her. Of course, I'd have to wear gloves...

As if she had read my thoughts, Dr. Speckle jerked her head up and fixed me with a beady glare. But before I could reassure her, Eli returned with a guy I presumed was Blake. Blake carefully wrapped the shovel in a paper shroud before lifting it down from the nails and carrying it out like it was made of glass.

"He doesn't want to knock any flakes of blood—" Eli broke off before he finished the sentence when he caught sight of my face. My stomach roiled and I felt my whole body tingle and go hot. A sweat broke out and dizziness overcame me. It felt like the worst hot flash I'd ever experienced, and I leaned against the tarp-covered car to steady myself.

"Maybe you should get some fresh air?"

I nodded and, after a few deep breaths, headed out into the sunlight. I hoped it would have a sanitizing effect on my fear—not that my fear was rational in any way. Even if the shovel was what had cracked Joe's skull, that was twenty years ago. It had nothing to do with me. Nothing had changed for me, not really. My coop plans might be delayed a bit, but I still had every chance to build my dream egg farm on this property, on my own terms.

But the sunlight did the opposite. It illuminated every corner of the farm, showing the acres of apple orchard I had no idea how to harvest or prune, the crumbling cottage, the potholed driveway, the barn that had seen better days, the forensics crew tearing out the posts I'd already set so they could dig a big hole right where I wanted to build. This vehicle was out of control and I was supposed to be driving, but it felt like I was going to crash the whole thing into a brick wall. Maybe Eli was right when he said the farm was too much for one little girl.

Too much for me.

"What's wrong?" Eli repeated.

"I just…I just feel really alone." Surprised by my own admission, I blinked back the tears that pricked my eyes.

"You're not," he said stoutly, and then, seeing my skeptical expression, added, "I'll prove it to you. Let's go. I'll drive."

"But I need to finish—"

"It can wait!" Eli tossed back over his shoulder. He was already halfway to his SUV. He turned to check if I was following and motioned me toward him. I glanced at the barn's gaping black maw of a doorway and then back at Eli's hopeful face. It wasn't much of a choice.

I threw my back into the barn door to close it and then trotted after him. He held the car door open for me—the door to the back seat. Unbelievable. And he knew it was obnoxious, because he was grinning at me.

"You're not serious."

"Department policy. My holster's on my right hip, so someone in the passenger seat could grab—"

"I'll be grabbing something else if you're not careful!" I said, sidestepping him to open the passenger door. "I can drive myself if you're so worried about being attacked." I slid into the seat and closed the door, pretending to ignore his slack-jawed face outside the window. He finally slammed the back door and jogged around to the driver's side.

"You know I'm going to get in trouble," he said mildly as he fastened his seatbelt. "They're all watching and someone's going to write me up."

"Where are we going?"

He put the SUV into gear and backed out of the parking spot. "I think you need to be among friends. I'm taking you to the Do or Dye."

I eyed him suspiciously. "You're not driving me to town just to chat with my girlfriends."

"I'm not?" He blinked innocently, his eyes trained on the highway as the Sutherlands' blueberry fields flicked by.

"I think you have an ulterior motive."

"I might." He gave a little shrug as he took the Curves like a pro, leaning into the turns.

I bit my lip to keep from grinning—I didn't want him to know how much I was enjoying the ride.

Chapter 15

"Can't you park around the corner?" I asked.

"Why would I do that?"

I craned my neck to see who'd see me exiting a sheriff's vehicle. Old Irene Wertheimer was down by the post office; she couldn't see past the end of the block so there was no danger there. A group of teenagers bunched at the corner, celebrating the freedom of the last day before school started with foot-high soft-serve cones. They were already darting looks at Eli's SUV, which meant that stories of Leona's scandalous arrest would be circulating within the hour. Better that than rumors of a budding romance, though.

"Thanks for the ride!" I said, and hopped out, letting the door fall closed behind me so I didn't hear Eli's reply. To my dismay, he followed me out of the car. The bells on the salon door jangled as I pushed inside, and Ruth looked up from a magazine where she was sitting under a roaring hair dryer.

She clicked it off and stood. "Nobody's here, so I thought I'd try out some of the new demi-perm colors," she said, pointing to the foils tucked into her springy hair. She hugged me and then stood back to take in my "Hens Before Mens" outfit before scrubbing the dirt off my forehead with a makeup wipe. I'd forgotten all about my barn-grime beauty treatment.

"What're you up to? Why the sheriff's escort?"

"I just needed to get out; it's been a crazy day. Eli offered me a ride because I was a little dizzy," I explained.

"I tagged along because I hoped to speak with Tambra," Eli added quickly. "Is she around?"

So that's what he was after—information about the case. I felt a little silly that I'd assumed his interest was romantic.

Ruth shook her head. "She's over at the park helping with the picnic."

"Guess that's where I'm headed, then." Eli gave me a brisk nod. "Hope a little girlfriend time helps you feel better, Leona."

After he left, Ruth looked at me, her face concerned. "Is everything OK? Are you sick?"

I shook my head. "It was just hot flashes, I think."

"Ah." Ruth nodded sagely. "You came to the right place, then! I have friendship, I have lavender face masks, I have turquoise and hot-pink hair dye." Ruth ticked off the options on her fingers. "All proven antidotes to menopause."

I chuckled. "No fun colors for me. That face mask sounds great, though. I could use a little relaxation."

"You got it." Ruth ushered me to a reclining chair and then bustled around the room gathering supplies. "I think I'll have one, too, if you don't mind. Fill me in on your day while I get everything ready."

I settled myself into the chair like I was at my fancy therapist's office in LA. "Well it all started when Anne Sutherland handed me a rooster in a box."

Ruth dropped something with a clatter. "What?!"

"I know. And I found out that Walt has been surveilling my place with a telescope. Apparently he's been doing it for years."

"Oh, yeah. I knew about that. Grandpa used to call him Neighborhood Botch behind his back because he was always up in everybody's business. You know, like 'Neighborhood Watch,' but *messed up.*"

I grinned and closed my eyes as Ruth wrapped a warm towel around my face, leaving my lips clear. The warmth radiated deep into my pores. Heaven. I heard her sit down in the chair beside me and let out a comfortable sigh.

"We're just going to do this for ten minutes or until the towels cool," she said, her voice slightly muffled. "Wake me up if I fall asleep. That's what Tambra does. What does Eli want with her, anyway?"

"This morning, she ID'd the dead guy in my yard. She really did know who it was. Oh yeah, and Eli thinks he was murdered."

"What?!" Ruth gasped and I heard her sit up, the foils in her hair crinkling.

"I told you, it's been a day." I pulled one corner of the towel off my face so I could peek at her. "It's Hobo Joe—remember him?"

Ruth looked sick. "Of course I do. Gosh, it's been so long, I'd totally forgotten about that guy. Grandpa was furious when he took off with the duck pond half-dug. We heard about it for years."

"Well, apparently he didn't take off. Someone cracked him on the head and buried him in the pond."

Ruth laid back in her chair and put the towel back on her face. "That's so awful. Poor man."

I fixed my towel, too. "He'd have been found earlier, but your grandpa decided to abandon the project. Any idea why he filled it in?"

"No, you'd have to ask Rusty. I was so busy getting the Do or Dye off the ground back then that I wasn't really paying attention to the farm, but Rusty was there every day. Grandpa was the brains of the operation, but Rusty was the muscle because Grandpa had a bad back."

"I did ask him. This morning."

I heard the crinkle of vinyl as Ruth sat up again. "You did?"

I pulled off my towel—it was cooling off anyway—and met her eyes. "Tambra told me Rusty had a fight with Joe at the last bonfire night, so I went to his trailer to ask him about it. I didn't tell Eli that, though," I added guiltily. "I didn't want to get your brother in trouble."

"I can't believe he and Joe were fighting. I thought they were friends!"

I nodded. "They were. He found out that Joe stole a telescope from Walt. Told him to return it or pay Walt back. But Joe refused, so they got into it. Rusty threatened to tell your grandfather, but Joe disappeared before he could do it."

Ruth's jaw dropped. "Oooh, yeah, Grandpa had zero tolerance for thieves. He forgave many a character defect, but that was not one of them. I wouldn't blame Joe for running off rather than dealing with my grandpa when he was angry."

"That's what Rusty said. Anyway, Amos told him to fill in the pond, so he did. He thought maybe it was just a project Amos invented so there was a reason to employ Joe to begin with."

"I could see that. Here, let's put these in the sink and move on to phase two—the mask!" Ruth gleefully snatched my towel away and returned with a bowl of purple gunk. She cackled as she smeared the gooey substance on my face. "This will get that dirt out of your pores! I know you think you want it there, but trust me…you'll thank me later. Even farm girls need to keep it fresh."

"I hope you're right." I could feel the purple goo crack as I moved my lips; it was already hardening on my face. It was also heating up…like, really heating up and tingling to an alarming degree. I clutched the arms of my chair. "Is this even safe?!"

Ruth flipped the sign on the door to "closed" and shut the blinds on the front window. "Deep breaths, Leona. Deep breaths."

She leaned toward the mirror and began applying the lavender mask to her own face. I tried to relax and follow her instructions, slowly breathing in the luscious scent of lavender essential oil and breathing out my stress and fear. I repeated a mantra over and over: *My farm will be fine. Eli will solve Joe's murder. I don't need to hide behind dirt to be a real farmer.*

I might have even dozed off, because I startled when a timer dinged.

"Let me get mine off and then I'll do yours." Ruth used a damp towel to remove most of her lavender mask and then, with a fresh towel, gently dabbed at my forehead. She still had a few thin smudges of purple around her eyebrows and temples.

"You missed a spot."

"I'll live. Just like you're going to live when I do your makeup." I started to protest, but she held up her hand. "Deep breaths. It's not going to kill you. This is *deep soul nurturing*—"

"But—!"

She shushed me again. "Not for you! For me. This is for me. Indulge me, as your friend. I am not gifting you; you are

106

gifting me. It's the gift of trust. Now, gimme."

I couldn't help breaking into a smile, despite the restrictive mask still on most of my face. "OK, fine! Do your worst. But then you'll owe me the same favor down the road." I rubbed my hands together as though I were hatching an evil plot.

"Of course." Ruth leaned over me to remove the mask under my chin, and I dutifully submitted to the rest of her ministrations—I didn't say a word, even when she applied sparkly, plum-colored eyeshadow!

OK, I might have said a curse word.

"For that, I'm doing your hair, too!" Ruth said, her eyes glittering as she snapped the clamp on a curling iron menacingly. "And no peeking until I'm done!"

She spun my chair around so I could no longer see in the mirror and turned on the radio. A Bangles song came on and we both belted out the chorus as she tortured my hair into obedience. The next song was one we recognized, too, and the third one had been the Prom song our senior year.

"Last curl," Ruth finally announced, rolling up the iron near my forehead. "Isn't it funny to think that this music is as old now as the Fifties stuff we listened to on the Oldies station was when we were in high school?"

"Hilarious," I said drily. "I love being an oldie. Can I look now?"

She stepped back to assess her work. "Yes, you look like a princess. Oh! I just had a thought!"

"What? It doesn't involve any more plucking, does it?" I checked myself out in the mirror. My face was hardly recognizable with its freckles hidden under a layer of paint, and my hair was—well, it was glorious. It was a dang golden halo. My grays looked like artful highlights rather than worn edges.

"Nooo." Her eyes danced, and she bit her lip eagerly. "Don't say no, just hear me out! Tambra has all her old beauty pageant stuff stored in the back room. Do me a favor and put on one of her tiaras. It'll be so fun!"

Ruth's idea of fun and mine seemed to be further apart than I remembered, but the look of childlike joy on her face was too pure to refuse. I was already painted and pasted up, so I might as well complete the illusion. I sighed. "I'll wear one if you wear one. As long as you're sure she won't mind."

"No, she'll love it. We'll take pictures for her." Ruth clapped her hands gleefully. She patted her head. "Let me rinse these out and then we can pillage the stash."

I watched, amused, as she leaned over the sink and shampooed her own head. Even wet, the purple streak looked great. Then, a turban towel wrapped around her damp curls, she tugged me into the back room. "This whole rack is hers. Crowns are in boxes up top, and these"—she gestured to the garment bags hanging below the boxes—"are the gowns! You won't believe all the crystals on them. Tambra said that one dress was easily a couple grand when she bought them. Look!" She unzipped a bag to show me one-shoulder red dress covered in Swarovski crystals that looked like a giant glittery lipstick.

"Wow. That's quite a look." I was suddenly glad I was several sizes too wide to squeeze into that sparkly tube, because judging from the look on Ruth's face, she would have tried otherwise.

"I know, it's not my style, either—I'm more of a leather-and-feathers gal—but you have to admit, that's a gorgeous piece of fashion." She zipped it back up and reached for another one.

"Look at this one! It's my favorite. If I were a goddess, this is what I'd wear."

I leaned around her to look at the next dress. A strapless number, it started out purple on the top and gradually transitioned to pale aqua at the hem. Lavender and turquoise chiffon butterflies fluttered all over the huge, tulle skirt. "Try it on!"

Ruth threw her head back and laughed. "Let's just say me and strapless don't get along!"

"Come on! You owe me one, right? I'm calling in my favor! You have to try it!" I pulled the garment bag's hanger off the rack and something clunked inside the voluminous dress.

Ruth winced. "I hope we didn't break anything." She stooped to feel around under the skirt and pulled out an acoustic guitar. As she turned it in her hands, I could see it was decorated within an inch of its life. The back of the guitar was covered with colorful stickers, and the front was hand painted with a colorful, swirling nighttime sky and the silhouette of fir trees.

"I didn't know Tambra was a musician," I said, relieved to see that the instrument didn't seem to be damaged by my careless handling. "Was that her pageant talent?"

"She's not," Ruth said, suddenly subdued. She flipped the guitar so I could see the name carved on the back of the its neck: *Joe.*

Adrenaline jolted through me. This had to be Hobo Joe's guitar...but why did Tambra have it? Ruth and I shared a panicked look.

"What should we do?" I whispered.

"We should put it back!" Ruth straightened and grabbed the hanger from me, placing it back on the rack. She tucked the guitar back under the dress and zipped up the garment bag. "I should have asked before going through her pageant things. I feel bad for invading her privacy."

I followed her out of the back room into the main salon. "That guitar isn't her pageant stuff, though. She was hiding it there!"

Ruth suddenly became very busy cleaning up the remnants of our lavender masks. She gathered up the damp towels and wiped down the chairs, then began rinsing out the bowls in the sink while I stood in the middle of the room, hands on my hips, watching her in disbelief.

"Ruth!"

She turned off the sink water. "What?"

"I know you want to, but we can't ignore it."

"We don't have to get involved," she said stoutly. "It's none of our business."

"The guy who owned that guitar is buried on my farm. The farm you sold to me. The farm where your brother worked for decades! We're *involved*. If we cover up evidence and it comes out, we could get in trouble!" I pleaded.

Ruth crossed her arms. "We don't even know what we're covering up. This is Tambra we're talking about here. She was a child back then—she didn't commit *murder*."

"I seem to remember you thought you were pretty grown when you were seventeen. Anyway, I don't think she killed anyone, either. But I do think she knows more about what happened to Joe twenty years ago than she's letting on. She wouldn't be hiding this guitar inside a pageant dress for no reason. We have to take it to Eli."

"Give me a minute to decide." Ruth fanned herself, took a few deep breaths, then went to the small mirror-topped table

110

filled with crystals, shells, and candles. She lit a yellow candle and stood back, her eyes closed.

"What's that for?"

"Clarity," she murmured. She picked up a stone from the table and rubbed in on the center of her forehead as she hummed a low tone.

This was all getting a little bit weird for me, so I retreated to Tambra's manicure station. Although plenty of my so-called friends in Beverly Hills had practiced wacky rituals like colonics, mushroom smoothies, and injecting fat from their rear ends into their faces, I'd never indulged in New Agey stuff to any degree. In fact, hanging up stockings at Christmas was about as religious and dogmatic as I got. Ruth had always been more inclined to seek spiritual guidance, though, whether from her church youth group when we were kids or the collection of crystals and candles on her salon's makeshift altar now. If that's what she needed to figure this out, so be it.

I only had a few more minutes to wait. After ringing a small gong, Ruth disappeared into the back room. When she rejoined me, she had Joe's guitar in hand and a beatific smile on her face. The candlelit forehead massage had done the trick, apparently.

"We're going to the picnic," she announced, grabbing her purple purse with her free hand. "Tambra can explain why she has the guitar before we throw her to the wolves."

"Eli's not a wolf," I protested, scurrying after her. "He's kind and fair."

"You think so? I guess that explains why you let him stay overnight at your place and then chauffeur you around town." Ruth grinned and handed me the guitar to hold while she locked the salon door behind us.

"How—" I broke off and rolled my eyes at the question I'd been about to ask. Of course Ruth had heard that Eli didn't go home last night; she heard everything. "We're just friends," I said firmly.

"Uh huh." Ruth swiped the guitar from me and laid it gently in the back seat of her car. Something inside the instrument made a dull clunk.

I froze at the sound. The last time something had mysteriously clunked on my watch, it turned out to be a dead guy's foot bones.

Chapter 16

I put my hand out to stop Ruth from closing the car door. "Wait. What was that noise?"

She cocked her head, listening. "I don't hear anything. Was it a freight train whistle?"

"No, the guitar! It made a noise when you set it down. I think it has something inside!"

Ruth slid the guitar back out and shook it gently. Something within the body of the guitar shifted from side to side.

"I told you."

She peered through the strings into the sound hole. "I can't see anything. It's too dark."

I pulled out my phone and turned the flashlight on, aiming it at an angle into the guitar's interior. "Now try."

"Ah, I see something!" She held up the guitar and jostled it gently until a white object showed at the edge of the sound hole, then squeezed her hand under the strings and nabbed it with two fingers. "Got it!"

She pulled out a roll of paper held closed with a blue rubber band and set the guitar down on the back seat again. "What do you think it is?"

"I don't know! Look and see!"

Ruth shook her head and held the paper tube behind her

back, out of my reach. "Let's talk to Tambra first. It could be private."

I wanted to scream with frustration. "Joe's dead, Ruth! He *wants* us to find out who killed him."

"Who says this belonged to Hobo Joe? Just because it's in his guitar doesn't mean he put it there." Ruth set her jaw stubbornly. She wasn't going to budge on this; the strength of her friendship with Tambra clearly outweighed any argument I could make.

I yanked open the car's passenger door and plopped in the seat. "Fine. Let's go."

"See? That wasn't so hard." Ruth tossed the paper roll into the back seat with the guitar and, sliding behind the wheel, started up the car.

It was only a two-minute drive to Honeytree Park, where the picnic was in full swing. Dozens of children swarmed the play equipment while adults mingled near the covered picnic area, chatting and eating corn on the cob. "It looks like everyone in town is here!" I said, my stomach rumbling at the sight of the barbecue buffet on the other side of the park.

Ruth pulled into a parking spot next to Tambra's Prius and nodded. "They are. Look, there's Tambra." She pointed to a picnic table under a tree, where Tambra's long red hair acted like a flag in the summer breeze.

I wasn't surprised to see that Tambra was talking to Eli. I'd assumed that when he left the salon, he'd come over here to the picnic. What was a surprise was their body language. I watched as he threw his head back and laughed uproariously, and Tambra reached out to touch his arm.

Ruth's eyes darted to me. "He's probably questioning her about Joe, following up on the lead you gave him."

"That doesn't look like an interrogation," I muttered. Why was anger fluttering under my skin? I had no reason to be angry at either of them. It wasn't anger, I quickly realized—it was jealousy. Stupid, petty jealousy.

I rolled my eyes; I had nothing to be jealous about. I must have absorbed Ruth's insinuation that Eli and I had something going on. Just because we dated forty years ago didn't make us an item, and I had no claim on his attention—thank goodness. I didn't want it anyway. I pushed open the car door and got out, and Ruth quickly followed.

When I reached for the door to the back seat to retrieve the guitar, she rushed to stop me. "Wait. Leave it in the car. If we flash that thing around the park, people will recognize it, and that means everyone will have questions. I want to talk to her before we turn it over to Eli, in case there's an innocent explanation for why she hid it inside her goddess dress."

I nodded, understanding fully the desire to avoid attracting the interest of Honeytree's citizens. I didn't even like the idea of parading my painted-and-curled self across the park, let alone showing off evidence in a murder investigation. It was better to stay under the radar for as long as possible.

Ruth put her hands to her mouth. "Tambra!" she shouted.

All heads swiveled toward us.

"Subtle," I said darkly. Ruth shrugged, unapologetic, and waved across the park at Tambra.

Tambra spotted us and waved back, leaving Eli's side to jog toward us. For a moment I was transported into the *Baywatch* intro, as Tambra's stride lengthened and she seemed to run in slow motion, her hair whipping back and forth. Half the adults in the park were in thrall watching her lithe movements—you can probably guess which half.

Tambra slowed as she reached us, slightly out of breath. "Well, shoot, you two look straight out of a magazine. I like the purple on you, Ruth. What's going on? Playing dress-up at the salon?"

Ruth shared a look with me. "Sort of. Get in the car."

Tambra checked on the playground over her shoulder where I assumed her kids were playing and then slid into the back. The second her cheeks hit the seat and she saw the guitar, she gasped. Ruth closed the door on her and, with another grim look at me, went around to the other side and got in. I took the front passenger side, leaning to see them both through the gap between the front seats.

"I didn't think anyone would look there," Tambra said quietly, running her fingers over the guitar's frets. She gently plucked one string and the sound thrummed through the car.

"We were just going to try on some of your pageant stuff. We didn't mean to pry. I'm sorry, hon." Ruth bit her lip.

I couldn't understand why she was dancing around the topic. "Listen, we need to know why you have it."

"Did Joe give it to you?" Ruth added, leaning toward Tambra in the back seat. I'd watched enough cop TV shows to know she was leading the witness. She must have sensed my disgust because she added. "What?! They were friends!"

Tambra twisted her hands, and tears, dark with mascara, began to leak down her face as she ducked her head. "Actually, I stole it from him." She scrubbed her cheeks, smearing her makeup so I could see that she did indeed have freckles like mine underneath the heavy layers of concealer and foundation.

"You stole the guitar from Joe?" Ruth's forehead furrowed. "Why'd you do that?"

116

"So he'd come get it back! But he didn't." Tambra's face crumpled again. "He didn't come. I should have known something bad had happened!"

Ruth rummaged in her purse and produced a pack of tissues that she handed to Tambra. "I don't understand, honey. Can you explain?"

Tambra dabbed her eyes and nose with the tissues. "I had a terrible crush on Joe. He wrote the most beautiful love songs and sang them when we all sat around the bonfire." She reached out and caressed the guitar again. "I was *sure* they were for me. I mean, I was *sure*. They were about how we couldn't be together, but he'd love me from a distance. He even looked at me when he sang, sometimes."

"It's understandable why you'd be smitten by that," Ruth murmured, nodding. "Did he know how you felt?"

Tambra lifted her head. "Oh, he knew. I confronted him one night and laid it all out there. I said I knew he'd written the songs for me and that I shared his feelings. I said I wanted to be with him. It sounds stupid now, but you have to remember I was seventeen. All I wanted was to be in love."

I swallowed, remembering my own seventeen-year-old dream—to leave my dumpy hometown behind and live a glamorous life in the big city. Look where that got me. "Be careful what you wish for, I guess," I said.

Tambra nodded. "Turned out he didn't feel the same way. I was fifteen years younger than him. He thought of me as a little sister. The songs weren't for me. He was so nice about it." A hiccupping little sob erupted from her throat and she smiled through her tears as she dabbed them away. "I was devastated, but he put his arm around me right there by the fire and just held me until I stopped crying. And then he thanked me."

"For loving him?" Ruth asked, her hand pressed to her chest and her eyes shiny with emotion.

"No, for telling him about it. He said my confession made him realize that he needed to tell the woman he loved about his true feelings. He was about to go see her when Rusty interrupted us. Joe set down the guitar next to me and went off to argue with him in private, and I saw my chance—I took it and left the bonfire."

"You thought he'd come after you to get it back," I said.

She nodded, chewing on her lower lip until her lilac lip gloss was nearly gone. "I told you, I was young and dumb. I wanted another shot to convince him that we were meant to be together before he told this other woman about his feelings. You know, because he couldn't sing to her without his guitar. I thought for sure he'd know I had it and show up on my doorstep looking for it." Tambra balled up the tissue in her fist and pain flashed across her face. "But he didn't. I never saw him again."

Ruth grabbed Tambra's other hand and squeezed. "I'm sorry, honey. That must have stung when he didn't come."

"I'm just mad I didn't make a fuss when he disappeared, you know? I *knew* he wouldn't leave town without that guitar. I knew it! Even *if* he went to the woman he loved without his guitar, he wouldn't take off without trying to get it back. And he had to know I was the one who took it because it was sitting right next to me at the bonfire. He'd at least come ask me about it, right?"

I couldn't imagine the guilt and grief that must have been running through Tambra's veins since Joe's skeleton was discovered. "You were just a kid. All these grownups were convinced he hopped a train, and there's no way you could have changed their minds. You couldn't have done anything."

"I could have told them about the guitar," she said quietly, her gaze locked on the crumpled tissue in her hand. "Maybe if I'd said something about the guitar, they would have believed me."

"Or maybe not," Ruth said. "Grown ups are pretty hard-headed sometimes. Don't beat yourself up about it."

Tambra sighed as she absentmindedly shredded the tissue. "I just wish I'd done more."

"Why *didn't* you tell anyone about the guitar?" I asked. Ruth shot me a look that said *shut your pie hole, Leona.*

Tambra shook her head. "It's OK, Ruth. It's a fair question. I didn't want to get in trouble for stealing it, so I didn't tell a soul. That guitar's been under my bed for the last twenty years—at least, until they pulled that guitar case out of the ground. Then I realized it could tie me to a murder, so I moved the guitar to the salon just until I could figure out what to do with it. I'm sorry, Ruth. I didn't mean to get you involved in anything, I just panicked."

"You have to give the guitar to Eli now," I said.

At my suggestion, Tambra's nostrils flared and her jaw tightened. "What if he thinks I had something to do with Joe's death? I can't think how the guitar will help them. I took it before Joe was killed, so it's not related to the murder."

"Maybe it will make you feel a little better to get rid of it," Ruth said gently. "Cleanse your aura of all that guilt you're feeling."

Tambra shook her head vehemently. "No...no. I already told Eli everything I remember about that night. I left out the guitar, but he knows everything else. The guitar is just a distraction—if I turn it over, Eli will tear apart my life, and you know I won't be able to put it back together again, not if everyone knows about it."

She was right—at least about how the stain of being a suspect in the investigation would stick to her forever in a town like Honeytree. I could picture the conversation now:

Where'd you get your nails done?

Oh, Tambra down at the Do or Dye—she's real good.

Is that the girl who killed the train-hopper who played the guitar? I heard that she and him had plans to run off, and when he changed his mind, she murdered him.

I don't know about that, but she sure can murder a manicure!

Tambra gnawed off the last of her lip gloss before she replied. "The cops shouldn't be looking at me. They should be looking at whoever Joe was in love with. She was probably the last person to see him alive."

"Did Joe tell you her name?" I asked.

Tambra shook her head. "No. And honestly, I was half convinced he just made her up to let me down easy. That's part of why I thought that taking the guitar would work. I was young and dumb, but I wasn't completely stupid." She cracked a rueful smile.

"Well, we're not here to make you do anything," Ruth said comfortingly, patting Tambra's hand before she released it.

"Yes, we are!" I blurted out. "That's why we brought the guitar with us—to turn it in. Even if it doesn't help with finding the killer, maybe it will help them identify Joe. I'm sure his family has been missing him all these years and would like to have it back."

Tambra's eyes welled with fresh tears, and Ruth scowled at me. "What good is dragging her through the mud, Leona? The poor thing has been through enough! Why don't we just say we found it at the salon, but we don't know who put it there? That way it can get back to Joe's family without causing problems."

"Why would Joe's guitar be in the salon?" I asked, incredulous, feeling the heat rise in my face. "Eli will see right through that—it'll either be on *you*, the person who owned the farm where the body was buried, or on Tambra, anyway. This isn't about dragging anyone through the mud, it's about doing what's right. Any time we're not doing what's right, we're doing what's wrong."

"Hm." Ruth sat back and stared straight ahead while she thought, and I rubbed my neck where a crick was developing from twisting to see them in the back seat.

"What's this?" Tambra leaned to pick up the roll of white paper from the floor of the car. I'd forgotten all about it in the excitement over the guitar.

"That's not yours?" Ruth asked. "We found it inside the guitar."

Tambra shook her head and I shot Ruth a triumphant look. I'd been right—they *were* Joe's papers. "See? All the more important that we turn the guitar in."

Tambra snapped off the rubber band and unrolled the papers. Her eyes widened as she looked at them. "It's music. It's his songs! I can't believe these were inside the guitar for so long."

She riffled through the pages incredulously and then turned them toward me so I could see more than the blank backside of each page. Sure enough, it was music, of a kind—scribbled lyrics with chord notations. Printed in pencil at the top of the first page in block letters was the title of the first song: "FOR ANNE."

A jolt ran through me. I pointed at the title. "Do you think that could be Anne Sutherland? Joe did a lot of work over at their place, didn't he?"

Ruth's jaw dropped. "No. Surely not. Anne's married."

"Since when did that ever stop anyone?" I asked. "It didn't stop my husband, that's for sure."

"Mine either," Tambra added as she scanned the pages. "Plus look at these lyrics—they're all about her quiet beauty and how the world was trying to keep them apart. It has to be her." She looked up from the papers and gave humorless laugh. "God, how did I think 'quiet beauty' was about me, with my sparkles and screaming-red hair? I really was deluded."

Ruth giggled. "Well, quiet beauty wouldn't have won you all those pageant crowns, would it?"

Tambra didn't laugh. "It might have won me Joe's heart."

Ruth's face fell. "Oh, Tambra. I didn't mean to be insensitive. I was trying to lighten the mood."

Tambra nodded. "It's fine, I just—" She broke off, startled, at the sound of a knock on the car window.

Chapter 17

I turned, my heart pounding until I saw it was just Eli grinning through the glass. I really do hate surprises. I frowned at him as I rolled down the window.

"Wow," he said, staring at me. "You look...different."

Just what a girl wants to hear after a two-hour makeover. *Different.* "What do you want?"

"Just letting Tambra know her little one scraped his knee on the teeter-totter, but I patched him up. In case she's curious where that Paw Patrol band-aid came from." His grin faded as he took in the three of us: me with a scowl, Ruth anxiously plucking at Tambra's arm, and Tambra clutching her damp tissue and staring at him with red-rimmed eyes. "Did I scare you? I didn't mean to sneak up on you."

"No," I snapped. "Although a little warning would have been nice. We were coming to see you anyway. We have evidence that might help in your investigation." Ignoring the two women in the back seat, I forged ahead. "I found Joe's guitar hidden in the barn. And it has something inside it that you might find interesting."

I heard Ruth's sharp intake of breath at my lie. I hadn't planned to lie to Eli, but in the moment I couldn't expose Tambra to any more trauma. Eli would have what he needed.

I just hoped he wouldn't ask when I'd found the instrument or how I'd smuggled it to town without him knowing about it. I got out of the car and waited until Tambra opened the back and handed me the guitar and the roll of papers.

"I dropped the rubber band on the floor, I think," she said, her voice apologetic as she leaned down to search for it.

I gave the guitar to Eli and waved the roll of papers. "These were inside the guitar. It's his guitar tabs and lyrics—you'll be interested to know he wrote his love songs to Anne Sutherland."

Eli's eyes widened as he took them from me. "Wait—Joe was in love with *Anne*?!"

"I think so. He spent a lot of time at their place, remember? She's no beauty queen"—I glanced at Tambra, who was still feeling around for the blue rubber band—"but she has her own appeal."

"When Anne serves her blueberry pie, I think any man could fall in love." Despite the joke, Eli's face was grim. "I think you ladies just may have cracked this case."

Ruth looked aghast. "What? You think Anne clobbered him with her cast-iron skillet or something? There's no way!"

"Eli doesn't mean Anne," I said, realization dawning. "He means Walt. If Joe confessed his love for Anne, Walt would never let him walk out of that house alive. Think about how he treats her. It's like she's his property! When she came over the other day to drop off that cobbler, she said Walt was watching her. I think that's what the telescope is all about. It's not about watching the neighbors, it's about watching his wife. Maybe that's why Joe stole it to begin with—to keep Walt from spying on Anne all the time!"

"Could very well be," Eli said. "I might have done the same

in Joe's shoes if I'd heard Walt talking about her the way he was this morning. I need to get over to the Sutherland place right now."

I nodded. "I'm coming with you."

He shook his head vehemently, backing away from Ruth's car. "No way. This could be dangerous."

"You have to give me a ride," I said, smirking at him. "You drove me to town, remember?"

#

"Stay in the car," Eli said as his SUV rolled to a stop in front of the Sutherlands' white farmhouse.

I rolled my eyes at him and got out anyway. He jogged around the car and caught my arm just as I reached the porch steps.

"I mean it, Leona! This is law enforcement business now, not just a friendly visit. You either wait in the car or walk home." He set his jaw and I could tell he wasn't making a suggestion, but Eli wasn't the only one who could dig in his heels. I was just about to make a smart remark when a meek voice drifted across the porch.

"Is he hurting you?"

When I turned toward the sound, I could see Anne's faint, grayed shape through the screen door. Eli instantly dropped his arm to his side and I shook my head. "No, everything's fine. We were just talking."

"Leona was just *leaving*," Eli added pointedly.

The screen door creaked open, revealing Anne in an apron that was covered with dark red splatters. Her rubber gloves were red, too, and she held them up like she was a doctor going into surgery. She held the door open with one leg as she eyed us appraisingly. After a moment, she seemed to decide that

I was telling the truth that Eli wasn't a threat to me. "Well, if you're looking for Walt, he's out in the shed. I'm up to my elbows processing the end-of-season berries for jelly."

"I'd like to speak to you first, if that's all right," Eli said, and I realized he was clutching Joe's sheet music in his other hand. "May I come inside?"

Anne's eyes darted nervously to the shed and then back to us. "I guess he won't mind if Leona's here, too."

I shot Eli a triumphant look over my shoulder as I headed up the steps and into Anne's kitchen. It was a homely place with worn linoleum on the floor and butcher block countertops. Crocheted potholders hung on the wall near the harvest-gold stove, where a large pot of something delicious-smelling was bubbling alongside a canner. The white cabinets had likely been there since the farmhouse was built, but they were as spotless as if they were new. A drop-leaf table with two chairs—the antique version of a kitchen island—stood in the center of the room, and behind it, bookshelves packed with cookbooks and paperback novels lined the walls.

Anne snapped off her gloves and threw them in the sink, then took off her berry-stained apron and motioned for us to take the two chairs. "Coffee? I know it's almost supper, but I can make a pot. I'd offer you a slice of pie, but it's still got another twenty minutes in the oven."

"Don't trouble yourself. We'll only be a minute." Eli took a seat, spreading the papers Ruth and I'd found inside the guitar out on the table in front of him. "Have you seen these before?"

Anne peered over his shoulder at the scribbled lyrics and her face paled even more than usual. Her hand went to her neck and she nervously flipped her locket over and over in her fingers.

126

"I'll take that as a yes," Eli said gravely.

Anne sank onto the stepstool nearby and passed her hand over her face. "No. I've never even heard them. He told me he wrote songs for me, though."

"Joe did?" I prompted, taking the chair nearest her.

She nodded. "He was nice, very friendly and hardworking. I was so surprised when I found out he took Walt's telescope. He didn't seem like the type—but then again, I had no idea that he had feelings for me, either. Maybe I'm a poor judge of character."

Her eyes flickered to the front door, and I wondered if she was thinking about her husband in the blueberry shed. She had to regret marrying someone so controlling and unkind, but perhaps Walt hadn't always been that way. I never could have predicted how Peterson would treat me twenty years down the line when we were college sweethearts. Of course, he'd say it was my fault—that if I'd taken care of myself, his feelings wouldn't have changed.

"You can't blame yourself. Joe was a man with many secrets," Eli said gently. "Can you walk me through that night? The night he told you how he felt?"

Anne's forehead furrowed. "It was so long ago."

"Just do your best." Eli put his phone on the table. "Is it OK if I record this?"

"I guess so," she said hesitantly, and Eli tapped a button on the screen. Anne took a deep breath. "I was making fruit-of-the-forest pie, I remember that. The apple harvest was in, and I had blueberries in the cooler and rhubarb canned from the spring. I was on my second batch of pies so it must have been after eleven o'clock at night when Joe knocked on the door."

"Was Walt home?" Eli asked.

She shook her head. "He was gone playing poker—his weekly game in Duma. Sometimes they play all night. I was alone."

"Who does he play with?"

"Mike Spence and his brother and some of their friends. They've had a game running for as long as I've been alive." Anne smiled faintly. "Walt has a real weakness for cards."

"So Joe came over," I said. "And you let him in because Walt wasn't home."

Anne nodded, and she shot another guilty look at the door. "He said he just wanted to talk, but he was so anxious. I thought maybe he was coming to confess to stealing, so I gave him a piece of warm pie and a beer to settle his nerves. I told him he could tell me anything. Well—"

"Be careful what you wish for," I said wryly. That was becoming the theme of the day. Maybe the theme of my life.

Anne nodded. "He took that as a sign that I felt the same way he did and spilled his guts. He said he knew from the first time he saw me that we were meant to be together. Then he asked me to run away with him." Her forehead creased and her hand fluttered to her locket again, tugging and twisting so hard that I thought she might break the chain. "He said he thought he could be patient and wait for me to end things with Walt, but he couldn't wait anymore. It had to be that night. I wanted to know why the rush, but he wouldn't explain it. Just said we were meant to be, and we had to go."

"Rusty was about to turn him in for stealing," I explained.

Anne looked up, her mouth a small "O" of surprise. "Rusty Chapman told him to come see me?"

I shook my head. "No, Joe came up with that on his own. Rusty just told Joe to leave town when he found out Joe had stolen from Walt. He knew his grandfather wouldn't tolerate a thief on his farm. That's why Joe came to see you—it was his last chance to tell you how he felt before he hit the road again."

Eli cleared his throat delicately, trying to steer the conversation back on track. "Joe confessed his feelings. You told him you didn't share those feelings. And then?"

"That's not what happened. I didn't have a chance to tell him anything." Anne shifted uncomfortably on her perch. "Joe didn't let me get a word in edgewise before he swooped in and kissed me! I just froze; I didn't know what to do." Blotchy pink patches rose in her cheeks as she stared at the floor to avoid looking at either of our faces.

"You did nothing wrong," I said reassuringly.

Anne looked up at me. "I did, though. I let him in, and I never should have. That's what Walt said, anyway. He said when you open a door, you get what you ask for. He chased Joe right out of here."

I whipped my head toward Eli to see if he'd heard what I heard. By his grim look, he had. "I'm sorry, I think I misheard you. You said Walt chased him out? But earlier you said Walt was playing poker with Mike Spence."

Anne pushed her stool back and went to the window to look out toward the blueberry shed. With her back to us, she said, "I was getting to that part—Walt came home while Joe was here. He'd blown his bankroll in the first half of the night and he wasn't ready to quit, so he came back to raid the sock drawer. He walked into the kitchen right when Joe planted one on me."

My guts twisted as I imagined Walt's face when he saw another man kissing Anne, and Anne doing nothing about it.

"He must have been furious."

She turned back toward us, her hands still on the sink edge, and nodded. "I thought Walt was going to kill him…" Her voice trailed off as she caught a glimpse of Eli's intent expression and seemed to remember who she was talking to. "Of course, he never would. He grabbed my kitchen knife and chased Joe outside."

"Then what?" I asked, leaning forward in my seat.

Anne shrugged. "Then Walt came in, gave me grief, got his money, and went back to his poker game."

"He didn't have any blood on him?" Eli asked. "Or on the knife?"

Anne shook her head. "I don't think Walt even left the porch. He just stood at the rail and yelled the most hateful things you've ever heard. And no, I won't repeat them." Anne glared at Eli's phone on the table, her voice the firmest it'd been during the whole conversation.

"And you never saw Joe again after that?"

Anne shook her head again. "No. Now, if you don't mind, I need to make the cornbread—Walt hates it when I forget the cornbread." She went to the cupboard and began pulling out ingredients—more ingredients than she needed to make cornbread, but I could tell she was flustered and emotional after recalling that traumatic night so long ago.

"I appreciate your help, Anne." Eli hit the pause button on his phone, then pushed back his chair and stood. I followed, and as soon as we were outside, he said in a low, urgent voice, "OK, now will you please listen to me this time? Go home. Right now. Cut straight across the field, hop the fence, and tell Blake or whoever's supervising that I need backup over here." The whole time he was talking, his eyes were trained

130

on the door of the blueberry shed.

"Are you going to arrest Walt for Joe's murder?" I asked.

He gave a terse nod. "Go get Blake," he said again, still watching the shed like a hawk. "Tell him to come in quiet. Go!"

I went. I'll admit it now—I hadn't been running in a good decade. I tried jogging back in my midforties, on the safety of my posh gym's treadmill, but I never enjoyed it. When the yearlong gym membership—another one of Peterson's birthday-gift fails—expired, I didn't renew it. Now, as I bumbled over the rocks and molehills in the blueberry rows, my thighs jiggling with every impact of my foot on the ground, my purse bouncing against my hip, and one arm across my chest to keep the girls from hitting me in the face, I regretted not sticking with the exercise. I could only be grateful that Eli was too busy watching the blueberry shed to catch a rear view.

The forensics crew saw me coming and one of them had the decency to hold the barbed-wire fence apart so I could shimmy through. Thank the lord I wore jeans and not leggings that could get snagged on the wire.

"Where's the fire?" one of them joked as I leaned forward with my hands braced on my thighs to catch my breath.

As soon as I had gulped enough air to form the words, I said, "Eli needs backup. He's going to arrest Walt for the murder. He said come in quiet, whatever that means."

The team shared a look of concern before Blake directed two deputies to take a car around while he and the remaining man, the one who'd held the fence for me, went back through the fence into the field. I didn't fully relax until I lost sight of them in the already-reddening leaves of the blueberry bushes.

The sweat on my forehead dried in the cool afternoon breeze, and I pondered what to do while the drama was going down next door. I'd go over and see Anne once Walt was hauled off to jail, of course, but until then, it was none of my business. I might as well finish clearing out the space for the chicks—who'd be arriving in less than twelve hours, I realized with a jolt.

I picked up the pace toward the barn but stopped in my tracks when I heard shouts echo down the hill from the Sutherland farmhouse. It didn't sound like regular cop shouting, confident and direct. It sounded like panic.

Chapter 18

My phone buzzed insistently inside my purse, and I automatically pulled it out to check the caller even though I was already on my way back through the fence. It was a text from Eli.

Stay put.

I froze, one leg in the blueberry field and the other one in my front yard, trying not to give myself a barbed-wire wedgie. Then my phone rang. It was Ruth.

"Eli says to stay put," she said breathlessly when I answered.

"What?"

"He called me and told me to call you and tell you to stay put. He said you probably wouldn't listen to him, but you'd listen to me."

With the phone pressed to my ear, I grunted the rest of the way through the fence, snagging my purse strap on the fence. After extricating it from the wire's greedy grasp, I moved along the row of blueberry shrubs, the Sutherlands' farmhouse grew larger in front of me and the deputies' shouts grew clearer.

"Call dispatch. We need forensics!" I heard Eli shout.

"We *are* forensics," Blake yelled back.

"Call anyway. We need the spatter guys!"

"What's going on?" Ruth said in my ear. I pushed aside

a blueberry branch so it wouldn't whip me in the face and peered at the scene in the Sutherlands' driveway. Eli stood in the doorway of the shed, his back to me as he looked inside. His head hung low and his shoulders slumped. What had he found inside?

When I didn't immediately answer her, Ruth sighed. "You didn't stay put, did you?"

I scoffed. "Of course not. If Eli thinks I shouldn't be here, that means I definitely should. He probably knows that, too—by telling me to stay put, he basically guaranteed that I wouldn't."

"Let me guess. If he told you to come over, you'd have stayed home?"

"Yep." I scooted to the next row and stood on tiptoe to see if I could get a better view inside the shed, but the interior was too dark for me to make out any detail, especially with Eli standing in the way. Suddenly, he turned around and I ducked behind a bush to avoid being spotted by him, but I was too slow. He frowned and started jogging toward me, and I braced myself for a sheriff-quality scolding. "Listen, Ruth—I should go."

"Call me later with an update! I—"

When Eli reached me, I panicked and hung up before Ruth could finish her sentence. He eyed the phone in my hand. "Didn't Ruth tell you to stay put? Those were my exact words."

"Yeah, but you know I'm not a very good listener. Plus, I deserve to know what's going on in my backyard. Did you find another skeleton in the shed or something?"

Eli shook his head, his jaw set. "We found Walt."

"Isn't that who you were looking…" I trailed off as I realized that what he was leaving out was more important that what

he'd said. He'd shouted for the forensics team, which meant...
I gasped. "Walt's dead?"

Eli gave a single nod. "He is."

My stomach sank. "Oh no—poor Anne!"

"I know, it's not a good day for her. I called her family to
come be with her, but they're not here yet. Since you're here
anyway, would you go in and sit with her?"

I nodded. "What happened to Walt? Was it some kind of
accident?"

"We're not exactly sure yet, but one thing's for certain—he
didn't die of natural causes. It's bad, Leona. Really bad."

"Do you think he somehow figured out that he was a suspect
and...you know, ended things?"

Eli closed his eyes momentarily and took a deep breath,
letting it out slowly. At first I thought he was upset with me
for asking, but then I realized that he was just calming his own
nerves. I hadn't even known Eli Ramirez *had* nerves. He was
always the type who laughed at ghost stories and jumped off
bridges into icy water for fun. Plus, any boy who could ride
in the passenger seat of my car when I was a teenage driver
had to have nerves of steel.

A few long moments later, he opened his eyes and looked at
me with a frank expression on his face. "I wish I could tell you
more, but honestly? You don't want to know. Trust me when
I say that nobody should have to carry the image of what's
inside that shed. I can tell you that Walt Sutherland definitely
did *not* do that to himself. Someone else did."

My eyes flickered toward the blueberry shed, where Blake
was setting up a perimeter of police tape and another member
of his team was donning a protective suit. Fifteen minutes
ago, I'd been certain that Walt was the only killer living in

Honeytree, Oregon, but clearly I'd been wrong. Someone was still killing here—brutally killing, if Eli's shaken demeanor was any indication.

"Do you think this is about Joe? Revenge for his murder, maybe?" I asked in a quiet voice.

Eli gave a tiny, helpless shrug. "Maybe. Or it could be unrelated. Anne said he's a gambler, right? Maybe he has debts. Maybe he ticked off the wrong cowboy. Nothing is clear. Well, not nothing. It's pretty clear that whoever killed Walt hated him. I mean, really hated him."

I swallowed. As much as curiosity pulled me toward the black maw of the open shed door, on this rare occasion, I wasn't feeling rebellious. "I'd better go see how Anne's doing."

Eli gave a shake of his head, like he was trying to wake from a bad dream. "Good. Good. And hey, Leona?"

"What?"

"Watch your back, OK?"

I nodded, my spine prickling at the warning as I made my way to Anne's front door.

Inside, the sweet scent of cornbread baking permeated the air. I found Anne pacing restlessly around the kitchen table, her hand over her mouth and her face drained of color. I had no idea what to say to her, so I went to the stove where the canner and a pot of soup were still simmering, a pie cooling on the counter nearby, and turned off the gas so the soup wouldn't scorch on the bottom. I refilled the empty kettle on the back burner in case Anne's relatives might want tea when they arrived; I could tell by looking that Anne didn't. She looked...broken.

"I'm so sorry about Walt," I murmured, for lack of anything better to say.

She stopped pacing abruptly and looked at me, her eyes narrowed to fierce slits. "I know I should be sad. But I'm not! I'm glad he's dead. I don't care if that makes me a terrible person."

Wow. I was not expecting that from meek, mousey Anne. "Um, I mean—I'm not here to tell you how to feel. You might want to phrase it a little differently for when you talk to Eli, though."

"No!" Anne smacked her hand down on the tabletop. "I am done phrasing things for other people's benefit. I'm glad he's dead, I'm glad he's dead, I'm glad he's dead. He's made my life miserable for the last thirty years, and I'm glad he can't do that anymore."

With a jolt, I recognized myself in her words. "You know what? You're right. He can't hurt you anymore." I pulled out a chair and sat down, patting across the table for her to join me. "You're free, and you're allowed to be happy about that."

Anne met my eyes for the first time as she sank into the chair opposite mine and grasped my hands in hers. "Did your husband hurt you, too? Is that why you moved back here?"

"He didn't leave bruises." I nodded to the blue bloom on the side of Anne's neck. "Not like those."

Anne brushed her hand lightly across the dark marks on her neck. "The physical pain isn't the worst part, is it?"

"No."

We sat together in silence for a few minutes, holding hands, watching out the darkening window as the lights from arriving sheriff's vehicles flicked in and out, red and blue, like neon bruises, until the kettle squealed. Anne rose to take it off the heat. She paused at the stove. "How would you like some pie?"

I grinned at her. "You know what? I skipped lunch, so I'd

like it a lot."

She set two plates of pie and two forks on the table and slid back into her seat. "Want to hear the worst thing Walt ever did?"

I nodded and let the first forkful of flaky crust melt on my tongue.

"He once bet a whole blueberry harvest on a hand of poker, and he lost."

"Bastard," I said with my mouth full.

One corner of her lips quirked upward. "That's not even the worst part. When the bills came due, he pawned all my jewelry to pay them. My wedding ring, my grandmother's locket, all of it. Like it didn't even matter." She touched her necklace and I noticed for the first time that she wasn't wearing a ring. It wasn't so unusual for married people to eschew wedding rings around here—they were expensive, for one thing, and they could be dangerous for those who worked with their hands. But Anne must have treasured hers, by the look on her face.

"I wanted to kill him for that"—her expression turned guilty—"but I didn't, obviously. That had to be twenty years ago."

"I'm glad you got your locket back, at least. I can tell it's important to you."

Anne's expression flickered. Surprise, wariness? My words had elicited some reaction, some memory. I couldn't tell what was going through her mind, but I could tell there was more story there. Her face settled into pale, smooth calm. "I'm glad, too." She pointed her fork at me. "Your turn. What's the worst thing yours did?"

I barked a laugh. "I can only pick one?"

She nodded and, through a mouthful of pie, said, "There

are things we can live with and things we can't. What was the moment when you knew it was all over? Was it the TV thing?"

I stiffened with surprise, although I don't know why I'd assumed Anne hadn't seen the clip. The whole world had seen it live on the *America Today* show. Then the video clip had gone viral, with over twenty-seven million views the last time I checked. I'd be surprised if anyone in Honeytree *hadn't* seen it. But so far, everyone had the decency to pretend the whole thing hadn't happened, so it was a shock to hear Anne mention it.

Anne winced at my expression. "You don't have to answer; I was just hoping for a distraction so I don't have to think about Walt out there. I'm so sorry."

Here I was, sitting across from a woman whose husband's murdered corpse was probably still warm in the shed, and she was apologizing to me for bringing up painful memories. "No, it's fine. I wish it was the TV thing. I should have walked off the soundstage the minute he brought out those photos of me in my underwear and carved them up with his Sharpie. I was just completely blindsided."

Anne gasped. "You didn't know?! I thought you must have had some inkling or you wouldn't have gone on the program."

"I had none." Peterson was there at *America Today* promoting his new reality TV show called *Then to Ten* that would document a woman through a yearlong plastic surgery makeover. I was along for the ride to play the part of supportive spouse—or so I thought. But the joke was on me; I was the first subject of his program. I was the walking, talking "before." The humiliated look on my face when Peterson showed those images is why the *America Today* video went viral, but that wasn't even the worst part.

139

"It was what he said backstage afterward that clinched it. That's when I knew that our marriage was over."

Anne leaned forward, her eyes widening. "What'd he say?"

"Well, at first I told him I wasn't going to do it. He was the one who wanted to be famous, not me. I had no interest in changing my appearance or in having cameras follow me 24/7 for an entire year. I told him to get another subject—one who *wanted* a makeover. One who didn't mind giving up her privacy. We lived in LA, for goodness sake, where there are a hundred thousand women who would jump at the opportunity!"

"I take it he didn't apologize." Anne looked at me with sympathy and clucked her tongue. "They never do."

I chuckled humorlessly. "Nope. He told me I was sabotaging his career with my quote-unquote 'willful indifference about my appearance.' He said nobody would hire a plastic surgeon whose wife looked like me. He said I was his best advertisement, and if I wouldn't play along, he wouldn't either. Our marriage would be over if I didn't go under the knife."

"No wonder you walked away." Anne crossed her arms over her apron. "I hope you took him for all he was worth."

"Nope. Pre-nup. Signed it when I was young and dumb and believed in true love."

"Sorry, Leona."

There she was, apologizing to me again. I'd meant to distract her from her own pain, not garner her sympathy. I forced a smile. "Don't be. If Peterson wasn't such a motherclucker, I'd have been stuck eating mediocre blueberry pie at hipster restaurants in LA forever!" I made a big show of shoveling a few bites into my mouth and was gratified to hear her chuckle.

I heard footsteps and muffled voices on the porch outside,

and Anne's face grew serious again when someone rapped gently at the door. I rose and took our empty plates to the sink, hiding the evidence of our enjoyment; for some reason I felt guilty about eating the pie, like we'd been sneaking dessert while the grownups weren't looking. Anne smoothed her dress and folded her hands in her lap.

"Ready?" I asked, and she nodded silently. I crossed the kitchen, conscious of my sneakers squeaking on the linoleum, and cracked open the door.

Eli's dark eyes met mine as he leaned into the doorframe. "Her family's here," he said, his voice low. "How's she doing?"

"Holding up." I opened the door wide and saw a few people with Anne's same wide pale face huddled like pigeons behind Eli. "Come on in. There's soup on the range, cornbread in the oven, hot water in the kettle, and pie on the counter."

Chapter 19

I woke in the early hours when it was still dark, not to the sound of Alarm Clock's crow, but to the sound of my phone ringing. I scrabbled it from the nightstand and held it to my ear.

"What is it?" I asked groggily. I hadn't gotten to bed until nearly midnight, and my eyes were still glued shut with sleep. "Who is this? Is everything OK?"

"Leona Davis?" A woman's voice I didn't recognize was on the line. "This is Stef at the post office. Your chicks are in. Can you be here in a half-hour?"

I sat up too fast and my head spun. I'd totally forgotten about the chicks in all the chaos after Walt's body was found. I hadn't even finished setting up the brooder in the barn. Heck, I was still wearing my "Hens Before Mens" shirt; I'd only bothered to take off my shoes and jeans before I collapsed into bed last night. My mother would be horrified that I'd slept in my street clothes, especially street clothes that had been worn while cleaning out a dusty old barn.

"Yeah, I'll be there. Just hold your nose when you hand over the box—I can't remember the last time I showered."

Stef snickered. "Will do. Come around the back of the building to the loading dock. The front door's locked for a few more hours."

"Gotcha. Thanks." I'd already pulled on one leg of a clean pair of cargo pants and, after I hung up the phone and dropped it on the bed, put them the rest of the way on and pulled a clean T-shirt over my head. This one was pink and said "World's Best Nana" in curly lavender script, a Mother's Day gift from my twin grandchildren, Isabella-Sophia and John-William, who lived in Chicago.

Well, actually, it was from my daughter Andrea. Isabella-Sophia and John-William were only two years old and hadn't yet mastered the art of ordering stuff from Amazon. I was pretty sure that I wasn't the world's best nana anyway, given that I'd only seen my grandkids once in their lives, back when they were still little pink-and-blue burritos. Andrea's fancy heart-surgeon husband moved in Chicago's "elite circles" and the children were already enrolled in a prestigious preschool that cost, if it can be believed, as much as Andrea's tuition at Northwestern had. The little darlings wore their little uniforms and never visited their grandparents because they couldn't miss a day for fear of falling behind their privileged classmates. As you can imagine, Peterson was very proud. I just missed them.

When the divorce papers were filed, I offered to move to Chicago to help out with the twins, but Andrea said no. The T-shirt was a consolation prize, I think. That said, it was very nice, thick and soft. Perfect for getting some work done around the farm. I thumped down the stairs two at a time, jammed my feet into my sneakers and a blueberry muffin into my mouth, grabbed my keys and purse from the hook by the door, and barreled out to the Suburban.

I skidded to a stop when I saw the black SUV parked behind

my car, "Douglas County Sheriff" glinting on the side in gold letters. Eli's head lolled back in the driver's seat. As I drew closer, I saw a string of drool trailing out of his mouth as he slept. He'd clearly been here all night—*again*.

I rapped on the window. He jerked awake, looking around with a panicked expression until his eyes lit on me and a smile spread lazily across his face. He motioned for me to step back and then opened the door, stretching as he got out into the chilly morning air.

"You surprised me."

"You need to move your rig," I said, motioning behind him. "I can't get out."

His face grew serious. "That's the plan. I don't want you going anywhere without me today. Not with a killer operating in the Flats."

I rolled my eyes. "I think I'll be safe on the way to the post office and back. Whoever killed Walt has nothing against me. Move your car, Eli!" I started toward the Suburban, but as I reached for the driver's door, Eli stepped smoothly between me and the handle.

"I'm not going to let you do that. I'll give you a ride, though."

"Give me one good reason why I need a chaperone." I glared at him and crossed my arms.

The smile dropped off his face and he leaned in close, bending down so his face was level with mine. "Because maybe Walt didn't kill Hobo Joe. Maybe he just saw who did it, and that person is still trying to cover up their crime. And you're the one going around asking questions about Joe's murder, so now you're on the killer's radar, too. Ever thought of that?"

I hadn't. He straightened up, a smug expression on his face. "I didn't think so."

"But nobody knows I've been asking—" I broke off and groaned. "Ruth. If she knows, all of Honeytree knows."

Eli nodded. "The whole sheriff's department is aware, too—everyone is interested in this case and word travels fast. There's not a corner of the county that doesn't know you found a skeleton in your yard, and that Walt might have seen something that morning twenty years ago. I'm starting to think he might not have been Joe's killer. He might have been telling the truth."

I leaned up against the Suburban. "Or he might have lied. From what Anne told me last night, Walt was abusive to her for years. He's a violent man. It's not crazy to think he was the one who killed Joe. And it's not crazy to think he was mixed up in some other sketchy stuff that led to his murder—stuff that has nothing to do with me or Joe. Now, my chicks are waiting for me at the post office and I've got"—I pulled my arm away from him and checked the time on my phone—"less than fifteen minutes to get there now. Could you *please* move your car?"

"Nope. I'll take you there."

"Fine! But you're being very silly about this." I threw up my hands and stormed around to the passenger side of his SUV. I took my seat and crossed my arms over the seatbelt, tapping my foot impatiently while he backed up and eased down the driveway. I could tell Eli was pleased that he'd managed to horn in on my errand, but he was smart enough keep his mouth shut about it.

We rode in silence all the way to Honeytree, until he pulled the SUV up to the curb in front of the post office and turned to look at me. "I know you're not taking this seriously, but you need to be careful. You didn't see what I saw in that blueberry shed. Someone very dangerous is at large."

I glanced out my window and saw the red *CLOSED* sign hanging in the window of the post office. "Back door."

He frowned. "You think someone used a back entrance of the shed to kill Walt? I don't think it has a back door."

"The post office. I'm supposed to pick up the chicks at the back entrance."

"Ah. That makes more sense." He grinned and pulled around the corner, edging his vehicle as close as possible near the loading dock where a mail truck was already parked.

"I'll just be a minute." I hopped out just as the back door of the post office, marked "Authorized Personnel Only" opened. A woman in a blue USPS hoodie stuck her head out. She had a narrow face and dark eyebrows that made her look angry at first glance, but on second look, her brown wavy hair framed a kind expression. I didn't recognize her, but she looked young enough that she probably wasn't even born the last time I lived in Honeytree.

"Leona?" she asked, arching one eyebrow.

I nodded. "That's me. Are you Stef?"

"Yup. Your peepers are peeping. I resisted the urge to open the boxes, but man, it was hard!" She chuckled. "They're so cute! We don't see many shipments of fall chicks. Usually we have a batch around Easter, though."

I nodded politely, my palms itching to get my hands on those boxes. I knew that the chicks would be fine without food and water for about three days after hatching, but they'd already been in transit for two days, so I was eager to get them home and settled in the barn.

"I want spring eggs," I explained. "Spring chicks don't lay until the fall, and then egg production goes down during the winter. You waste a whole laying season if you get spring chicks."

"I figured you had a farm, with the size of those boxes. Let me grab them for you." Stef ducked back inside and returned with two large, shallow boxes that had air holes punched in all sides, one stacked on top of the other. "I'll put them in your car so—" She stopped short as she took in Eli's SUV and realized it was a sheriff's vehicle.

"A friend gave me a ride." I knocked on the back and Eli popped the rear door from the front seat, giving Stef and me a glimpse of the masses of equipment stored in the back. Luckily there was plenty of space remaining for my babies.

Stef gently set the boxes down and I quickly moved the top box so it was sitting flat on the floor of the car, too, so the air holes in the top of the lower box weren't blocked for the ride home. "Do I need to sign for these?"

Stef wrinkled her nose. "No worries—I'll initial for you. But, um…most people want to check the chicks in case…well…I don't want to say it. We'll call it shipping damage."

I nodded. As callous as it sounded, I didn't expect all the chicks to make the trip. I actually ordered an extra dozen to compensate for mortality. I slid my fingernail underneath the tape on the side of the first box, silently apologizing to Tambra for the scar it left in my orange polish. When I flipped open the lid of the first box, I saw what I expected—a tightly-packed huddle of fuzzy golden bodies separated into four quadrants with cardboard dividers. And I also saw what I didn't expect—several chicks with brown stripes down their backs. I groaned. The hatchery had included "bonus" chicks for cushioning and warmth. Just what I needed in my life, more random chickens.

147

"What?" Stef asked. "They all look OK to me."

I pointed to the offending baby birds. "They sent extras."

"And that's a problem?" Her expressive eyebrows knitted together.

I sighed. "It means I'm stuck with birds I don't want. And I already ordered extras in case some died in the mail." I popped open the other box and saw the same thing—a handful of randomly colored chicks marred my otherwise perfect little flock. "See, I wanted to have four dozen laying hens next spring, so I ordered sixty chicks. And then they included an extra"—I counted quickly—"ten. And the chicks are all healthy. So now I have seventy chicks when I only planned for forty-eight. And the extras are probably all cockerels or some weird heritage breed that only lays twice a week."

I glared at the boxes, where the chicks were huddling even more closely together, peeping from the influx of cool morning air. It was hard to stay angry at the sight of so many cute little fluffballs, though.

Stef chuckled. "Guess you'll be having a few chicken dinners. Not the worst thing in the world."

It was hard to argue with that. I replaced the lids to the boxes and smiled crookedly at Stef. "Sorry to complain. They look great; thanks for the gentle handling."

"Any time, Leona." Stef jammed her hands in her hoodie pockets. "Good luck with your chicks! Maybe I'll stop by when I'm on my route to see the little guys."

"Gals," I corrected. "And please do. I want them handled as much as possible so they're not afraid of people, so if you're into chick-cuddling, you're invited."

"I'm into chick-cuddling," Eli said from the front seat, his eyes twinkling at me in the rearview mirror. I snorted and closed the tailgate, giving Stef a wave as she headed back inside before I opened the passenger door.

"That's not what I meant." I slid back into my seat, suddenly conscious of my unwashed hair and baggy cargo pants. Surely, he wouldn't consider me a chick, anyway. His non-reaction to my hair and makeup efforts yesterday made that pretty clear. What did he say? I looked *different*. Not pretty. Not even *better*.

Eli blinked innocently. "What? I love baby animals."

"Sure you do." Especially the petite, long-legged kind like Stef—the kind I'd been back in the day. I crossed my arms over my grandma shirt, another reminder that I was more than a little past my prime.

As Eli put the SUV in reverse, I wondered why I cared what he thought, anyway. I'd spent the last few days rebuffing him at every opportunity, and I should be annoyed that he bullied me into accepting a ride to the post office. I wasn't interested in having a serious relationship ever again, and especially not with some boy I dated thirty years ago. But I had to admit that I was susceptible to him; it had been so long since I'd spent time around a *nice* man that it was hard not to confuse kindness with romantic interest. What I'd interpreted as Eli's flirtation was probably just him being a good friend for old time's sake, and friendship was something I needed.

I glanced over at him as he studiously watched the backup camera. "Thanks for the ride. You're not so bad, you know."

"Oh no!" His face registered shock and he slammed on the brakes, jerking my head forward.

Chapter 20

"What is it?" I squinted at the backup camera to see what Eli had been trying to avoid, but nothing was visible on the screen.

He waited a beat before grinning at me. "I think you might like me."

I pursed my lips and glared at him. "I think you gave me whiplash."

"I doubt it," he said merrily as he headed back toward the highway. "I was only going about three miles per hour."

"Hmph." I rubbed the back of my neck to make my point and stared out the window as businesses and then houses and then trees flicked by, feeling slightly foolish for showing my hand. It was funny how I was the same person here I'd been in high school—albeit far less likely to squeeze into a pleated miniskirt—as though the intervening decades hadn't really happened. I felt just as silly, nervous, and self-conscious as I had as a giggly teenager planning for the Homecoming Dance.

What does he mean? Does he like me? Is he just teasing?

Stupid.

The peeping in the back of the SUV intensified as we took the Curves in silence. When we got back to the farm, I was grateful to see the white forensics van parked by the part of my yard cordoned off with crime scene tape. The three guys crawling around the giant pile of dirt meant that I wouldn't have to endure another awkward conversation with Eli. Between this crime scene and the one next door, he'd be in work mode instead of torture-Leona mode.

"Bye!" I said over my shoulder as I bolted out of the car and went around to the back to collect my babies. I gingerly picked up the first box, trying not to jostle them as I did so.

To my chagrin, Eli joined me and scooped up the second box with equal care. Apparently he wasn't as focused on work as he ought to have been, judging from the annoyed look his colleague Blake shot him from over by the van.

"Where to?"

With an apologetic shrug to Blake, I led Eli toward the barn and used my back to slide open the heavy door, careful to keep my little box of fluffs level. The comforting smell of the barn enveloped me as soon as we stepped inside and somehow it seemed that the chorus of peeps grew louder. Maybe the little gals knew they were home.

I set my box on an empty section of workbench behind my shrouded car and cleared a space next to it so Eli could do the same. It was then that I noticed Dr. Speckle's bucket was empty. Not only had she abandoned the nest, but it looked like all the eggs were gone, too! Had a raccoon gotten into the barn? Just what I needed…nasty rotten eggs strewn everywhere. I stooped to get a better look inside the bucket and gasped in horror.

"What is it?" Eli dropped down beside me.

I could barely answer. "The eggs. They're…"

"Hatched? Ah, here they are!" Eli stood and peered behind the bucket, chuckling as he nudged aside a pile of empty coffee cans to reveal a clucking, scratching Dr. Speckle and at least a dozen multi-colored, wobbly chicks. Behind her, Alarm Clock arched a concerned neck toward us to ensure we weren't there to molest "his" babies. Eli licked his lower lip as he scanned the group, counting. "I get fourteen. You?"

I confirmed his count and fell back onto my seat in the barn dust and groaned. "Eighty-six!"

"You ready to bail on this whole place, huh?" Eli grinned at me.

"No, I mean now I have eighty-six chickens. Sixty that I ordered—sixty that I *thought* would turn into forty-eight—but between the packing-peanut chicks and these barnyard mutts and their parents, now I have eighty-six." I wanted to cry. Eighty-six chickens and the coop wasn't even started.

"You seem a little overwhelmed. Why don't I give you a hand getting these little ones settled?" Eli reached down to pat my shoulder, but I shrugged him off and struggled to my feet, dusting off the seat of my cargos.

"I'm fine. This will be fine." I jutted out my chin and willed my words to be true. "I just have to wrap my head around it. I wanted a chicken farm, right? And the universe is saying, 'Here you go. Start farming.'"

"Be careful what you wish for." Eli winked at me.

"Hey, that's my line."

He ducked his head, grinning. "If you change your mind..."

"I know, I know." I waved him out and set to work clearing out the remaining few items from the back corner of the barn. Then I swept out the inside of a large stock tank and put a layer of straw in the bottom. I hung a heat lamp so it warmed one end of the tank, added food and electrolyte-laced water to the opposite end, and then the makeshift brooder was ready for the babies.

I moved the first box of chicks to the floor and gently ferried the chicks two-by-two into their new habitat. Right away, they scrambled around exploring the tank, discovering the food and water by quite literally stumbling into it. The chicks I'd ordered all looked pretty much identical—pale golden with faint red stripes down their backs. They'd grow into petite, efficient layers who didn't eat much and produced a large, quality egg every day like clockwork.

The half-dozen "bonus" chicks in this box were another story. They were every color of the rainbow—black, light yellow, brown with racing stripes, even pale gray—and some stood a head taller than the rest of the flock. I didn't know if they were male or female, nor if they were layers, meat birds, or dual-purpose—a fancy word that just meant a chicken that grew too slow to be an efficient meat bird and didn't lay enough to make it worth the feed. I'd already decided that dual-purpose wasn't for me—I wanted the predictable numbers and quality that came with the layers bred for commercial production—but here I was with two-dozen wildcards, ten from the hatchery and fourteen from the dear Dr. Speckle.

"I'll feed you until I find you new homes," I said, rising to fetch the remaining box of chicks. If enough of them were female, I might even be able to sell them and recoup my investment in the chicks; so-called "started pullets" could fetch five or six times the cost of a day-old chick.

I emptied the second box of peeping pompoms and then went to deal with the barnyard brood. I felt a little guilty stealing the babies from their parents, but they'd be safer and better-fed in the brooder with the other chicks. The first few were easy to grab, but as their frantic cheeping rose, like any good mother hen, Dr. Speckle squawked and flapped at me, trying to deter my thieving talons. As far as she was concerned, I wasn't a concerned caretaker, I was just a hawk with an orange manicure.

And Alarm Clock wasn't there to play either. Like a swirling storm of feathers, he hurled himself at me, spurs-first. I put the chicks down and grabbed the lid of the garbage-can-cum-feed-bin just in time to use it as a shield. The angry rooster glanced off but returned for a second pass, Dr. Speckle on his heels. As the remaining babies scattered around me, I realized that I'd have to contain the parents before I could pilfer their brood.

When Alarm Clock made another move, this time aiming for my ankles, I clamped the garbage can lid down on top of him, pinning him until I could clasp him firmly under one arm. Dr. Speckle clucked and called her babies, shoving them beneath her wings to keep them safe from my predation. With an apology, I popped Alarm Clock into an empty bucket and shut the lid on it. Then I gently shooed Dr. Speckle into her old nest, making sure all the chicks followed her inside.

She trilled and fussed over them until they were all safely underneath her, and once they were settled, I lifted the whole shebang into the stock tank. "Gotcha!"

I dusted my hands and let Alarm Clock out of his bucket. He seemed properly chagrined and pretended to be very interested in pecking at the dust around my feet. I debated whether to leave him loose in the barn with so many chicks—from my research, I knew that occasionally a rooster would kill babies that weren't his—but Alarm Clock had been so gentle and protective of Dr. Speckles' hatchlings that I was pretty sure he'd accept the new babies as his own. Plus, he'd deter any thieves—human or otherwise—that might enter the barn.

I set an alarm on my phone to check on the chicks in a few hours and headed back to the house to clean up and have another cup of coffee. But as soon as I shut the barn door, I saw Eli wave to me. I pretended not to see him and made a beeline for the porch, but he jogged ahead and met me at the bottom of the stairs.

"No," I said.

He looked hurt. "You didn't even hear what I had to say."

"Are you done, need any help, blah blah blah." I made a talky motion with my hand.

"Wrong." He squared his shoulders and cleared his throat, arranging his face into the picture of professional detachment. "Actually, *ma'am*, I'm here to inform you that we'll clear out of your yard by tomorrow morning. Our investigation on your property is wrapping up."

My jaw dropped and I gripped the porch post in surprise. "I thought you were going to dig up the whole yard. It was supposed to take a week, minimum!"

"We've expended about as much effort as we can. County's pulling the team off this case now that a more pressing investigation is underway." His eyes slid toward the fence and beyond to the Sutherlands' property.

"But they could be related," I protested, although why I was arguing for the sheriff's department to continue clucking up my yard was beyond me. I should have been thrilled. I should have been thinking about how to get my coop finished before the bad weather started.

He sighed. "Our chances of solving a fresh case are about a thousand percent higher than solving a twenty-year-old cold case. It'd be one thing if we'd investigated Joe's disappearance back then, but we didn't, so we have almost nothing to go on. It's just a matter of practicality. Better to catch a murderer who's operating in the present than one who killed in the past. Heck, Joe's killer might be dead already—but we know Walt's is alive and well."

"Guess I'll have to get back to building my coop." I forced a smile, even though the thought of any killer alive and well in my neighborhood was unsettling to say the least. I'd have to console myself with the fact that my coop-building schedule would only be delayed a few days instead of a few weeks. Then again, if I employed some power tools, I might not be behind schedule at all. Suddenly I felt wide-awake, no coffee necessary.

I poked Eli in the arm. "Can you move your vehicle, please? You're blocking me in."

A frown darkened Eli's expression. "Why do you need the car? I thought you were going inside the house."

I crossed my arms defiantly, annoyed that I had to explain myself. It was my dang car and my dang driveway, and I could drive up and down it all day for kicks if I wanted to! "If you must know, I'm going to borrow a trencher from Mike Spence so I can get working as soon as your guys clear out tomorrow. Not that it's any of your business." Eli's face lit up and I groaned. "Why are you happy about that? Don't tell me that you're—"

"Coming with you!" he finished triumphantly.

"No thanks, I've had enough supervision for one day."

"For once, this isn't about you. I need to talk to Mike Spence, too, about Walt's poker connections. We'll save gas. It's better for the environment!"

This man was impossible. Any time we had a conversation,

my eyes felt like they were permanently on the "roll" setting. "Fine, but move your rig anyway. I'm going to drive."

"Sorry, I've gotta drive my official sheriff's vehicle while on official business." He shrugged, clearly not sorry at all.

I shrugged right back at him. "Guess you'll have to keep up with me, then."

Chapter 21

I kept the gas pedal almost to the floor for most of the drive up Briggs Road, stomping the clutch to take the hairpin turns and then hitting the gas again as soon as I could do it without tipping the Suburban. This car couldn't beat Eli's Interceptor on a straight stretch of highway, but I sure could beat him at this kind of driving. He was a full half-mile behind me by the time I pulled down the narrow driveway to the Spences' log cabin.

Mike Spence and his twin brother Bob had lived there since birth; the cabin had been built by a Spence ancestor back when Briggs Road was more of a deer trail than anything else. Everyone referred to it as Mike's house, probably because he was the more outgoing brother, the one who went to town to collect gas for the chainsaw and milk for the fridge. Bob was more of a homebody, but both were the kind of men who lived off the land, shooting deer and collecting mushrooms in the woods that surrounded their home. The outside of their log cabin was studded with the antlers of their hunting spoils.

A figure flashed in briefly in the front window, but I waited until Eli parked beside me to get out of the car. Eli pushed open his door, looking a little green around the gills.

"I'll write you a reckless driving ticket later," he said.

My mood suddenly improved by a factor of three or four. I pressed my lips together to keep from giggling. "Did you have trouble keeping up?"

He growled and, slamming his door shut, marched toward the front door. I tagged behind him, taking a little guilty pleasure in the rear view of Eli's impressive physique. Even if I didn't want to buy, window-shopping wasn't against the rules, was it? A moment later, the figure inside the cabin peered out the window at us again and then opened the front door just as Eli was about to knock.

"Well, I'll be. The law has finally made it to Briggs Road," Mike Spence drawled, leaning outside. A small, wiry man, he still looked the same as he had when he'd help my dad clear brush out of our back forty. Same tanned, leathery face, same deep lines around his eyes that spoke of a man who laughed more than he cried. He'd seemed like an old man to me back then, but here he was, forty-odd years later just as wrinkled, gray, and spry. I had a feeling if I challenged him to a tree-climbing contest, he'd beat me. "You here to lock up Bob?"

Eli glanced at me, bewildered. "Why, what did Bob do?"

Mike's face nearly cracked in half, his grin was so wide. "Nothin'. I was just pulling your leg. Although sometimes his cooking is criminal. He burned the toast again this morning. Can you smell it?" He sucked in a deep draft of morning air through his nose.

Eli chuckled and slapped him on the shoulder. "No laws against bad cooking—at least, not that I'm aware!"

"Well, there should be," Mike said, glancing back into the house. "Hear that, Bob? There should be!"

"I heard you." Bob's doleful voice filtered out to the porch. He was definitely the Eeyore to Mike's Tigger. "Maybe ask him what he wants instead of horsing around. Don't waste the man's time."

"There's a lady, too," Mike said sourly, as if my presence was some kind of retort to Bob's criticism.

"I'm Leona Davis—my dad was Bud Landers." I stuck out my hand and Mike grasped it in his hard, calloused paw, nodding.

"Oh, yes, I remember those yellow curls chasing Bud's chickens all over tarnation." His eyes misted over and he brushed them with the back of his hand. "I was sorry to hear about your folks, real sorry. They've been gone a while now, haven't they? You still living at their place?"

I shook my head, swallowing away the wash of grief at the mention of my parents. "We sold it about ten years ago. I just moved into the Chapman farm. Actually, that's why I'm here. I wanted to ask you—any chance I could borrow your power trencher? Walt Sutherland said you and Bob had one, and I need to dig a foundation for my new chicken coop."

Mike's face didn't change at the mention of Walt's name. He clearly hadn't heard the news of Walt's death. "Oh, sure, sure. Bob! Get the trencher out of the shed, would you? Bud's girl needs to borrow it." Inside, Bob grumbled, but I heard the sound of a chair scraping back and then the back door slammed.

"Thanks. I'll keep you in eggs in the spring, once my girls are laying," I promised. "They'll go great with your burned toast."

"Happy to help. You tell Walt to stop loaning out my stuff, though!" Mike flashed me a tobacco-stained smile and winked.

"Actually, Walt's why I'm here," Eli said, stepping forward. "I hate to be the one to tell you, but he's dead, Mike. He was

160

killed yesterday."

The color drained from Mike's face and he sagged against the doorframe. "Killed, you say? Was it some kind of accident?"

Eli grimaced slightly. I guess even a sheriff doesn't get used to delivering bad news. "I'm afraid not. I'm looking for any information about troubles he might have been having. Figured you knew him well so you might have some leads."

Mike shook his head, his eyes downcast. "I wouldn't say I knew him well. I'm not sure anyone knew him well except his wife."

"I thought he played poker with you every week!" I blurted out.

Mike shifted where he stood, his expression suddenly wary. "Well, sure. Bob and I run a regular game on Friday nights. But it's not a stitch-and-bitch circle, it's five-card stud. We don't chitchat, we play cards. Walt's been playing with us—oh, I don't know, it's got to be forty years now."

Forty years of weekly get-togethers and he didn't know Walt very well? *Men.*

"Who all plays with you?" Eli asked, his voice a whole lot more patient than I felt.

Mike grunted. "People come and go. We try to keep it small. Me, Bob, Walt, and then whoever. Zeke, Sherm. Some others who've passed away or moved away."

Eli's ears perked up at the names, and he slid a small notebook out of his shirt pocket and flipped it open to jot them down. "So that's Zeke Jones and Sherman Dice?"

"Don't know anybody else by those names, no." Mike Spence's goodwill was clearly evaporating. "Can't recall the others over the years off the top of my head."

"Do you guys take attendance at your games? Maybe you have a list somewhere of people who have played up here?"

Mike snorted so hard he choked. "Not a chance. And even if I did, I wouldn't give it to you. More than one fellow has used a weekly poker game as an alibi for time spent away from the missus." He winked at us. "Sorry, kids."

My heart stilled at his mention of wives as I thought of Anne Sutherland alone in her quiet farmhouse. I knew Eli didn't think Joe and Walt's deaths were necessarily connected, but could it be more than a coincidence that Joe's murder took place on a poker night, the perfect excuse for Walt to be out of the house?

"Did Walt ever use the game as an alibi?" I asked, keeping my voice as light and innocent as possible.

"Naw. He took his cards real serious. Rarely missed a game unless he was ill or out of cash. Gosh, I still can't believe that old goat is gone." He shook his head.

"Did he ever leave the table to get more money and then not come back?" I pressed. "I'm thinking twenty years ago or so?"

Mike squinted at me. "You've got a lot of faith in the memory of an old man. I can't say I recall a time when Walt went on tilt and didn't finish out the night. Course if I did, I wouldn't tell you that, either."

The gravel scraped behind us and I turned to see Bob, Mike's identical but more somber and pale double, pausing near the tailgate of the Suburban with the power trencher in tow. The body of it was bright yellow and it looked for all the world like a rototiller with a chainsaw attached to the front. I swallowed hard. If I was going to run my farm by myself, I was going to have to master intimidating equipment like that, I reminded myself.

"Pop the back," Bob said gruffly. "I got my hands full here."

I jogged over and opened the rear doors, and he and Mike heaved the power tool inside with the affection of men who love their tools more than anything. "Thanks," I said. "I'll take good care of it."

"Welcome." Bob gave a noncommittal nod.

After Bob and Mike had both disappeared back inside the cabin, Eli and I stood by our cars as the sun slipped behind a cloud.

"Got me some leads," he said, thwacking his notebook before putting it back in his pocket and clicking his pen triumphantly.

"Got me some trenches to dig." I mimicked his tone. "I guess here's where we part ways. You going to write me that ticket?"

"Thanks for reminding me." He clicked the pen and filled out the top sheet of his ticket booklet before ripping it off and handing it to me with a flourish.

I waited until he was out of sight down the driveway before I looked at the damage. He'd filled it out this time. I scanned past my name, address, offense—reckless speeding—to the ticket value.

It was his dang phone number again.

Motherclucker.

Chapter 22

I took the Briggs Road switchbacks more slowly on the way home; for some reason downhill always feels more dangerous, like when you have a crush on someone and instead of holding back, you just let yourself fall head over heels, dignity be damned. Well, I wasn't about to give into that feeling, so I crept down the hill to the highway like a little old lady who'd forgotten her glasses.

When I finally pulled the Suburban into my driveway, I was so distracted by my daydreaming that I almost crashed into the red truck that was parked in my spot next to the house. Rusty Chapman hopped out, waving his hands apologetically and making a cranking motion. I rolled down the window a crack to hear what he had to say.

"Sorry! I should have pulled up further. Old habits die hard."

"Don't worry about it." I eased my car around the tailgate of his truck and parked on the other side. Before I could even get the window up, he was at my door, opening it for me. I was immediately suspicious—chivalry was not a word in Rusty's vocabulary. Anyway, I could open my own feather-fluffing door.

"What're you doing here?" Maybe not my most gracious approach. I rephrased. "What brings you to the old farm?"

"Well, I was watching the team work." Rusty nodded toward the van and the excavation site where half the forensics team was swarming, his curls bobbing. "Looks like they're making quite a mess. I was thinking you might need some help getting things cleared up."

I followed his gaze to the future site of my dream coop. The enormous pile of dirt that the forensics team was sifting through for pieces of Joe loomed next to the hole where he'd been exhumed—a hole that had grown from person-size to roughly elephant-size. Equipment was everywhere, including the lights, cameras, sifters, makeshift workstations, and dozens of digging tools. If they were planning to finish their work and pack everything up by tomorrow, it was pretty clear they weren't going to fill in the hole before they left.

But Rusty wasn't here to watch the forensics team—he couldn't have known that the team would finish tomorrow because I'd only known about it for an hour or two myself! And he wouldn't have known that they'd leave a mess, either. He had some other motive for his visit—checking up on "his" farm, probably. I narrowed my eyes. "What's the real reason? I know it wasn't about Mount Dirtpile over there. You couldn't have known about that until you got here."

He sighed. "OK, you're right. But Ruth told me—"

"Of course, Ruth. Wait, how did she know?"

"Ruth told *me* that Stef told *her* that you got your chicks in this morning and the hatchery gave you extras. She figured you might need a hand getting things set up for them, so I came over," he explained patiently. "To help."

"Out of the goodness of your heart. I don't buy it."

He grimaced. "OK. The truth. I've been working for Walt over at his place, but now that he's gone…well. I could use a paycheck, if you're hiring."

Now that was the real story. Rusty sensed my vulnerability as a single woman running a farm for the first time and figured he could squeeze a few bucks out of the deal, pluck the fruit of my ignorance. If I didn't have a gaping hole in my yard, I might even be mad about it. "Fine. They're going to finish up tomorrow morning. Once the van is gone, you can level the dirt for me. But the timeclock doesn't start until they leave!"

"OK." He nodded absentmindedly, staring at something over my shoulder, and stepped around me to pluck an apple off the tree nearest to the house. He took a bite and spat the piece into the hydrangea bush by the porch, then handed me the bitten apple.

I was hungry, but not that hungry. I handed it back. "No thanks, I'm good."

He grinned at me and proffered the apple again. "Don't eat it; it's still too sour anyway. But look"—he pointed to the missing chunk—"the seeds are browning, there's hardly any green in the flesh near the peel. That's how you know the apples are almost ready."

I took the apple and turned it in my hand, studying it. I never would have noticed those things—or even thought to check. I looked up at Rusty and the acres of orchard that stretched out behind him. It was only a piece of paper that said I was their owner. The trees were fifty years old if they were a day and had been nurtured by generations of Chapmans. No wonder Rusty felt responsible for the place even though his family didn't live here anymore. I'd forgotten that he wasn't just a handyman here—he was an expert.

"After you fill in the hole, I'd appreciate your advice about the apples. Maybe I can hire you as an orchard consultant?"

He laughed, wrinkling his upturned nose. "Consultant sounds a little too fancy a word for someone who's going to tell you to pick the apples when they're ripe."

"There's more to it than that and you know it. I could muddle through with internet searches and library books, or you could come show me the way you've always done it. The right way. I don't have a ton of money right now." That was an understatement, I reflected. I hoped the harvest itself would pay his wages; the only lines I had in the budget until spring were groceries, property taxes, and chicken feed. "But I will scrounge up enough to pay you for your expertise."

He ducked his head, looking pleased. "I'm no expert, but I'll do what I can. First piece of advice is free. Don't try to sell this year's harvest."

My mouth fell open. "What?!"

He met my eyes earnestly. "They're too small and scabbed. You'll waste a lot of time trying to find a buyer. I'd juice 'em if they were mine—"

"Well, they're not!" I snapped, panic rising in my chest. "I have to sell them whole; I can't afford to hire a pressing crew. Heck, I can't hire *you* if I don't sell the apples. And I can't sell the apples if I don't hire you. I'm kind of stuck here!"

He rubbed his forehead as though I'd given him a migraine. "Why are you ladies always so difficult? It's like no matter what I say, you don't believe—"

"Oh, here we go! Suddenly you're not my employee, you're my boss!" I put my hands on my hips and leaned in, whatever guilt I felt about purchasing the farm evaporating in an instant. "What 'ladies' are being difficult, Rusty? Your sister, who lets you live in her backyard for free? Me, the person who just offered you a job when you needed one? Grow up!" My voice rose in volume until I was nearly shouting. By the end of my outburst, I realized that even Blake and his forensics team had stopped their work to stare at me.

"I was just trying to say—" Rusty broke off as my purse began chiming—or more accurately, my phone inside my purse began chiming. I recognized the tone; it was my baby chick alarm.

"I have to go check on the birds," I said. "Just. Please. Let's not make this about ladies getting you down. You can shovel that manure elsewhere. I just need you to shovel dirt, OK?"

"OK," Rusty mumbled, his cheeks flaming. He glanced up at the forensics crew, who seemed to remember they were in a rush to finish and resumed their activity, loading the last of the garbage bags into the back of the van. Then he asked meekly, "Do you really want me to use a shovel? That's a lot of dirt. It'd be faster to use a trac—"

"Tractor's broken. Shovel's been taken in as evidence. Do you have your own you can bring?"

Rusty took a step back and swallowed. "Evidence of what?"

"Joe's murder, obviously," I said. "I found it when I was cleaning out the barn. It had what looked like dried blood on the handle. Eli thinks he was probably killed with it."

Rusty seemed shaken by the news. "I thought we sold all the tools."

"I'm sure you sold the good ones. This one was pretty decrepit and hidden in the back corner behind a bunch of junk. In any case, it's gone now—so either you have tools you can bring or you're digging with your hands."

Rusty licked his lips and gave a nervous laugh. "Guess I better fix the tractor today, then. Is that in your budget, boss?"

I grinned at him over my shoulder, feeling slightly sheepish that I'd lost my temper earlier. "Well, a new tractor sure isn't. You can give it a shot, but don't spend too much time on a lost cause, if you know what I mean."

He followed me inside the barn and located the dusty tractor, then began shoving aside boxes and tools so he could access all sides. "What's wrong with it?"

"It won't start. If I knew what was wrong with it, I would have fixed it. Don't *you* know? Watch the car," I added, nodding toward my tarped Porsche as I passed on the way to the brooder.

"I've got no idea." He shook his head, surprising me. "We sold off the good tractor when Granddad passed. That's the one I used the most. This one was kind of the backup tractor. It's a good make, though—worth fixing. It'll get you through a few years at least. First off, it needs fresh gas. You got any?"

"Mhm." I motioned toward a gas can on the workbench as I checked the food and water in the brooder, only half-listening to Rusty ramble on about tractor models. The chicks had already managed to dirty the water, so I emptied it out and refilled it, adding a scoop of electrolytes to help rehydrate them after the stressful shipping process.

A few of the chicks were sprawled out limply in the straw, probably sleeping. I couldn't help giving each one a nudge just to make sure they were still breathing. They all hopped to their feet right away, peeping loudly at my rudeness, which sent Dr. Speckle into a frenzy of motherly clucks as she ushered the affronted chicks under her wings.

All except one.

When I nudged the last one, a little yellow layer, she struggled to stand, then lost her footing and toppled over again and stayed there still. I picked her up and gently dipped

169

her beak into the electrolyte water. She sipped it, but when I tried to prop her up on her feet, she tipped over again. It was then that I noticed her crooked toe and splayed legs.

I cussed under my breath. A genetic defect. She probably wasn't going to make it. The humane thing to do was end her life now, before I made a huge investment in time and feed.

"What?" Rusty asked over his shoulder.

"Nothing." This was part of farming, losing animals. I'd planned for this loss, I reminded myself. I knew what I was getting into and that's why I ordered extra chicks. But as I watched the wobbly little critter try to stand up, I couldn't stomach culling her—not when she so clearly wanted to live. Besides, she wasn't going to pass this defect on to her offspring because she wasn't going to have any offspring. If she could lay eggs, she could be a productive member of the flock. I just needed to correct her splayed legs enough for her to walk. And in the meantime…

I scooped up the little chick and tucked her inside my bra, careful not to crush her. She snuggled in just as she might under Dr. Speckle's warm, feathered wing. I looked up to see Rusty's openmouthed, wide-eyed expression.

"*What* in the H-E-double-hockeysticks are you doing?!" He looked both horrified and delighted, like he'd caught me picking my nose.

I flushed. "I'm just keeping her warm until I get her inside. She needs a little doctoring, that's all."

"I've never heard of the cleavage cure." Rusty snickered, staring at my grandma shirt—or at my chick-cradling boobs underneath it. "But I have to say, I'm all for it!"

"The only thing you need to cure is that tractor," I snapped. Rusty Chapman could keep his eyes and opinions to himself.

Chapter 23

At the comfort of my kitchen table, I gingerly taped a band-aid around the chick's legs to hold them together and still provide some range of motion. I set her on the table and she wobbled but stayed upright! She immediately began pecking at a chip in the enamel tabletop, so I sprinkled a pinch of the chick starter I'd stashed in one of my cargo pockets on the table a few inches in front of her. She hopped toward it and gobbled most of it up in less than a minute, then cocked her head and stared at me with one beady eye, looking for more.

Satisfaction surged over me. "Good job, little one. I think you've got a shot."

I peered closer at her crooked toes. They were curling backward pretty badly; she'd have a hard time roosting when she grew up, which meant she was doomed to occupy the bottom of the pecking order. Those that roosted higher had higher status; only the lowliest of low hens would sleep on the floor. I used pieces of another bandage and a cut-up toothpick to splint her feet into the proper position.

The little chick pecked at her new booties—they made her look like a duckling instead of a chick—and then when they proved inedible, turned her attention to the fresh batch of starter crumbles in front of her.

Hop, hop, hop.

I was so engrossed in watching the chick's progress that I didn't hear Ruth come in until her voice came from right behind me. "Rusty said you had a house chicken. I guess he wasn't lying."

I shrieked and jumped out of my seat. "Don't you people knock?!"

At my sudden movement, the little chick flattened herself on the tabletop as though I were a swooping hawk, but when I picked her up, she nestled against the warmth of my palm, her eyes fluttering closed.

"I've never knocked at the door to this house." Ruth's voice was unusually subdued. "I'll remember next time."

"I'm sorry," I said instantly. "I didn't mean that; I was just startled. You don't have to knock—you and Rusty are always welcome here. Wait, he called you? How in the world did you get here so fast?"

Ruth pulled out a chair and sat down next to me. "I was already next door, dropping off dinner for Anne and her family, and I figured I'd swing by and see the new chicks. Rusty caught me in the driveway and said you'd just taken one of the babies inside."

"This one had splay leg." I passed her the chick and a smile spread across her face as she examined the chick's feet and legs.

"You should call her Boots. How are you, little Boots?" Ruth cupped the chick close to her, and Boots closed her eyes again, her head nodding down as she fell asleep in Ruth's hands. "Precious. If I could bottle this feeling and make a spa treatment out of it, I'd earn a fortune."

"Somehow I think 'the baby chicken facial' wouldn't be a huge seller." I giggled.

"I don't know. People are asking for snail-slime facials all the time."

"No!"

She shrugged as she stroked Boots's sleeping head with one finger. "It's true. It's a thing. You can look it up on the internet."

I shuddered and tried to quell the image of a snail trail across my face. "How's Anne doing?"

"You know. She's a mess, as we all would be in her situation. The sheriff's department is swarming her place, tearing it apart looking for clues about who might have had something against Walt. They pulled everything out of the blueberry shed and everything out of every closet and drawer inside the house. I hate to think how they're going to leave it. Hopefully Anne's sisters can help her put it back together."

I nodded. "Tell me about it—I'm worried about how they're going to leave my yard, too. It looks like Crater Lake out there."

"Maybe you should put in that duck pond my grandpa had planned," Ruth said wryly. "I'm only half kidding. That's a big hole. It'll take forever to fill it back in."

I grinned. "Nah, Rusty's going to fix the tractor and use that to move most of the dirt. Thanks for telling him to show up, by the way. He'll be a big help."

Ruth frowned. "I didn't tell him to do that. All I said was your chicks came in. I guess coming over to help was his idea. I didn't know he had a thoughtful bone in his body." Ruth looked at me appraisingly. "I hadn't considered it before, but maybe he's interested in you."

173

I snorted and pointed to my "World's Best Nana" shirt. "Rusty has a thing for grandmas, huh?"

"Well, he's our age, isn't he?" Ruth asked. "And you're cute as a bug. Lots of guys are checking you out. I saw how Eli looked at you at the park the other day."

"Yeah, like I'm *different*." I rolled my eyes, remembering his comment. "I think Rusty's more interested in making money. He said he was expecting a paycheck from Walt but now—"

"Yeah." Ruth nodded. "Now he's got to get his ducks in a row."

"Or chickens, in this case." I grinned at her.

"I wish he wouldn't work here," she said abruptly.

I swallowed. I didn't blame Ruth for feeling that way; my own feelings were complicated enough. She'd sold the family farm to someone who wasn't family despite Rusty's protests, which I'm sure weighed heavily on her conscience. "I'm sorry. I should have turned him down. I just thought it was what you wanted, since he said you sent him. I'll let him know that—"

"No." She shook her head, her eyes welling up a little. "Really, it's fine. He has to find his own path. I hoped that once you moved in over here, he'd spread his wings a little, figure out what he wants to do with his life. But a week or two of work over here will pay some bills, and goodness knows he needs that, too. Just don't let him take over and pretend like he's still running it. He's got to remember that the farm is in new hands and he isn't the only one who can do the job. Make sure you boss him."

I grinned. "No worries—bossing is my forte. Just ask Eli."

Ruth's expression turned to amusement. "I told you. That man's been tagging after you like a dog after dinner. Stef said he drove you to the post office this morning."

I nodded. "He's trying to keep an eye on me, you know, because of a killer active in the neighborhood, *blah blah blah*."

"Surely he didn't think someone was going to murder you on the way to the post office? Oh, yuck, she pooped!" Ruth wrinkled her nose and handed Boots back to me, then rose to get a paper towel from the holder by the sink.

I stroked Boots's pale yellow fluff with one finger as she settled back into my cupped palm. "He's just worried that Walt's killer might come after me because I've been asking around about Joe's murder."

"He thinks the murders are related?" Ruth's eyes nearly bugged out of her skull. "How could they be? I thought Walt killed Joe because he was jealous!"

I shrugged. "No way to know now. But Eli thinks it's possible Walt wasn't the killer. He thinks it's possible Walt was telling the truth that he saw the killer burying Joe's body. When I dug up Joe's bones and word got out, the killer might have decided to get rid of the potential witness."

"Do you think Eli's right?" Ruth asked worriedly.

"Nah. I mean, we could come up with a million theories of the crime. Let's say Walt killed Joe. Word gets around that Walt knew the skeleton was buried in my yard. Someone from Joe's family goes to the blueberry shed and exacts revenge. 'Hello, my name is Toronto Montoya. You killed my son, prepare to die.'"

Ruth chuckled despite the grim subject matter. "I think we'd notice if any Canadians were hanging around town. They have funny accents." Ruth tossed the paper towel in the garbage and squeezed a blue dollop of dish soap into her palm before vigorously scrubbing her hands like she was going into surgery.

I giggled at her. "A Honeytree girl who's afraid of a little chicken plop?"

Ruth rinsed her hands and flicked the excess water back into the sink. "Hey, I touch people's faces all day. I can't run the Salmonella Salon."

"Oh, right. No baby chick facials for you. Snail-slime spa treatments only."

She swatted me with the back of her hand as she sat down again. "Yelena swears by them."

"Well, she is very well-preserved for someone her age," I admitted, and then I stopped short, remembering the conversation I'd had with Yelena in my kitchen just a few days earlier. "She moved here after she retired, right? She said it was fifteen years ago. Do you know where she lived before?"

Ruth shrugged. "I assume Russia."

"Because of the funny accent," I said, grinning. For some reason I got a kick out of pointing a finger at the least likely suspect on the planet. It proved my point—there was no way to know who had it out for Walt. He was nearly eighty, after all, and he must have collecting plenty of enemies over those eight decades, given his stellar personality.

Ruth blew a curl out of her face and rolled her eyes. "Oh, please! Yelena hasn't been faking a Russian accent for fifteen years to hide her true Canadian identity. That's just ridiculous."

"Of course not. But maybe she raised her children in Toronto. Maybe her son Joe rode the rails around the US before he disappeared twenty years ago. Maybe she tracked him here to Honeytree, where the trail went cold, and she's been waiting here ever since, hoping that he'd show up. Then when I moved here, he did show up—or at least, his bones did. Cue revenge killing." I shrugged.

"You think Yelena went on a murderous rampage?" Ruth looked skeptical. I couldn't blame her. Little old Yelena with her braids wrapped around her head was hardly the picture of a calculating woman bent on revenge.

"I know I would if someone hurt Andrea. You'd better believe I'd stab the plop out of someone who took her life, whether it was twenty minutes ago or twenty years ago."

Ruth tilted her head to the side, considering. "She *was* pretty keen on coming out here to the farm even though her hair was only half-done. Tambra said she basically insisted, and it's not like her conditioning treatment couldn't have waited until the next day."

"And that night I told everyone that Walt seemed to know the body was buried there." My voice came out barely above a whisper. I was just being stupid suggesting Yelena was a potential suspect, but suddenly my wild theory didn't seem so crazy.

Ruth pulled out her phone and scrolled quickly through a few menus before holding it to her ear. "I'm calling Eli," she said to me.

I nodded. While she filled him in on our suspicions about Yelena, Boots the baby chick and I went to find a heating pad. Though my dad had never brooded chicks this way, I'd read that I could use a heating pad to stand in for a mama hen. Boots needed a few days with her braces on before I could put her back in with gen-pop, so I had to make her a warm place to snuggle that wasn't down the front of my shirt.

I located the heating pad in the bottom drawer of the bathroom and dumped out a Rubbermaid tote of sky-high heels—when was I going to wear *those* again, anyway?—to house Boots in. A ratty hand towel spread in the bottom of the bin, a desk organizer with the heating pad clipped to the top to make a cozy cave, and two mayonnaise-jar lids to hold food and water, and Boots was happily hopping about and pecking in her new home. I admired her pluck—it took me a little longer than thirty seconds to feel at home after my move.

"Eli says he'll look into it," Ruth said behind me.

"Cheese and rice, you scared me again!" I pressed my hand to my thudding heart in an attempt to calm it to merely cardiac-arrest level.

"Sorry not sorry." She giggled at my expression. "You look like you've seen a ghost!"

I held out my hand and she helped me to my feet. "Two days ago, I dug up a dead guy. Yesterday, my neighbor was brutally stabbed. Forgive me if I'm a little jumpy."

She clucked her tongue. "I know, it's a lot. But Rusty's out front, I'm here, and Eli's taking care of business. You can lean on us. Heck, if you want to come stay with me for a while, that's fine."

"Be careful, I might take you up on that." I forced a grin. "I mean, I would if it weren't for the chicks. I need to check on them throughout the day while they're so vulnerable." I motioned to the plastic tote, where Boots was standing in a corner, peeping mournfully. My heart, which had finally slowed to a reasonable speed, panged with sympathy for the little chick.

Ruth leaned over the tote to get a better view of Boots, frowning. "What's wrong with her? She was so happy a minute ago."

"She's lonely."

"How can you tell?"

"Process of elimination. She's got food, water, warmth—everything but company."

"Well, that's unacceptable!" Ruth declared, and marched out of the bedroom. She grabbed her purse from the kitchen table on her way to the front door.

I tagged after her. "Where are you going?"

She looked at me like I was crazy for asking. "To the barn. We're going to pick her out a friend."

I should have known. "We better make it two, then. Because—" I paused, not wanting to say the real reason aloud—that the chicks had a not-insignificant risk of death in these first weeks. "Well, because why have one friend when you can have more."

Chapter 24

Outside, I was shocked to hear the chug of the tractor drowning out the sound of the forensics team working. Rusty had somehow resurrected it in the barn and was already testing it out in the driveway. He waved at us triumphantly from his seat and in the same moment, the tractor lurched forward. His comical grimace and mad grab for the wheel sent Ruth into a gale of giggles.

"Ride 'em, cowboy!" she called to him, her hands around her mouth like the megaphones we used as cheerleaders on the sidelines of Friday night football games.

He grinned and yelled back over the tractor's grumble, "Hey, I've had a good ten seconds in the saddle. I'm calling that a victory!"

I gave him a thumbs-up as I ducked inside the barn. "The brooder is in the back," I said over my shoulder to Ruth.

She rubbed her hands together greedily as she followed me to the stock tank. "I can't wait to get my hands on these cute little cotton balls!" She reached in and scooped out a couple of chicks, nuzzling them before popping them into her cleavage and grabbing a couple more. She plopped down on a straw bale next to the tank, beaming.

"Huh. I only fit one in mine," I said, motioning to her boob-nest.

She glanced down and smirked. "Honey, I can fit two tacos and a Corona in here, plus chips and guac in an emergency." To prove her point, she tucked the other two chicks into her shirt and they quickly snuggled in with their sisters.

"I see how it is—you've stashed your buffalo wing appetizer in there for later." I smirked right back at her.

Ruth cracked up. "That's right. Gotta have my drinks and snacks. Let's get these little ones settled in the house."

We went back inside, and, as I had predicted, Boots's frantic peeping settled down immediately when she was surrounded by four of her sisters. The five chicks snuggled under the heading pad and crashed out almost immediately. "See? We get by with a little help from our friends."

Ruth nodded as she rested on her heels beside the Rubbermaid tub, watching the babies sleep. "We need to do what we can for Anne," she said thoughtfully. "Especially once her family goes back home. She'll need friends."

"I'll be sure to check on her, since I'm right next door." I didn't know Anne well, but I certainly sympathized with her situation. Friendships could be forged in all kinds of circumstances, and sometimes the strongest ones came out of adversity. "I can give you a daily update on how she's doing, if you want, and we'll go from there."

"Perfect. We'll need to assemble a casserole crew, too. It's tough to eat when you're grieving, but it's nice to have food on hand when you can stomach it."

"I'm in. I can take her something tomorrow."

Ruth shook her head. "Yelena already said she's bringing something over tomorrow. You can do the next day. We'll set up a schedule for everyone else to sign up."

My forehead creased, thinking of the suspicions we'd voiced earlier. "Yelena's going to visit Anne tomorrow? Is that really a good idea, given what she might have done to Walt?"

Ruth stood up abruptly. "You know as well as I do that Yelena didn't kill anyone. I just felt we had to pass along any possibilities to Eli. You were right—we don't know Yelena as well as other folks who have lived here longer. We can't be sure she's trustworthy. The sheriff's department needs to be looking at all the possibilities. All the outsiders."

I swallowed. "Outsiders like me?"

"Of course not. You're from here." She rolled her eyes and held out her hand to help me up, but I struggled to my feet on my own.

"I live next door to Walt and Anne," I reminded her. "I could have killed him."

"You were in town with me and Tambra," she said stubbornly. "I was with you."

"You don't know that. You don't know what I was doing before noon. Actually, Tambra could have done it, too."

"She was at the back-to-school picnic!" Ruth crossed her arms, her expression bewildered.

"Was she?" I arched an eyebrow and stepped toward her. "You weren't there. We didn't take the guitar to the park until after two o'clock."

Ruth backed up so quickly, she hit her shoulder on the door frame. "Eli saw her! As soon as he dropped you off, he went over to the picnic."

"Did he? Or did he drive over to the Sutherlands' and exact a little vigilante justice?"

Ruth's chin began to wobble. "What are you trying to do, Leona? I don't understand why you're accusing everyone we know!"

I rubbed my forehead. I honestly didn't know why I was badgering Ruth like this. Maybe it was her comment about outsiders that had rubbed me the wrong way. "Sorry. I just think we shouldn't rule out possibilities. Nobody should get a pass when it's something so serious. Not even me. Not even Anne, for goodness sake! Wouldn't you want to kill Walt if he was your husband?"

Ruth rolled her eyes and tossed up her hands. "Now you've gone too far. One second you're bringing her casseroles, the next you're saying lock her up because she had an unhappy marriage."

"No, hear me out. Maybe Anne and Joe were having an actual affair and Walt caught them doing more than kissing. That'd explain why Walt was so angry—maybe it was more than a first kiss. The day after their relationship is exposed, Joe just disappears. For twenty years, Anne thinks he left her without saying goodbye. He abandoned her. But then when I dug up his skeleton, she realizes Walt murdered him. Her lover's body has been right under her nose for decades. She'd be angry. I know I would be."

Ruth nodded. "More than angry. I'd be livid. It all falls apart when you think about Anne as a person though, doesn't it? I can believe Walt is a killer, but Anne? Her own husband? She just doesn't have it in her." Ruth squinted into the distance as though she could see the Sutherland farmhouse through the cottage wall.

"Believe me, I could kill my ex easier than just about anybody on planet Earth," I muttered. "The fact that Walt is her husband makes it *more* plausible, not less. Did you know he's been beating up on her for years?"

Ruth's frown deepened. "How do you know that? Walt's a bit of a curmudgeon and not someone I'd want to marry, but so is pretty much every other man of his generation around here. I've never seen him act violent."

"I saw the bruises on her neck last night. She said as much."

"Huh." Ruth's tone was skeptical. "How'd you notice something after living here three weeks that I didn't see in thirty years?"

I shrugged. "I guess you never know what's going on inside someone else's marriage unless you see it really close up. My relationship with Peterson looked perfect on the outside, right? TV-perfect. Like a shiny red apple with unblemished skin that's all rotten on the inside. You wouldn't know anything was wrong. Even Andrea didn't know—she's still mad at me because she thinks I didn't try hard enough to repair things after the *America Today* incident. She didn't realize that I'd been struggling to fix our relationship for at least a decade." I sighed, thinking of those grandbabies.

"I'm sorry," Ruth said quietly. "I mean, sorry that you had to go through that. That you still are going through it. I'm sure Andrea will come around with some time." She paused, and then said hesitantly, "Now, don't take this the wrong way, but maybe you're projecting your personal feelings about marriage onto Anne a little bit? I mean—you've always had a lot of fire, Leona. And even *you* didn't kill Peterson when you probably should have."

"Ha!" My laugh startled the puddle of sleeping chicks, who peeped and ran around the tub before settling back down again.

Ruth grinned as she watched the babies nod off again. "Anne's not that kind of woman. I know her, and she's a decent human being."

"Even decent humans have a breaking point." I raised an eyebrow.

"But I know her. This is a small town!"

"You know her, but you don't *know* her," I said.

"Rusty does, though," Ruth said stubbornly. "He's spent his whole life working on this farm right next door to the Sutherlands, and he and Walt were real friends."

I stopped short. "Let's ask him, then."

"What?"

"Let's ask Rusty about Joe and Anne's relationship. He knew the Sutherlands well and he worked side-by-side with Joe. He saw them both up close. He'd be the one to know if they had an affair back then—if it was more than just a one-sided crush. Come on."

Chapter 25

I moved past Ruth, through the tiny living room toward the front door.

Ruth followed me out of the bedroom. "And what if Joe and Anne did have an affair? What would that prove, anyway?"

"It wouldn't prove anything, but it might explain why Anne snapped and killed Walt when she realized he was Joe's murderer." I opened the front door and squinted out. Rusty was steering the tractor carefully back toward the barn. I started down the steps toward him.

"She's not a killer!" Ruth yelped as she trotted after me. "You can't just say stuff like that about people without a whole lot of caveats just because you have a wild hair. The poor woman just lost her husband! Don't get Rusty to say something he'll regret."

"Rusty!" I hollered, waving my arms to get his attention. He turned down the throttle when he saw me and waved back. I jogged ahead of Ruth. "Hey, I have a question!"

"Oh yeah?" He turned the tractor all the way off and ran a hand through his bushy hair so it stood straight up. "What's up? What do you think of my progress? The tractor's running good, right?"

"I'm impressed. I was wondering—you worked on the

Sutherland place quite a bit over the years, didn't you?"

"Sure I did," he said, looking wary.

Ruth drew up next to me, panting and holding an arm across her chest. "You gotta warn me at least twenty-four hours in advance that we're going to run. I'm wearing the wrong bra for this nonsense."

"Nobody told you to chase me across the yard."

"I'm just trying to keep my brother out of trouble," she said, shooting Rusty a meaningful look.

"Trouble? What kind of trouble?" Rusty looked back and forth between us.

I rolled my eyes. "Imaginary trouble. I just want to know—was Anne sleeping with Hobo Joe? Be honest."

His jaw dropped. "No!"

"Do you think they could have been doing it in secret? Did he talk about her a lot or meet with her alone?"

Rusty's face crumpled. "No! What? Why would you ask something like that?"

"See?" Ruth said, grabbing my arm. "Leave him out of it."

I shook off Ruth's hand and ignored her, addressing Rusty. "Joe never mentioned Anne in all the hours you worked together? You never guessed all his bonfire songs were written for her?"

"I mean—he mentioned her name," Rusty mumbled. "We talked about the Sutherlands because we did jobs over there. But Anne would never stoop to sleep with someone like Joe. You shouldn't say stuff like that." He grimaced at the thought.

"That's what I said." Ruth pursed her lips at me. "It's not a good idea to cast aspersions, Leona."

For some reason their reluctance to talk about it made me even more determined to get answers. "What do you mean, 'someone like Joe'? A Canadian? A musician? I thought everyone liked him."

"They did," Rusty said darkly. "Too much if you ask me. But he was a hobo, a train-hopper. He didn't understand loyalty. He could disappear overnight, anytime—and he *did*. Who wants a relationship with someone like that? Not a woman like Anne."

"Rusty," Ruth said slowly, her forehead creasing deeply. "You do realize that Joe disappeared overnight because he was killed, right? Not because of his flawed character. For all we know, Joe might have settled down in Honeytree if someone hadn't ended his life."

"Of course I know that now. But I didn't know back then, when I filled in the duck pond." Rusty's shoulders sagged as he motioned to the broken earth nearby where Joe's skeleton had been buried. "I just thought he took off and left us all behind."

Ruth clucked her tongue sympathetically and reached out to squeeze Rusty's shoulder. My heart, which had been beating a mile a minute, stilled. Of course, filling in this hole in my front yard would be like déjà vu for Rusty. He'd unknowingly filled in a grave in this exact location twenty years ago. How could I have been so insensitive to ask him to do the same task?

"I'm sorry," I said, shaking my head. Ruth looked at me with *I told you so* written all over her face. She knew exactly why I was feeling chagrined. "I guess I got ahead of myself. I thought if Anne and Joe were having an affair, that could explain why Walt was angry enough to kill him—and why Anne might take revenge twenty years later. I didn't mean to bring up bad memories for you."

Rather than its intended effect, my apology made Rusty's

face turned redder than a rooster's comb, and I thought he might burst into tears. He opened his mouth to say something, then stopped himself, then blurted out angrily, "First Anne's hooking up with hobos, and now she's a murderer?"

"It's just a theory..." I trailed off when I saw Ruth's face crumple in disappointment.

"You can't say things like that, Leona. You could really hurt someone."

"What are you talking about?" I held out my hands toward her, bewildered. "A few minutes ago, you called Eli because you were suspicious of Yelena, and now you're getting mad at me for being suspicious of Anne? When did you become such a hypocrite?"

"There's a big difference between telling the sheriff a piece of information that might be relevant in a case and spreading malicious rumors."

"That's a laugh—half the rumors in town come straight out of the Do or Dye," I said, stung by her accusation.

Ruth paused, shaking her head sadly as she backed away from me toward where her car was parked. "You're not the person I thought you were." She whirled and, without a backward glance, got into her car and sped down the driveway, pausing only for a split-second before turning onto the highway and barreling back toward Honeytree.

My heart felt like stone, sinking from my chest to somewhere deep in my belly. My only true friend left in the world, Ruth was the last person I wanted to alienate. Before I opened my big fat mouth and accused my neighbor of murder, I should have remembered that town loyalties run deep—and so do town grudges. I needed to make amends, and fast, if I wanted to have any hope of recovering from my gaffe.

"I didn't mean it," I said to Rusty, embarrassed to make eye contact with him. "I was just talking and not thinking. I won't hold it against you if you can't finish the project, though. Come on in the house while I write you a check for the magic you worked today on the tractor."

"I didn't do anything." Rusty kicked a clod of dirt, the deep red color in his cheeks fading to pink. "Doesn't take magic to tinker a little bit."

"Only a wizard could get that old tractor up and running in less than a half-hour, though." I was gratified to see the corner of his mouth turn up and his shoulders straighten. "Let me pay you for your trouble."

He shook his head. "I won't take a check for a job left undone. Granddad wouldn't have it. I'll be back in the morning to help you fill in the hole after the county boys leave. You can pay me then."

Gratitude for his generosity flooded my chest, buoying my heart back up where it belonged. "I appreciate it, Rusty. And I appreciate all your advice about the apples, too—I didn't want to hear it, but I swear I'm listening."

He nodded absentmindedly, his attention already back on the tractor as he fired up the engine.

"You'll tell Ruth that I'm sorry?"

He looked up momentarily. "You better tell her yourself. She doesn't believe anything 'less it comes from the source."

He was right—as much as Ruth gossiped with her hairdressing clients, I'd never heard her share a rumor that wasn't true. Certainly not one that was malicious or hurtful. I pulled my phone out and sent her a text, even though I knew she was probably still driving.

"I'm sorry," I wrote. "Forgive me?"

I waited there a minute or two, standing there in the driveway with her brother, but no answer came.

Chapter 26

That night, I tossed and turned in my attic bedroom, jumping at every little creak and cricket chirp. The background hum of the generator powering the crime scene lights outside buzzed louder and louder in my ears until I stuffed my pillow over my head and moaned. But even after I heard the techs shut off the generator and their vehicles crunch down the driveway when their shift ended, I couldn't sleep. All I could think about was the hurt look on Ruth's face when she left my house.

I checked my phone. Still no reply from her.

After staring at the ceiling for another solid five minutes, I gave up and got out of bed. There was no point in wasting wakeful hours—I might as well go check on the chickens. I pulled on a pair of sweatpants under my short nightgown even though I didn't expect anyone to see me, mostly because the sweatpants had pockets that could hold my phone. First I stopped by Boots's bin and then, seeing all the chicks snuggled peacefully under the mama heating pad, headed out to the barn, nightgown flapping.

I winced as the barn door squealed open. A gentle chorus of sleepy clucks came from the stock tank in the back of the barn. It was a good sound, the sound of a peacefully sleeping hen and rooster who were only slightly disturbed. Apparently I was the only one on this farm who couldn't get a good night of sleep. I almost wished Eli was parked out in the driveway so I could wake him up and have someone to talk to.

Not really. Really I wished I could call Ruth. She was the kind of friend who wouldn't get upset if you called her late at night. The kind of friend I couldn't really afford to lose. My head started to ache. I leaned against the tarp-covered Porsche and rubbed my forehead as I wracked my brain trying to figure out how I could I get Ruth to forgive me. I'd accused her of malicious gossip and hypocrisy, accused her friends of adultery and murder. No wonder she was done with me. But obviously she wasn't accepting a simple apology.

I checked my phone again, but it didn't have any text notifications—just the time, two o'clock in the morning, the double-zeroes glaring at me from the screen. Nobody should be awake at this hour. Even highway patrol was off duty at two a.m., according to Eli.

I jerked my head up. Highway patrol was off duty. Why hadn't I thought of it before? There was no better way to clear my mind than a drive. Whisking the tarp off the Porsche, I admired the sleek lines of the little convertible. Poor girl, she hadn't had a good run since the move. I'd been starting her up to keep the battery charged every so often, but she hadn't been out on the highway and stretched her legs—and she had long legs.

The driver's seat felt like an embrace from an old friend, almost as good as one of Ruth's hugs. The car started up and purred like a kitten, and I backed out of the barn right away to let her warm up in the driveway, so the exhaust wouldn't affect the sensitive little chicks. A few minutes later, and I was out on the open road, the wind twisting my bedhead into crazy corkscrews as I accelerated down the Flats.

As the car slipped past the Sutherland place, I caught a glimpse of spotlights still on near the blueberry shed. The forensics team must be working through the night. Was Eli there? Is that why he hadn't camped out in my driveway? Or had I finally run him off?

Oh, who cared. I shook my head and let the car go full-out. She didn't let me down—she gripped the highway and a few seconds later I was pressed against my seat. I only had a few seconds to enjoy the straightaway before I spotted the Curves ahead. I let off the gas a little and focused on what came next—steering into the turn at just the right moment, adjusting the speed using the accelerator instead of the brake. My mind settled, anxiety lifting as I prepared for the challenge. Ruth had her incense and crystals, but this was my meditation, taking these shadowed turns with pure focus on the pavement.

Meditation was supposed to be lonely, right?

The moon the only witness to my driving prowess, I slowed as I came into town and pulled into the parking lot of the sawmill. Plenty of cars were there for the graveyard shift, but otherwise the town was deserted. Nobody saw me turn around and head back, eager to regain the focus and momentum I'd felt in the Curves.

But the way home felt different. The focus that had come so easily on the drive toward Honeytree eluded me. I pushed harder through the turns, anticipating the Flats where I'd be able to let the little car demonstrate her full horsepower, but the moonlit shadows of the trees that arched over the road suddenly felt ominous. Distracting. I shook my head and took the next turn harder, pushing the car to its limits around the tight curve.

Something flickered in my peripheral vision and I slammed on the brakes, skidding to a stop just milliseconds before a three-point buck leaped across the road in front of me.

Close call. Too close.

I waited there on the dark, empty highway until I caught my breath and then crept the rest of the way through the Curves, staying well under the speed limit, paranoid that another deer might emerge from the underbrush. When I made it to the Flats where the farmland on either side meant fewer hiding places for wild animals, my shoulders relaxed a little. I was almost home, and now that my adrenaline had come down a notch, I was suddenly very, very tired.

I was so tired that I didn't even balk when headlights flashed at me from the end of the Sutherland driveway. I knew it was Eli. I pulled over and waited for him to walk to my car.

"I wasn't speeding this time." I was sure of it, even if I hadn't glanced at the speedometer. I looked up at him and saw eyes as tired as mine felt. "You've been working late."

He nodded, stifling a yawn. "You, too. I saw the light on in the barn earlier."

"Couldn't sleep," I said. "Too much on my mind."

"You want me to stay over? I'm getting used to crashing in my front seat."

I shook my head. "No—I'll be fine."

He looked a little relieved and stretched his arms over his head, then used both hands to crack his neck. "My back says thank you. Plus, I could really use a shower." He grinned.

"No kidding." I waved my hand in front of my nose and kept my face deadpan.

His eyes crinkled around the edges. "OK. I'll swing by in

the morning to sign off on your crime scene. Blake says all they have left to do is pack up the last of the sifting setup."

"Can't say I'm sorry to see you all go."

"Goodnight, Leona." He paused. "Just curious…how fast did you get her up to?"

I grinned at him and motioned to his badge that glinted in the glow of the headlights. "You know I can't tell you that."

Chapter 27

I woke to the sound of someone hammering on my front door. I opened my eyes blearily, checked the time on my phone, and then when I saw it was after nine, I jumped out of bed so fast that it made me dizzy. I hadn't slept in this late since high school.

Stumbling to the closet, I located the pair of cargo pants I'd worn yesterday and a shirt that passed the sniff test and pulled them on as I headed downstairs. I yanked the T-shirt down over my stomach and twisted my hair up into a bun before I opened the front door, squinting in the bright sun that seemed to shoot daggers into my skull. I felt like I had a hangover and I hadn't even been drinking.

Rusty's eyes bugged out as he took in my appearance. "Did I wake you up?"

"No," I lied, surreptitiously sweeping the sleep grains out of my eyes.

"Then what happened to you?" He leaned closer to me, scrutinizing my face.

My fingers went unconsciously to my cheeks, where I felt the telltale lines of pillowcase wrinkles pressed into them. "OK, maybe I was asleep. I had a late night."

Rusty grinned broadly, clearly making some assumptions.

"Good for you." He bumped the handle of the shovel he was holding on the porch floor. He'd made good on his word and brought his own tools. "Looks like the county guys cleared out already so I just wanted to check in with you before I got started." He turned, affording me a view of the little tractor he'd already pulled out of the barn parked on the other side of the driveway next to the dirt pile.

The dirt pile looked even bigger now that the enormous forensics van wasn't next to it. A few of my original stakes remained upright in the ground beyond it, the ends of crime scene tape fluttering from them, but I'd need to re-mark the rest of the chicken coop foundation once the ground was leveled. "How long do you think it'll take to get it all leveled out?" I asked.

He squinted one eye, calculating. "I guess about a day, maybe two if the tractor's ornery."

I nodded, stifling a yawn. "I'll let you get to it then. I'm going to make some coffee. You want some?"

"I'll never say no to a fresh pot of coffee. Double sugar, no cream." He flashed me a rakish smile, the kind he'd been famous for in school when he was voted class clown. It was something else to see his fifty-something face look fifteen for a second, and I felt a squeeze of love for him and his family. For Ruth. The two of them had been a part of my life for so long, they felt more like cousins than friends.

That's it, I wasn't letting Ruth off the hook so easy. You couldn't just walk away from family, even if they were acting like a chicken turd. I made some quick pour-over coffee, sweetened it to cavity-causing levels, and took a mug of it out to Rusty, who, to my surprise, wasn't working. He was standing next to the hole staring back at the house. At my

Suburban, to be exact.

I turned to see what he was looking at and almost dropped the coffee.

Scratched into the paint on the passenger-side door was a message.

GO HOME. Then a word that I won't repeat, but it wasn't polite.

The blood drained from my face and I stood there, frozen, until Rusty gently coaxed one mug from my grip. "I need some coffee to deal with this." He tossed back a long swill, wincing as the hot liquid hit his throat. "What do you think it means?"

"I guess someone's not too happy that I'm back in town," I said coolly, even though my insides were a storm of emotions. Who'd taken the time to sneak up my driveway in the middle of the night to vandalize my car? The eerie feeling someone was watching me crawled up my back, but I shook off the urge to check over my shoulder. I wasn't going to let anyone see me crack. "Oh well, their problem, not mine."

"Too bad about that. Gonna cost a penny to repaint."

"Guess so." I swallowed hard. It was either that, or drive around with an NC-17 message on the side of my car all day. All the moms in Honeytree were going to love that. Maybe Tambra had some nail polish that matched my paint job and would help me touch it up.

"Oh, I almost forgot! There's a little surprise for you in the barn!" Rusty said.

Hoping for a distraction from the unsettling message, I headed into the barn, where I noticed I'd forgotten to pull the tarp back over the Porsche after my late-night drive. I started to pull it back over the car when I stopped in my tracks.

"What the cluck?!"

Perched on the headrests of my beloved convertible were two damp, bedraggled full-grown hens, one white and one black. They were missing half the feathers on their backs but had more than their share on their heads. In fact, they looked like Vegas showgirls wearing giant feathered headdresses.

"Rusty!" I screeched, storming out of the barn with my fists clenched. Rusty was already using the tractor to push the nearest section of the dirt pile into the hole, but when he caught sight of me, his eyes widened and he cut the tractor's engine.

"What's wrong?"

I planted my fists on my hips. "If this is some kind of joke, it's really not funny!"

He shook his head, his expression bewildered. "You want me to move the dirt somewhere else?"

"Not the dirt, the chickens! Did you bring them over to prank me?"

He chuckled and shook his head. "Nah, a few minutes ago some station wagon slowed down long enough to toss those two biddies into the ditch by the highway. I stuck 'em under your lamp to dry off."

Well, they weren't under the lamp anymore. I rubbed my face in frustration. "You've got to be kidding me."

"I was just trying to help." His face reddened, and instantly I was sorry for yelling at him, even though the two bedraggled birds could be bringing all kinds of disease into my flock. He'd been operating from a place of compassion, not malice.

I sighed. "I'm not talking about you. You did the right thing. I'm talking about whoever dumped their hens in my lap."

He beat a thoughtful rhythm on the tractor steering wheel. "Someone probably heard you're starting up a chicken farm and thought you'd give their laying hens a good home. They're trying to help."

I snorted. They were helping my farm by dumping birds like whoever vandalized the Suburban was helping keep it clean by scratching the paint. "People are trying to unload their manure is what you mean. Those two birds could be spent, sick, who knows what. You saw them—they're a mess. I've got a falling-down farm, a coop for eighty-six chickens to build, and a different dead guy popping up every day. The last thing I need is random dirty birds getting thrown into the mix."

Ignoring my rant, Rusty started up the tractor again, and his face lit up when it roared to life. "Will you listen to that? Turned right over! I didn't even have to crank it. I'm kinda proud of myself on this one."

"Nice work," I said, sighing. "I'll let you get back to it."

"You know," he said, his voice raised over the engine sounds so he was shouting at me even though I was standing two feet away, "I wouldn't put the coop here. You want to put it closer to the barn, I think, so you're not having to constantly haul feed and water back and forth."

I shook my head and motioned to my right ear. "Sorry, I can't hear you over the tractor!" I lied, then turned and speed-walked back to the barn before he could yell his unnecessary opinions at me again.

Rusty didn't know that I'd spent more than a few hours picking out the perfect coop site. The spot I'd chosen got exactly the right combination of shade and sun, had the perfect drainage and the least cover for predators, and—perhaps most importantly—gave me the best view of the coop from the kitchen window. Those chickens were going to be my livelihood during my retirement, and I wasn't going to compromise their safety to save myself a few yards of walking.

I wasn't going to compromise their health, either. I might not have the heart to toss the two interlopers back in the ditch out front, but I had enough sense to quarantine them from the rest of my vulnerable flock.

Back in the barn, I checked the brooder. Dr. Speckle was dozing peacefully with dozens of babies squirming underneath her, Alarm Clock had hopped inside the brooder and was gobbling up the chick starter, and the chicks that couldn't squeeze beneath Dr. Speckle or perch on her back were back under the heat lamp. But the new hens were nowhere to be seen.

They weren't in any buckets or hiding behind the straw bales, either. I looked above my head and spied a telltale tail feather peeking out from the edge of a beam. "Ah ha!"

I grabbed a ladder that was leaning against the back wall of the barn and set it against the beam, but as soon as I ascended, the hens squawked and fluttered to a new location. I groaned and slumped on the top of the ladder. How was I supposed to get them down when every time I got near them, they flew away? I needed to stop chasing and start luring.

I climbed down and, patting my cargo pocket to make sure I still had a few crumbles of chick starter in there left over from yesterday, climbed the steep stairs to the loft that extended over half the barn. A few small scattered piles of hay gave away its intended purpose—Amos Chapman had used the loft to store hay for his livestock. But the back corner also had a rusty old spring bedframe pushed up against the wall. This was where Joe must have slept when he was living and working at the farm.

Dropping to my knees, I scooted toward the beam where the hens were huddled just beyond my reach, careful not to get too close to the edge. I sprinkled a little bit of crumble on the edge of the beam and then moved back so they would feel safer approaching, clucking softly with my tongue. "Here, chicky-chickies."

The hens turned their ridiculous poofy heads toward me and clucked softly to themselves, but they didn't make a move to eat the food. They had no idea what was going on. Maybe their silly feathered hairdos were blocking their vision. I tapped softly near the small pile of chick starter, as though my fingers were a beak. That was how mother hens showed their chicks where to find food. "Here chicky-chicks. Come and eat. This is for you."

Tap, tap, tap.

The white hen cocked her head and sidled a couple of feet toward me. I tapped again, and she scooted the rest of the way to the food and began pecking at it. At the sound of her friend gobbling up the starter, the black hen pushed her way to the loft and joined in on the feast, her back to me. I didn't wait—I snatched her before she had her guard up again and, holding her wings firmly at her sides so she couldn't flap away, took her downstairs.

With an apology, I stuffed the black hen into a temporary holding tank, also known as the five-gallon bucket with a lid I'd used to contain Alarm Clock, then went back for her sister. The white hen, now savvy to my hawkish predation, heard me approach and took off flapping. Thankfully she chose to fly left instead of right, perching on the wrought-iron headboard of the old bed instead of way out somewhere on a beam where I couldn't reach her.

I slowly crept toward the bed, leaning to avoid bumping my head on the slanted ceiling and hardly daring to breathe. The hen turned around on her perch nervously, seemingly unaware whether she faced into the wall or toward an escape route. I waited until her head was pointed toward the corner before I lunged and grabbed her. I missed her wings but caught her by the leg and reeled her in, flapping and hollering, until I could clamp her under my arm and quiet her.

Success. I clutched her grimly, wiping the sweat off my forehead with my forearm. As I turned to go back downstairs, I forgot to duck and clocked my head against the rafters. I moaned in pain and rubbed the growing egg above my right eye with my free hand.

"I'm fine!" I reflexively said to no one. "I just hit my head on…" My voice trailed off as I caught sight of the offending rafter. It was crowded with generations of carved names, dark with age. Instinctively, I reached up and ran my finger over the ones I recognized.

Ruth. Rusty. Amos. Anne 4-Ever. Anne's name had a heart around it. I traced the heart with my free hand. Joe must have carved it when he lived up here. He must have been pretty obsessed with her if he was spending his free time writing songs about her and carving her name into the wood where he could stare at it every night.

So Joe definitely had more than a casual crush on Anne Sutherland, and it made me wonder—would he carve "4-Ever" about someone who didn't even know he liked her? Forever meant something was going on between them, right? Something that Joe wanted to last. Maybe my wild theories about Joe and Anne having a real affair weren't so crazy after all. I just needed to find a way to bring it up to Eli without ticking

Ruth off any further.

I pulled out my phone and thumb-typed, "I know you're mad at me, but we really need to talk."

The chicken under my arm tried to wriggle free and I clamped her there more firmly while I sent the text and headed down the steep loft stairs. I picked up a second lidded bucket and popped the white hen inside until I could find a proper place to quarantine both birds. Maybe I'd be able to convert one of the old horse stalls into a temporary holding cell until I was sure the two hens were healthy.

But first, coffee.

Chapter 28

I caught sight of a black sheriff's SUV turning off the highway as I was heading back into the house. I stopped in my tracks and groaned. Just what I needed, Eli here to stir up the drama that had just settled to the bottom of the proverbial bucket. I glanced at my phone to see if Ruth had responded to my text yet, but she hadn't, and I cursed under my breath. OK, maybe it wasn't under my breath.

"What's wrong?" Rusty looked up from the tractor's seat, his brow furrowed with concern, and saw Eli getting out of the truck, balancing two giant cups of Dutch Brothers coffee. Rusty shut off the engine. "Do you want me to get rid of him?"

By then, Eli was close enough to catch the tail end of the question. "You can't get rid of me. I'm here on police business." He handed me one of the coffees and added, "Creamer, no sugar, right?" He was right. I took a grateful sip, scalding my tongue in the process.

Before I could say thanks, Rusty swung his leg off the tractor and got dangerously close to Eli. "Oh really? What business is that? Stalking women you have a crush on?"

To my surprise, Eli took a step back and put up his free hand, as though Rusty were the one with a gun on his belt. "Hey man, I'm just doing my job. I have a case to investigate, and

Leona's an integral part of that. I need her help."

Rusty crossed his arms and tipped his head back to scan Eli from head to toe, skepticism seeping from his every pore. "Please. We've known each other our whole lives and you're not fooling anybody. You're hanging around here, bribing her with gifts, hoping to rekindle a fire that went out thirty-odd years ago, but Leona needs you like a hole in the head. If she wanted you, she would have married you back in the day. Her priority is the orchard now, not solving some cold case. She needs to focus on the farm."

This time, Eli didn't step back. Instead, he pointed a finger at Rusty's chest, his jaw tight. "The orchard is *your* priority, Chapman. *I'm* hanging around here, living in the past? You're the one who's telling Leona what to do like your family still owns the farm and she's just a sharecropping tenant. She doesn't want to be an apple farmer! She never did. What she wants—"

"Enough!" I said sharply. Both their heads swiveled toward me, their faces registering shock as though they'd forgotten I was there even though they were arguing about me. "Neither of you have any business deciding what I want or don't want, need or don't need. I'm the one who decides that. You can both take a hike."

They stood there, frozen, staring at me with open mouths. I stamped my foot and pointed at the highway. "I mean it. Go!"

"But I'm not done," Rusty protested, gesturing to the remaining dirt pile behind him. "I've barely even started."

"I'll finish the rest on my own," I said stiffly. "It's dirt, not impossible."

"I can help with the work," Eli began, but I silenced him with a cutting look.

"I don't need your help. In case I wasn't clear before, I'm not interested in your opinions, either. Don't you have a case to solve? Go talk to people who might actually know who killed Walt, because I don't." Then to Rusty, I added, "Hang on, I'll get you your money."

I let the front door bang shut behind me, my brain buzzing angrily as I rummaged through my purse and all the pockets in the jackets hanging by the door. How dare Rusty say Eli had a crush on me—that was humiliating to us both! And how dare Eli speak for me about what I wanted for my own farm like he was my dad or something. He needed to mind his own business. I located a few crumpled bills—not enough to pay Rusty fairly for resurrecting the tractor and getting a third of the dirt put back where it belonged.

I went to raid the emergency fund I kept in the cookie jar on the deep windowsill above the kitchen sink. It was shaped like a Barred Rock hen and made me smile every time I looked at it.

As I lifted the head off the chicken and reached for the bills inside the jar, out the window I noticed Rusty and Eli were exchanging some choice words in the middle of the driveway. *My* driveway, I wanted to remind them. If they were still arguing about what I should do or shouldn't do, they could save their breath. And if they got so hot that they came to blows—at this rate, it didn't look unlikely—I was going to turn the hose on them.

Eli seemed to hear my thoughts. He turned his back on Rusty and stormed over to the porch steps. Apparently, his strategy to win the argument was to be the first to intercept me on my way out. Rusty took a different tack. He returned to the dirt pile and, rather than firing up the tractor, channeled his anger into shoveling as much dirt as possible, as quickly as possible back into the hole. I froze, my hand still inside the chicken-shaped cookie jar.

Maybe Eli was right. Maybe Walt told me the truth about seeing a man burying the body early that morning, twenty years ago. I'd assumed it was a story he'd invented to cast suspicion on Amos and away from himself. I thought his story was thin—everyone knew Amos had a bad back and couldn't have buried a body himself. But maybe both things could be true. Maybe Walt wasn't the killer and Amos didn't bury the body.

Because one other person would have seemed perfectly at home shoveling dirt on the Chapman farm in the wee hours of the morning—Rusty. Tambra had seen Rusty and Joe arguing that night at the bonfire, I remembered. Did their argument continue after Walt chased Joe back to the Chapman farm?

Out the window, Rusty planted his shovel in the dirt to catch his breath, and the chill sunk deeper into my bones. A shovel just like that was the weapon that had killed Joe. I stuffed the bills from the cookie jar into my pocket and rubbed my upper arms to get rid of the goosebumps that had prickled to the surface. The more I thought about it, the more probable it seemed.

There was no way around it—I had to ask him about it. And lucky me, the cops were already here. Stalkerish or not, never had I been more thankful to have gun-toting Eli hanging around in front of my house.

"Rusty!" I called as soon as I stepped out the front door. I thudded down the porch stairs two at a time, jerking my head at Eli to let him know that he should follow me. "I'm just curious—when was the last time you saw Hobo Joe alive?"

The blood drained from Rusty's cheeks and he stood there stiffly, one arm balanced on the shovel's short handle like a scarecrow in a field. It took a few moments for his mouth to form the words. "I—I—why do you ask?"

Beside me, Eli put his hands on his hips. "The question is, why aren't you answering her? When was it, Rusty?"

Suddenly Rusty became very interested in shoveling dirt again. Then, seeming to realize that shoveling dirt could look incriminating, he put down the shovel and headed toward the tractor. But before he took a seat on it, he stopped short and turned back toward us. "You already know when it was. It was at the bonfire," he said. "That's why I paused. I wondered why you were asking."

I realized he wasn't going to admit anything in front of Eli—not if I made it seem like I suspected him of any wrongdoing. I softened my approach. "I've done a little more digging since we talked about it last time," I explained. "Anne told me that Walt chased Joe off their property that night. I thought you might have seen Joe when he came back here to the farm. It would have been late, maybe midnight."

Rusty shook his head, his eyes trained stubbornly on the ground. "I never saw him alive again."

Something about his wording caught my attention. He didn't say that he never saw Joe again—he said he never saw him *alive*. Was he just echoing my original question? Or did he mean something more sinister?

"You didn't see him *alive*," I said slowly, gauging his expression as I spoke. His face turned toward me, his eyes widening. "Does that mean you saw him—"

"Dead?" Eli finished, taking a step toward Rusty and slightly in front of me, partially blocking him from my view.

I swatted Eli on the arm with the back of my hand and stepped back in front of him. "Was it *you* Walt saw filling in the duck pond at five o'clock in the morning? Did you bury Joe?"

Rusty's chin wobbled and he squeezed his eyes shut.

"It's OK, you can tell us," Eli said reassuringly from behind me. "Let it out, man. You've been holding this in too long."

"Yeah," Rusty finally choked out. "It was me. I drove out early in the morning to clean up all the cans and bottles from the bonfire so Granddad wouldn't be ticked off about the trash in his yard. But when I got here, I found Joe lying on the ground with his head bashed in. It was horrible..." He leaned forward and put his hands on his knees, his back wracked with silent sobs as he tried to hold in his tears.

"Why didn't you call the sheriff when you found Joe's body?" Eli asked, his voice almost a whisper like Rusty was a deer he didn't want to spook.

Rusty stood and rubbed his forehead and then squeezed the bridge of his nose. His voice cracked as he answered. "I felt responsible, I guess. Guilty."

I frowned as I tried to understand. "Why would you feel guilty if you didn't kill him?"

He sighed heavily. "After the bonfire, I went to the house and told Granddad that Joe was a thief, that he was the one who stole Walt's telescope. The next morning, when I saw Joe there in the half-dug pond, I knew Granddad had killed him because of what I'd said. I should have kept it to myself and none of this would have ha—ha—" He broke down in sobs again, sinking to his knees in the dirt.

In an instant I was next to him, my arm around his shoulders. "It's OK. It's not your fault. You panicked," I murmured.

211

Eli looked at me, wide-eyed with alarm, and motioned for me to move away from Rusty, but I just patted Rusty's back comfortingly. "You were protecting your grandfather."

Rusty hung his head. "I was trying to. I got Joe's clothes and guitar case from the barn and buried them with him at the bottom of the duck pond. It was a stupid place—it was just the quickest and easiest because of all the loose dirt. And of course Granddad didn't argue about filling in the pond."

"And you told everyone Joe hitched a train back to Canada," Eli added.

Rusty nodded. "I was surprised at how easy they believed it. Nobody even questioned it. Nobody wondered why he didn't say goodbye."

Tambra did, I thought. But she was the only one. It seemed everyone else went on with their lives like Joe had never been there. Eli reached out and put his hand on my upper arm, gently urging me to stand. I could tell he wanted me to move away from Rusty, so I ignored him. I knew Rusty wasn't dangerous—he was devastated. I leaned my head toward his. "I'm so sorry you were put in such a bad position."

Rusty shifted so he could look me in the eye, his brows knit worriedly together. "I'm the one who's sorry. I put *you* in a tough position. I knew Joe was buried here and I didn't warn you."

"That's why you didn't want to keep the farm yourself, though," Eli said thoughtfully. "I've been wondering—everyone's been wondering—why you'd let this place go. I guess I know why now: cowardice."

Abruptly, Rusty stood, his eyes blazing. "Who are you calling a coward?!"

"You. You were afraid to live here because you knew Joe

212

was there, under the ground. You pawned off the dead guy on Leona rather than face what you did."

I took Rusty's arm protectively, shielding him from Eli's insults with my body like I knew Ruth would want me to. "Don't be mean! He made a poor choice twenty years ago, but he shouldn't be punished for it forever. He was just trying to do the right thing for his family."

"Well, it was the wrong thing, not the right thing." Eli set his jaw stubbornly and pulled a set of handcuffs from his belt pouch. "I'm afraid I have to take you in, Rusty. Improper burial is against the law. So is obstructing an investigation by withholding information. You're accountable for those crimes. You need to pay your debt to society, even twenty years later."

"Isn't it enough that he sacrificed this farm? How much more do you want him to give up?" I clutched Rusty's arm protectively, but Eli just started reading Rusty his Miranda rights as he moved around behind us and clapped the handcuff on Rusty's free wrist. To Rusty's credit, he didn't even try to struggle. He pulled his arm away from my grasp with a regretful look and held it out for Eli to shackle.

I watched helplessly as Eli loaded Rusty into the back of his SUV and drove off toward Honeytree, where I assumed he'd book Rusty into the town's single holding cell—usually only used as an overnight drunk tank—until Rusty could be transported to the jail in Roseburg.

"Rusty just got arrested," I texted Ruth. "I thought you'd want to know. I have some cash I owe him if you need it to help with bail."

I put my phone away, feeling sick about how Ruth would react when she found out her grandfather was a killer. But oddly, once I settled my stomach with a few deep breaths, the overwhelming sensation I felt was one of relief. I wasn't scared anymore. Because if Amos Chapman killed Joe, that meant Walt's murder probably wasn't related to my investigation of Joe's death. It was related to something else in Walt's life—something that didn't have anything to do with me. Rusty had probably scratched the message in the side of my car when he arrived this morning, before he woke me up. And ironically, now I could follow his instructions and mind my own business. And my business was my chickens.

With a jolt, I remembered that the two Polish hens were still stuck in their buckets—without air holes! I hightailed it into the barn and was relieved when I could hear indignant clucking coming from inside the buckets. I quickly nailed some chicken wire over the frame of one of the stall doors, spread some hay on the floor, and filled some old dog dishes I found on a shelf with food and water. Then I gently moved the buckets into the stall, careful not to jostle the birds inside, and cracked open the lids.

The two Polish hens, sensing freedom at last, flapped out of the buckets straight into my face. I ducked to avoid their flying feathers and surprisingly sharp toenails. "You ungrateful, feather-headed, bony-breasted, freeloading—"

I broke off and fell onto my butt right there in the straw, laughing my sass off, when I saw what was at the bottom of the buckets. Both of those mothercluckers had laid eggs.

Chapter 29

I gave the two hens—who I named Cher and Phyllis in honor of their extravagant hairdos—a quick once-over for parasites. Thankfully, they didn't have any little bugs crawling around on them. Their main problem, besides the feathers obstructing their vision, seemed to be simple malnutrition. Maybe it was worms, maybe it was lack of good feed. Some people around here felt that livestock should forage for their feed, otherwise what was the point.

"I'll shoot 'em when I want to eat 'em" was the general sentiment.

I was glad Cher and Phyllis were going to escape that fate. Whoever had dumped them on my doorstep had picked the right farm after all. "I'll find you a home where you'll be spoiled rotten," I promised them. "But first we've gotta fatten you up and grow some of those feathers back."

I nabbed the still-warm eggs from the bottom of the buckets and carefully latched the stall door behind me, marveling as the perfect, smooth feel of the eggs in my palm. My farm's first eggs. I'd imagined this moment for months now, since the day I submitted the paperwork for my legal separation from Peterson and moved into the guest suite of our sprawling mansion. The day I let myself dream.

Of course, I'd imagined it differently, with orderly rows of laying hens obediently laying identical large, brown eggs in cozy nest boxes. I didn't think it'd be two crazy-headed Polish birds with half their feathers missing popping out eggs in the bottom of a bucket. But I also didn't imagine how good it would feel to make breakfast—two over-easy eggs on a bed of steamed spinach with a sprinkle of parmesan and a squeeze of lemon—with eggs from my own flock. Heaven on earth. And just what I needed to power the rest of the day.

I spent the next eight hours mastering the art of tractor-driving—it wasn't as easy as Rusty made it look—and I managed to get the hole most of the way filled in before the tractor ran out of gas. I figured that was a sign from the universe that it was time call it a day, although the yard was as bumpy as the potholed driveway.

The next morning, after finishing breakfast and chicken chores that involved changing out all the straw in the brooder tank because the chicks had tipped their water over during the night, I decided to go to town to pick up some protein supplements and dewormer for the adult chickens and some gas for the tractor. I started for the Suburban, but then remembered the terrible message carved into the paint. I didn't really want to flash that all over town and draw attention—attention that might remind people that I didn't belong in Honeytree. Someone clearly didn't want me here.

Had Rusty been the one who scratched *GO HOME* on my car? He had been there early in the morning, before I was awake. He could have written the message before he knocked on the door to wake me. Maybe his jealousy and resentment over me buying the farm had finally spilled over. Just a stupid, impulsive move, not a real threat. That made me feel a little

216

better, but it didn't change the fact that my car was messed up.

The only other option was my little red convertible. Of course, that would draw attention, too. People would say I was still a city girl. That I wasn't fit for farming. But that kind of attention would at least avoid the question of who hated me enough to vandalize my car—or in Rusty's case, who'd been dumb enough to make such a desperate move. He didn't need any more negative attention, either.

The Porsche it was.

#

I got my gas can filled at the station and then headed to the feed store. Sherman wasn't at the counter when I walked in. I guessed he was out back, smoking—good intentions only got you so far when it came to kicking a cigarette habit. The morning sun illuminated golden dust motes floating among the rafters as I made my way to the poultry aisle and began reading labels on the assortment of bottles that lined the shelves. I found antiseptic, antibiotics, electrolytes, vitamin crumbles, insecticide, and an assortment of other pills and potions before I located the protein booster I was looking for, a so-called "feather fixer" designed for molting show birds.

I held the five-pound sack on my hip like a baby while I searched for a good poultry dewormer, but there were none on the shelf. I glanced toward the counter to see if Sherman had returned from his smoke break, but he was still missing. I plunked the sack of feather fixer on the counter and headed for the rear entrance, where I could see the back door was cracked open. As I drew closer, I could hear the sound of voices outside.

"The colony's full," I heard Sherman insist, as he had when I tried to drop off Alarm Clock. "Full up to overflowing—and even if I had room, I don't take hens. Put them on Craigslist."

"I don't know Craig," a woman's voice with a thick Russian accent protested. I poked my head outside and saw Yelena in a green wool coat with her arms crossed as tightly as the braids on her head, glaring up at Sherman. "You have coop, I have chickens—what's the problem?"

"If I put a coupla hens in with these cockerels, the poor girls will get torn apart," Sherman drawled. He shifted a toothpick—perhaps the smoking-cessation trick of the day—to the other side of his mouth.

"Never in my days did I see a rooster kill a hen," Yelena said stubbornly. She caught sight of me and tried to recruit me to her team. "Leona, you have a chicken farm. Have you ever seen a rooster kill a hen?"

Sherman looked at me expectantly, clearly believing my answer would come down on his side, whether because he was right or because he knew his was the only feed store in town and I depended on him for my livelihood, I couldn't tell. "My chicken farming career is about three days old, so I doubt I'm the expert here," I said, hoping to wriggle out from under the question.

Yelena wasn't letting me off so easy. "Really, Leona. Even in books, this doesn't happen."

Sherman shifted his toothpick again, shaking his shoulders like a bug was crawling up his back rather than simple impatience. "Here's how it will go. My boys have things all worked out, see? Because they don't have hens to argue over. But the second I put your birds in there, half of those roosters will be fighting and half of them will be mating. Your hens will get beat all to heck. And when blood is drawn, the flock gets ruthless. Doesn't matter whether the roosters do it or their sisters, see? The point is, your hens will be over-mated and then pecked to death. I'm not putting them in there."

"What am I to do then?!" Yelena put her hands on her hips and channeled Disappointed Grandmother so well that I thought she might demand that Sherman bend over to be switched. Sherman reached for his back pocket and, finding it empty of cigarette packs, adjusted his toothpick and ground it between his teeth until it splintered.

"Why are you getting rid of your chickens?" I asked Yelena, hoping to defuse the tension. "I thought you enjoyed keeping them."

Her mouth puckered up like she'd bitten a lemon. "My sister Roza is sick and her husband is worthless, so I'm going back home to care for her. I don't know how long I will stay, so the birds must go."

"I'm sorry," I said automatically.

Yelena shrugged. "We do what we must for our family. And our *friends*," she said pointedly. Sherman rolled his eyes and edged toward the back door.

"Where does your sister live?" I asked, giving him time to make his escape.

"Canada," Yelena said. "We emigrated there together with our families—oh, it must have been fifty years ago if it was a day."

My eyebrows nearly hit my hairline. So much had happened that I'd forgotten about my stupid joke that Yelena had killed Walt, the one that Ruth had taken too far and reported to the sheriff's office. But maybe Yelena *had* moved to Honeytree to track down her missing son, and then taken revenge on his supposed killer when I cast suspicion on Walt. I tried to

219

picture Yelena attacking Walt with a weapon, but I just couldn't picture the adorable babushka in front of me channeling that kind of rage.

It was probably just a coincidence, I told myself. Canada was a big country. "Whereabouts in Canada?" I asked, keeping my voice casual.

"B.C.," she said. "A little bit outside Vancouver."

Hm, not Toronto. But Joe could have moved there on his own, as an adult. "You said your families came too? Do you have children?"

A wistful expression crossed her face. "Not anymore. My sister has two girls about your age, though. One is a nurse and the other makes quilts. They're not the kind for beds, they hang on the walls. Isn't that strange? Why put in stuffing if it's not to keep someone warm? But she likes it and she makes a living, so…" Yelena shrugged. "What can I say?"

"They sound like interesting people," I said politely. The truth was, I wasn't interested in her nieces at all. It was her comment about not having children *anymore* that piqued my curiosity. "You said you don't have—"

"This your feather fixer, Leona?" Sherman asked from the back door, holding the bag I'd left on the counter.

I nodded. "Someone dumped a couple of hens in bad condition in the ditch in front of my place, so I'm trying to perk them up before I find them new homes."

Sherman chuckled. "I guess the word's out that you're cooking up a chicken farm."

A smile cracked Yelena's weathered cheeks. She clasped her hands gleefully. "Of course! Why didn't I think of that?" she crowed.

"What?" I asked. Sherman chuckled; apparently he was in

on the joke that I still didn't get.

"They're in the back of my station wagon. I'll go move them over." Yelena started around the building and then stopped, turning back to me. "Is your car unlocked?"

"Yeah, it's a convertible and the top is down—wait, are you saying…" But Yelena had already disappeared. I stared at the point where her green woolen sleeve had vanished past the weathered gray siding of the feed store. "Did I just volunteer to take her hens?"

Sherman nodded.

I groaned. "I'm not even going to *ask* how many she's got crammed in the back of her Subaru."

"She told me three. But could be more; you know how it is." He crossed his arms, grinning. "Chicken math."

I frowned. "Chicken math?"

"It's like, you want six birds, so you buy eight in case a couple die…then one turns out to be a rooster and a secret stash of eggs later, you've got a dozen chicks running around and instead of six chickens you have twenty."

"Eighty-nine," I croaked.

"Pardon?" Sherman cupped a hand to his ear.

"I'll have eighty-nine. I wanted forty-eight."

Sherman's eyes twinkled as he gave a satisfied nod. "See? Chicken math. Happens every time. I'll ring you up if you're ready?"

"Dewormer," I said as I followed him back to the register. "I couldn't find it."

Sherman swiped something off a shelf as we passed and handed it to me. It had a picture of a bleating goat on the front.

"Goat and sheep dewormer?" I asked, puzzled.

"Works for birds, too," he said. "No egg withdrawal period. Just watch the dosage—I'll write it down for you." At the counter, he flipped over a sheet of paper and scribbled a few numbers in pencil on it before handing it to me. "Don't mind the stuff on the back. I was just working out the tournament pairing for the bowling league."

"You don't need it?" I proffered the paper.

He shook his head. "Nah. I passed it off to someone else—I'm thinking of quitting the sport. Too many smokers in the league. Bad for the old willpower. Maybe I'll take up poker again now that Walt's spot at the table is open." He gave me an apologetic grimace and rubbed the stubble on his chin. "Sorry—I know you were neighbors with him. I was just thinking out loud. Walt and I used to play cards together back in the day; I'll miss the old coot, too."

I nodded sympathetically. I didn't miss Walt, but I wasn't unaffected by his death, either. Like everybody in town, I wanted to know what happened and why. "Any idea who had something against him?"

Sherman bumped the brim of his cap back with his knuckle as though it'd give him a better view of the situation. "I can't say, really. I haven't spent much time with him since I quit playing maybe fifteen years back. He's always been cantankerous, though. Heck, that's why I left the Spence game—I couldn't stand how he and Zeke would get into it every week. So I get why someone would be ticked off at a guy like him, but I can't understand who'd go so far as to kill him."

My ears perked up at the mention of Zeke's name. "What do you mean, they'd get into it?

"Oh, just arguing over who owed who and who owed what.

Walt would lose his shirt and Zeke would let him pawn his trousers. Then the next week, Walt'd be salty because Zeke sold 'em before he could buy them back. It got to where it wasn't even fun to be in the game, so I shuffled off to Buffalo and picked up bowling." Sherman adjusted his hat, settling it onto his head so the brim rested on his impressively bushy eyebrows. "If I wanted to bicker for hours every Saturday night, I'd stay home with Marilyn! Plus, bowling is cheaper." He winked at me.

I grinned in spite of myself. "Well, good to know. I'll be interested to hear what Zeke has to say about it. I think Eli's already got him on the list to interview."

At the mention of Eli's name, Sherman stiffened, his face growing still and masklike. "That was all a long time ago. You don't need to go digging up hard feelings. I thought we were speaking as friends or I wouldn't have said anything. Didn't realize you were cozy with the sheriff."

"We're not cozy," I said automatically. "He's just an old friend."

Sherman didn't soften at my explanation. "Well, Zeke and Walt were old friends, too. Buddies argue now and then, but that's the end of it."

"You don't know what's happened between them in the last fifteen years," I pointed out. "You said so yourself."

His frown deepened. "Keep my name out of it, anyway. Have a nice day, now."

"Will do." It was clear he was done with the conversation. As I moved to leave, I noticed a pair of the pillow-top gloves Tambra had recommended hanging on a wire hook near the beef jerky and chewing gum. I grabbed a pair and put them on top of my pile. "Can you add those to my tab?"

Sherman jerked his head in the affirmative, and I slid my purchases off the counter, bracing myself for what I'd find in my Porsche. I didn't even know if Yelena had her hens in a box or if they were in a wire crate. I quickened my step. While my little car wasn't fresh off the lot, I wasn't a fan of chicken turds on my upholstery, either.

Out in the gravel parking area, I was relieved to see Yelena with a cat carrier in each hand, hefting them into the backseat of my car. She turned to me, dusting her hands and then the front of her wool coat.

"They're all yours," she said, beaming. I dumped the items I was carrying into the frunk and shut the hood.

"Great." My blatant lack of enthusiasm was bordering on rudeness, so I quickly added, "Can you tell me more about them?"

"*Da*. They aren't too old, less than two years. They're good girls, lay eggs every day. I'm sorry to say goodbye to them." The corners of her eyes crinkled deeply as she smiled. "Their name is Magda."

"That's the breed?" I asked, squinting at the cat carriers as I attempted to glimpse the chickens inside. I was imagining some rare Russian heritage birds, but Yelena laughed and shook her head.

"They're just plain red chickens. It's impossible to distinguish them from one another, so I call them all Magda. They don't mind."

"I'm going to steal that idea for my flock." I grinned, imagining the challenge of coming up with distinct names for all sixty of my layers. I wondered if Yelena's "plain red" hens were the same production breed as mine or if they were an older breed like Rhode Island Reds. Either way, between

224

these three and the two Polish hens, I'd have plenty of eggs to eat during the winter while I waited for the chicks to mature. Maybe I didn't need to find them new homes, after all. I could have a production flock for egg sales and a personal flock for less perfectly matched eggs.

Yelena held up her finger as though she'd just remembered something. "I have something else if you don't mind!" With surprising quickness given her age, she darted to her silver Subaru station wagon and returned with a towel-wrapped bundle that had a black handle sticking out of it. Pressing it into my hands, she said, "It's for Anne. Will you drop it off for me?"

"A casserole?" I guessed, judging by the warmth seeping through the towel onto my hands, and the rich, savory scent that rose from the dish a few seconds later and made my mouth water. Then my stomach turned—I'd forgotten that not ten minutes ago, I'd suspected Yelena of murdering Walt in a fit of misguided revenge for her son's death.

Yelena nodded. "Potatoes and eggs casserole. Good any time of day, breakfast or dinner. I thought Anne might like it; it's very hard to cook and eat when you're grieving. It was my daughter's favorite—so comforting."

She'd said daughter, not son. My shoulder's sagged in relief. I set the casserole in the passenger seat and buckled the seatbelt around the dish. "I didn't know you had a daughter."

Yelena tilted her head, her expression softening as her eyes grew misty. "Yes, she passed away when she was only sixteen. My only child."

"I'm so sorry," I said, reaching out to touch her shoulder. My heart ached at the thought of losing my own daughter at that age. Whatever grudge I held toward Andrea for criticizing my

225

choice to leave her dad dissipated in an instant. It was stupid to let the divorce mean distance from her and the grandkids, too. I should be grateful that I have time left on earth to spend with her, grateful that she thought of me enough to send a silly pink nana shirt from Amazon. I was ashamed of my own ingratitude now that I knew Yelena wasn't lucky enough to have grandchildren.

Her eyes came into focus on my face and she smiled kindly at me. "She was born very early and was never very healthy. She had breathing problems. I brought her to Canada to help her but"—she clucked her tongue—"I think it was too late. I should have come sooner."

I swallowed and pulled her into a hug. "You did your best, Yelena. You literally crossed the globe and left everything behind to help her get well."

She patted my cheeks and then clasped my face and planted a kiss on my forehead. "Aren't you a good girl? I think she'd have been like you if she'd had a chance to grow up. Well, I'm glad my chickens will live with you so I don't have to worry about them while I'm gone. I know you'll find Magda a good home," she added.

"I'll keep them until you get back," I said impulsively. "They'll be waiting for you."

She waved her hands dismissively. "No, no, that's too much to ask."

I shook my head. "It isn't too much. It's just right."

Chapter 30

As I turned out of the feed store parking lot, I spotted Ruth marching along the sidewalk. Her hair was pulled up into a frizzy ponytail and she wore leggings and a *Flashdance*-style sweatshirt that left one shoulder and a bra strap showing. Cute, but not Ruth's usual glamorous-hippie style. She looked like she'd just rolled out of bed. I slowed to a stop in the middle of the road.

"Did you get my message?" I called to her. She pretended not to hear me, her arms pumping faster as she speed-walked toward downtown. I leaned on the horn, letting it blare until she finally stopped and planted her hands on her hips.

"Yes, I got it! Happy?" Her face twisted with rage—rage at me, I realized with a shock.

I put the Porsche in park in the middle of the lane and hit the emergency flashers. "Why the heck would I be happy?"

Ruth marched over to my side of the car just as a truck came up behind me, and I watched nervously in the rearview as it swerved into the oncoming lane and navigated around us both.

"Maybe we should get out of the street," I said.

"Of course, you always know what's best." Ruth's voice was defiantly sarcastic.

I rolled my eyes. "Just get in the car. I'll give you a ride wherever you're going." I wasn't sure she was going to take me up on it, but after a moment of consideration, she walked around the front. She waited impatiently as I moved the casserole to the floorboards and then got into the passenger seat.

"I had to sell my car to raise Rusty's bail," she explained. "I was just heading down to the sheriff's office to pay it."

I flipped a U-turn and drove the speed limit toward downtown so we'd have more time to talk. "You know I didn't mean for Rusty to get in trouble."

"Oh, Rusty got himself in trouble when he buried that hobo instead of calling the cops! But to accuse my grandpa of killing a man? Really?!" She whacked me on the shoulder with the back of her hand. "He wouldn't hurt a fly. He didn't even eat meat; did you know that? Because he couldn't bear the thought of hurting a living creature for his own benefit. He didn't kill Joe."

My mouth dropped open in protest. "I didn't say he did—Rusty said that! Your brother's the one who was so sure your grandpa killed Joe over stealing the telescope that he buried a dead body to protect him! Maybe you just didn't see the angry side of Amos because you didn't spend as much time on the farm."

"He was *principled*," Ruth said, crossing her arms over her seatbelt. "Not angry. I told you not to throw people under the bus unless you know what you're talking about. It's damaging!"

I pulled the car up to the curb and looked over at her, hoping the hard shell she'd developed would crack a little and let me in. "Amos Chapman doesn't have a reputation to protect anymore.

He's gone."

"His family name isn't!" she blazed. I could feel the anger snapping out of her and sizzling along her curls like electricity. "The Chapmans might not have their orchard anymore, but they still live here. They still exist! You can't point fingers unless you know for sure what happened. And you don't know, Leona! You don't." Her voice cracked at the end of her sentence and her eyes, red-rimmed and bloodshot, welled with tears.

"Oh, don't cry, Ruthie." I reached out and squeezed her forearm. "I just want to help. I promise, I didn't make any accusations against your grandpa. Eli just happened to be there when Rusty confessed to burying Joe. He said your grandpa probably killed him, but that doesn't mean he did. He was just giving Eli his best guess, but that doesn't mean he was right. Like you called Eli about Yelena, right? It's no different."

"No." She held up one finger to correct me. "I called Eli because I thought he should know that Yelena might be from Toronto. Not because I thought she killed anyone."

"Come on now—isn't that the same thing? It just feels different because Yelena's not your family. She's from Vancouver, by the way, not Toronto. And she didn't have a son—she had a daughter." I swallowed hard, thinking of my own family and how we were spread so thin across the country. It didn't feel healthy to be so far apart from Andrea and the twins. Yelena was doing the right thing, rushing to her sister's side, and Ruth was in the right, too, as she so staunchly defended her grandfather and brother. "I get that you're mad. I'm sorry for buying your farm, I really am. I should have found a way to help you keep it instead. You're my best friend, and I can't

229

stand it if you're angry with me."

Ruth sighed and used the sleeve of her sweatshirt to wipe the tears from her eyes. "Don't be stupid. You saved our butts by coming in with cash. Nobody else could get a mortgage for the place because of its condition. Oh my word, what is that *smell*?"

The Magdas in the back had been so quiet that I'd forgotten all about them until that moment. "I have Yelena's hens in the backseat, and I think they pooped their temporary coops. I'm keeping them until she gets back."

Ruth's head swiveled toward me. "Where's she going?"

"Her sister's sick; she's going up to Vancouver to help."

"Kind of convenient that she's running away to Canada right after Walt gets killed, don't you think?"

My eyes opened wide—how could she toss out something like that right after our conversation about throwing around wild accusations? But then I saw her smirk.

"See?" she asked triumphantly. "I told you—it's just not cool."

I shook my head. "Too soon. Too soon. Go bail out your brother." I nudged her and she opened the door to the sidewalk.

"Thanks for the ride. I was just upset earlier and didn't mean what I said—don't hold it against me, OK?"

"We've been friends for too long." I waved her out and she slammed the door. The abrupt noise made the Magdas chuckle and fuss in their carriers. It was time to get them home. I watched Ruth's back disappear into the sheriff's office and then headed out of town with my three restless passengers. As I wound my way through the Curves, I wondered if I'd be able to go twenty-four hours in this town without picking up another batch of lucky clucks.

Well, it was all the more motivation to get the coop finished. And the plans I'd drawn up originally—plans to house four dozen layers this year and that many again next year—would need to be expanded. Maybe doubled. In a way, it was lucky that I'd dug up a skeleton and slowed my coop-construction schedule. If I'd proceeded as planned, I'd be short on space by a long shot.

I was so lost in thought by the time I hit the Flats that I didn't notice the flashing lights behind me until Eli—of course, it was Eli—hit the siren.

I jerked the Porsche over to the shoulder and rolled down my window. "Seriously?" I asked as soon as he approached. "I thought I washed you out of my hair!"

"I followed you out of town," he said.

"Obviously."

"License and proof of insurance?"

"Isn't this harassment? I don't think I was even speeding." That was a lie. I probably had been, but I wasn't paying attention to the speedometer. I was pretty sure Eli would have pulled me over whether or not I was speeding, though. I rummaged in my purse and handed him my ID.

He didn't even glance at my license, just held it pinched between his fingers. "Actually, I wanted to apologize."

I squinted at him. "You pulled me over to say you're sorry? For what?"

"I broke my promise. I said I wouldn't hold it against you if you pushed me away, and I did. I took it personally, and I might have left you in danger." He shook his head, his eyes darting to the Sutherland blueberry farm on the other side of the ditch and then back to me as though a murderer might

231

jump out at any moment.

I rolled my eyes at him. "First off, I wasn't in danger. Rusty is a dope, not a killer. And secondly, why can't you act like a normal person and just come by the house?"

He handed my driver's license back to me and smirked when I swiped it out of his hand. "Admit it—you wouldn't have listened. You'd shut the door in my face. I have to hold your ID hostage to get you to stop for a second."

"I'm going to run your foot over in a second if you don't step back from my car."

Eli shook his head. "No, you're not. Because you promised you wouldn't hold it against me, either, remember? Let me come help you, Leona. You need the extra pair of hands now that Rusty's locked up."

"Ruth is bailing him out right now," I said stubbornly.

"It'll take hours to process him. Might as well get a foundation trench dug while you wait for him to show up—*if* he shows up. You don't want to get behind schedule." He winked at me.

Irritation prickled under my skin. He couldn't use my own schedule against me! "I'll be fine. Worry about your job, not mine. Now, if you'll excuse me, I have a casserole to deliver." I started rolling up my window, but he put his hand on the glass to stop me.

"My job is to keep you safe," he said, leaning close enough that I could smell the Doublemint gum on his breath, same as he chewed in high school. Some things never changed. Back then, he'd tear a stick in half and give me one piece when we were done with football and cheerleading practice. The rush of mint, the rush of meeting in secret behind the bleachers, the rush of kissing him flooded my senses. Had it ever been that intense with Peterson? I doubted it.

I flushed, angry that I was so affected by the vivid memory. "I don't see what that has to do with my kissing coop!" I snapped, heat blooming behind my collarbone—great timing for a stupid hot flash. I blew air up to cool my forehead and fanned myself with my hand.

"Kissing coop?" His forehead furrowed as he tried to work out my meaning.

"Chicken!" I said. "Chicken coop!"

A slow smile spread across his face. "Why were you thinking about kissing, Lee?"

"I wasn't!" I turned the key in the ignition. "I'm going now."

"I'll follow you in," he drawled, still grinning.

"Don't you have a murder to investigate?" I asked tartly. "Keeping tabs on me isn't going to solve it."

His cheeky smile disappeared. "But it'll keep you safe."

"Just let me go already. Keeping me safe doesn't keep Honeytree safe!" I pointed at his badge. "I'm just one person, but you have a whole county of people to protect."

He set his jaw stubbornly. "I let you go once, thinking you were just one girl, and I was wrong. I'm not going to lose you again."

My heart, that I thought I had hardened like a rock, turned out to be more of an eggshell than a piece of granite and cracked slightly at the pain in his words. But he was being stupid. I was just going home, not entering a murderer's den.

"Are you going to write me a ticket?"

"Of course not. Unless you need my number again?" He jokingly reached for his ticket pad.

"Then I have work to do." I put the Porsche in gear, waited a half-second so he could get his foot out of the way of my back tires, and peeled out, making a sharp turn down Anne's driveway. I sidestepped the busy forensics team to knock at the door, but nobody answered, so I left the casserole on Walt's chair on the porch. Maybe Anne wasn't in a talking mood. I didn't blame her.

When I turned down my own driveway a couple hundred yards down the road, I was annoyed to see Eli's SUV follow and turn in behind me. I pulled up to the house and put the car into park, grabbed the chicken carriers from the back, and tried to make it into the barn before he caught up, but he was too quick for me, darting between me and the barn door.

I saw his face change as he took in the view behind me: my Porsche and the Suburban next to each other in front of the house. From this angle, he could clearly see the *GO HOME* scratched into the Suburban's paint. His face went pale.

"Go away, Eli." I tried to step around him, but he blocked me and I let out a frustrated screech. "I know what you're going to say. You're worried. But it's *fine.* I'm *fine.*"

"You don't know that," he said stubbornly. "When did this happen? Last night?"

"Night before," I mumbled.

He gaped at me. "You knew about it the last time I was here? When I took Rusty into custody? Why didn't you tell me?"

"Because I didn't want you to be like *this.*" I gave him a pointed look.

"I could kick myself for letting you talk me out of staying here. I can't believe I listened to you when you were receiving death threats!" He cursed under his breath and began pacing back and forth in front of the barn door, muttering half-sentences. "Trying to keep her safe…never listens. What's the point? Lost cause…standing guard…"

Oh, brother. I didn't have time to deal with his drama. "People have their opinions. It's not a death threat—it just says I should get out of here, and to which I'm not going to pay any mind. If you want to guard my property, you can do it at the end of the driveway. The *other* end," I added pointedly. "You're in my way."

He stopped and held out his hands pleadingly. "I can't just sit there! I'll go crazy."

"Then go do your job."

"I can't!" he burst out suddenly. "I have no leads in the case. I have nothing. Zero. Nada. What am I supposed to do? Go sit at a desk in my office and twiddle my thumbs and wait for the forensics report to come back?"

"Well, you're not going to find any leads here, just a bunch of chickens and dirt and chores that aren't done because I've been caught up in doing your job for you." He opened his mouth, stunned, and I finally maneuvered around him, carefully balancing the two chicken carriers so their passengers wouldn't be jostled too much. I set my back against the sliding barn door to open it, but of course it didn't budge.

He reached above my head to add his weight to the door and it finally creaked open. He followed me inside the barn, hovering as I added the Magdas to the stall with Cher and Phyllis. "Doing my job? How do you figure?"

The Polish hens didn't even seem to notice that the Magdas had joined them, at least not until the Magdas began exclaiming over the dish of layer crumbles. Then they rushed over and tried to defend their dragon hoard but spent most of the time crashing into the wall behind the food dish while the Magdas ignored them, happily filling their crops with feed.

Satisfied that the two groups of hens weren't going to

murder each other, I turned back to him. "Well, I don't know, Eli. How is it that you have zero leads, but I have one?"

His eyebrows nearly hit his hairline. "You do?"

"Yep." I leaned back against one of the barn posts and enjoyed the look on his face for a little longer than necessary. "Wanna hear it?"

His breath, which he'd apparently been holding, flooded out. "Yes, of course."

"Remember how Mike Spence said Sherman Dice used to play poker with them? Well, I found out that he quit the game because he was tired of how much Zeke and Walt argued all the time. Apparently, they really got into it."

He gaped at me. "How'd you find that out?"

"I was at the feed store this morning getting chicken stuff and Sherman told me."

"I asked him about Walt yesterday afternoon, and he didn't have a thing to say! Neither did Zeke at the pawn shop, for that matter." Eli crossed his arms indignantly, frowning at the memory of his failed questioning. "Guess I need to have another chat with Zeke. Actually"—he narrowed his eyes at me thoughtfully—"*you're* going to have a chat with Zeke. I'm just going to listen in. It's pretty clear that these old farts aren't going to open up to me. But a pretty lady like you…"

"Oh, no," I said. I backed away and busying myself with refilling the chicks' feeder, my cheeks burning at the implied compliment. He didn't mean anything by it, but for some reason it still made me blush. "I don't have time to play detective just because you're bad at it, mister."

"Oh, yes you are! You're going to help me out and then you're going to let me help you out. Even-steven." Eli grinned triumphantly. "You know you can't run that trencher by yourself. Your trench is going to be all wackadoo if you try. And you have no idea if Rusty is even going to show up. Plus, my services are free." To underline his point, he pushed up one of his uniform sleeves and flexed, wiggling his eyebrows for extra effect.

I couldn't help giggling at his ridiculous expression. And I had to admit he was right. I couldn't count on Rusty and I'd have to trench by hand if I went it alone. Now that my dream coop had to be larger than my original plans, that meant a lot more linear feet of foundation—and a lot more blisters on my palms.

"Do we have a deal?" Eli asked.

I sighed. "Fine. We have a deal."

Chapter 31

Unlike Honeytree, with its quaint, compact downtown, Duma had no town center. Instead, a series of short streets were strung out along the highway for a mile, like legs on a centipede—a centipede with a fifty-five mile-per-hour speed limit. I took the speed limit more as a suggestion and kept the Porsche's accelerator pressed nearly to the floorboards all the way to the pawn shop, enjoying the feel of the wind in my hair and leaving Eli in the dust. What was he going to do, pull me over?

I parked in front of Zeke's Antiques, where a sign in the cloudy window read "Buy, Sell, Trade." I didn't wait for Eli to get there. If he wanted me to be his undercover agent, surely he didn't want me to hold hands with him on the way through the door. I didn't know Zeke, but I knew pawn brokers made their business on sniffing out shysters and cops.

An electronic beep sounded when I stepped through the door, and right away I noticed security cameras all over the store. Unlike most local businesses, Zeke's Antiques had apparently joined the twenty-first century. I pretended to be interested in a display of vintage cameras until a man approached me from the side, leaning into my field of vision. He wore thick glasses with large, outdated frames, brown wide-wale corduroy pants, and a wooly cardigan that uncannily matched his mahogany skin tone, giving him the appearance of a nearsighted bear.

"Are you a photographer?" he asked, blinking drowsily.

"Oh, no. I'm just browsing. I've never been in here before, so I thought I'd stop by."

"New in town or just passing through?" He folded his hands over his comfortable belly and leaned back to get a better look at me. "I'm Zeke, by the way."

I held out my hand to shake. "Leona Davis. Used to be Landers? My dad had a chicken farm on the other side of Honeytree thirty, forty years ago."

He grasped my hand and squeezed warmly. "Of course, I remember your dad. Did some business with him now and again. I thought that place sold a while back, though."

I nodded. "It did, when Dad passed. I just bought the old Chapman farm. You know, the apple orchard on the Flats? It's next to the Sutherland U-pick."

Sadness flashed across Zeke's face. "Pity about your neighbor."

"You knew Walt?" I kept the question light and moved on from the cameras to the jewelry case so he couldn't see my expression.

"I sure did. He's an old timer; we go way back. Played cards together for years, and he pawned stuff here occasionally, too."

"Oh?" I smiled in what I hoped was a neutral, pleasant way, even though my heart was hammering in my chest. Where the heck was Eli? He was always around when I didn't need him and missing when I did. "Had Walt been in recently?"

"As a matter of fact, he was." Zeke adjusted his glasses and frowned. "Why do you ask?"

I froze. *I asked because I wanted to know if you got in an argument with him and possibly killed the guy.* I couldn't really say that, though, could I? I decided to lay it on thick. "Well, I'm good friends with Anne, actually, and I thought that if Walt had pawned something recently, maybe I could buy it back for her. You know, as a memento."

"Funny you should say that." Zeke gave me a puzzled look and, never taking his eyes off me, walked around to stand behind the counter, where shelves held rows of fat ledgers labeled by year, price-tagged items that hadn't yet been put out on the shelves, and shoeboxes with last names scrawled in Sharpie that presumably held items to be picked up. I wished desperately that I could see his hands—were they still in the pockets of his fuzzy sweater, or were they reaching for a weapon under the counter? Suddenly this nearsighted bear didn't seem so harmless.

I swallowed hard, blinking as innocently as I could. "What's funny?"

I was relieved to hear an electronic beep behind me. Zeke looked past me and nodded to Eli, who gave him a half wave and headed for a display of clocks that was near enough to eavesdrop on our conversation at the counter.

Zeke turned his attention back to me. "Well, funny because the reason Walt came in was sort of about Anne, too. He wanted to know if I'd sold a telescope that belonged to him maybe twenty years ago. He said it was stolen off his porch. You know he liked stargazing," he added, giving me a sad smile.

I nodded. I didn't know about stars, but Walt definitely liked neighbor-gazing.

"Anyway, I told him I don't pass stolen goods. Not then, not now. I don't run that kind of shop." Zeke directed this last statement very pointedly in Eli's direction. "I told you that yesterday, Sheriff."

Eli laughed and stopped pretending to be interested in the clocks. Shrugging, he said, "I'm glad to hear it, Zeke. Leona, you really shouldn't have started without me."

Zeke took off his glasses to peer at me and then put them back on again. "Huh. I guess I'm not as sharp as I used to be. I thought you came to shop; I didn't peg you as a snitch."

"I'm not," I said, suddenly irritated. I'd been getting somewhere with Zeke until Eli flubbed his part. "This guy just follows me around."

Zeke smirked, but the humor didn't reach his eyes. "Lucky you. Well, if you're not going to buy anything…" He made a walking motion with his fingers. "I got nothing more to say."

Eli nodded sheepishly. "We'll let you get back to business."

"Wait. You said Walt came in asking about his stolen telescope?" I shook off Eli's hand on my arm and leaned over the counter, resting my elbows on it.

"I did say that." Zeke stepped back warily. "So what?"

"And you also said it had to do with Anne. I don't follow."

Zeke waggled a finger at me. "Oh no. Oh no. You aren't going to pull me into this. How am I going to remember some twenty-year-old deal?"

I pointed to the shelf of ledgers behind the counter. The labeled years went back three decades or more. "Looks like you keep excellent records."

"How am I supposed to keep a record of something I didn't sell?" Zeke set his chin stubbornly, the loose skin of his neck wobbling slightly as he shook his head disbelievingly. I shared his disbelief—despite his claims of innocence, Zeke was definitely hiding something.

241

"Then you won't mind me looking at your books?" Eli asked gently. "I mean, if it's not there, it's not there, right?"

Sweat beaded on Zeke's forehead and he quickly swiped it away with the sleeve of his sweater. "I don't have to show you anything without a warrant. Go on now, Sheriff. You know that."

"Sure, I can get a warrant. But that means I'll be taking all your records and going through them with a fine-tooth comb. It won't just be one year of records, either…I'll see if anything on your books has been reported stolen going back to when the shop opened."

Zeke rolled his eyes and threw up his hands exasperatedly. "I don't even know what you want to see!"

"Yes, you do," I said. "We want to see whatever transaction Walt looked at. It would have been this time of year, twenty years ago. A telescope. Surely not too many of those cross your counter. Walt must have been pretty upset when he saw you sold his telescope, knowing it was his."

Zeke slapped his hand down on the counter, his eyes blazing at me. "I told you, I didn't sell it!"

"But…?" I knew there was more to the story. Zeke just glared at me, his lip buttoned tightly.

"Guess I'm calling it in!" Eli said cheerfully, pulling out his phone. "I'll just hang out here until one of the deputies brings by the search warrant. You can start boxing up all those books now, though." He waved a hand at the ledgers behind the counter. "And you won't be able to move goods through the shop until our investigation is finished, in case any of them are stolen." He strode across the small shop and flipped the sign in the door to "CLOSED," then made his call.

"Suit yourself." Zeke disappeared into the back room and re-emerged with a cardboard box that he began angrily tossing ledgers into. "I'm not getting involved in this mess."

"Don't you want to help figure out what happened to Walt?" I asked, watching Zeke's profile closely as he filled the box with books. "I thought you went way back."

"We do." Zeke snapped. He paused for a moment, stooped over the box. Then he stood up, rubbing his lower back, and gave a heavy sigh. "All right. *All right.* I'll show you what I showed Walt. I don't know what this has to do with him getting killed, but if it'll get the sheriff off my back…"

Eli gave me a look that was both surprised and pleased. "Nevermind," he said into his phone. "Strike that; a warrant won't be necessary."

Zeke grumbled as he slid a ledger from underneath the counter. Unlike the green books on his shelf, this one was blue. On the front, printed in black Sharpie on the canvas cover, was the word *TRADES.*

"I see," Eli said. "You didn't *sell* Walt's stolen telescope."

Zeke peered through his Coke-bottle glasses at Eli, his expression blank. "Do you want to see it or not?" When Eli wisely didn't answer, Zeke turned back to the book, taking his time perusing the records page by page. Maybe he was hoping we'd lose interest, and I'll be honest, after the first ten minutes, I very nearly did. I yawned so widely my jaw hurt, and Eli shrugged at me, his right leg jiggling impatiently.

"Here it is," Zeke finally said, his finger pointing to a line. He looked up at Eli and narrowed his eyes. "If I show you this, do you promise you're not going to tear apart my shop? This is it?"

"Yeah. Not today, anyway."

Zeke pursed his lips and pushed the book across the counter.

Eli spun it around, and we both leaned forward to read the entry, knocking our skulls together as we did so.

"Ow!" I said, rubbing my head where a goose-egg was already forming.

Eli rubbed his temple where a blue bruise was blooming and smirked at me. "You always did have a hard head, Leona."

Zeke snorted. "This is like a bad TV show where Sherlock and Watson are played by circus clowns. Hurry up and get your sorry selves out of my shop. That sheriff's rig out front is bad for my business."

I bent forward—more carefully this time— and found the line Zeke had indicated. It showed the date and what I expected. One telescope, large. Not pawned for cash or gold but traded for one antique silver locket.

"That must be Anne's locket! The one Walt pawned after he bet their whole blueberry harvest—"

"On a poker game," Zeke said. "I was there. I told him not to do it, but Walt never listened to sense. I bought a bunch of jewelry off of him to help the guy out."

Eli leaned on the counter, considering the new information. "Then Joe, in love with Anne, stole the telescope from Walt to get the locket back for her," he mused. "It's kind of romantic, isn't it?"

"Joe? Joe who?" Zeke asked.

I scanned the entry, looking for Joe's name. His identity would no longer be a mystery if his last name was recorded as part of the transaction. But the only name I saw was "Chapman, R." I pointed to it. "This doesn't make sense."

Zeke pulled the book toward him and turned it around, raising his glasses slightly so he could look at the book without them. "Sure it does. 'R' is for Rusty. You know, Amos

Chapman's grandson. He's the one who traded the telescope for Anne's necklace."

Chapter 32

My jaw dropped at the mention of Rusty's name.

"Holy Toledo," Eli breathed.

"I think you mean 'Holy Toronto,'" I said. "No wonder Rusty has been wracked with guilt all these years. He stole the telescope! He lied and blamed it on Joe, and that's why Joe was killed. Joe wasn't a thief at all—he was just a convenient scapegoat. That's why Rusty felt bad enough to cover up a murder: it really *was* his fault that his grandfather killed Joe."

Eli blinked, shaking his head. "Wow. Did not see that coming."

"Wow," Zeke echoed. "Unbelievable."

I nodded. "I know. People can make really bad decisions in a moment of panic, though."

Zeke barked a laugh. "No, I mean it's actually not believable. There's no way Amos Chapman killed someone. He wouldn't hurt a fly."

Zeke wasn't the first person who'd used that exact phrase to describe Amos Chapman. That's what Ruth said, too. But I knew better than anyone that people can have secrets so deep that you can live with them for decades and still be wrong about them. "It doesn't matter what anyone thinks now. Back then, Rusty believed it. He wouldn't have buried the body if he didn't."

Zeke flipped the blue ledger shut and slid it back into its place under the counter. "Oh, I'm sure he had a reason for burying the body. I just don't think it was that one."

"What's your theory of the crime, then?" I asked, eyeing Zeke skeptically.

He shrugged. "That's not my line of work. I just wouldn't bury no body because I *thought* I knew who killed him. I'd have to be a lot more sure than that."

I gasped. "You think Rusty *witnessed* the murder? You think he saw Joe being killed?!"

"Leona." Eli gripped my arm. "What if it's more than that? What if he did it?"

"No," I declared automatically. "Why would he kill Joe?"

Eli tapped the counter where the ledger had been. "Wrong question. First, ask why Rusty would steal Walt's telescope and trade it for Anne's necklace."

My jaw dropped. "*Rusty* was in love with Anne."

A smug smile spread across Zeke's face. "Now you're getting somewhere."

"How do you know?" Eli looked Zeke up and down and his hand unconsciously went to the handcuffs on his belt. "How are you involved?"

Zeke took a step backward and took his hands out of his cardigan pockets, waving them in front of his belly to show his innocence. "I'm not involved, man. All I know is that Walt came looking for the same thing you all did. He's a smart guy, and when he saw Rusty's name there in the records, he blew his stack. Said he should have known. Said she's been lying to him this whole time."

My head jerked toward him. "She? Don't you mean 'he'? Rusty?"

Zeke shook his head. "Naw, he meant Anne. About the necklace. How she got it back."

"She told him Joe gave it back to her and really it was Rusty?" Eli asked.

"Worse than that." Zeke opened his eyes wide behind his thick lenses. "She told him she bought it back with her own money. She said she earned it by doing housecleaning for Amos. That's what Walt said when he saw the trade." Zeke put on a growl, mimicking Walt's tone. "'Why was she over at the Chapman place for an hour every week if she wasn't cleaning house?' is what he said."

Eli and I exchanged a knowing look and heat crept into my cheeks. I remembered all too well how I'd tell my dad that I was going to do community service with the cheerleading squad in order to sneak over to Eli's house and make out. Had Anne used the housecleaning excuse to have an affair—not with Joe, but with Rusty?!

"Maybe Walt wasn't crazy-jealous," Eli murmured. "Maybe he was just regular jealous."

"Maybe Rusty was the crazy-jealous one," I added, nodding. "Maybe he killed Joe because he was jealous of the attention Joe was giving Anne. Or because Joe planned to tell Walt that it was Rusty who stole the telescope, and he wouldn't be able to spend time over at their farm anymore…close to Anne."

Zeke clucked his tongue. "All I know is I wouldn't want to be Rusty when Walt found out. He was ready to erupt when he left my shop. And believe you me, I've been on the receiving end of Walt's temper more than a few times. I wouldn't wish it on anyone."

"Walt found out," I breathed. "All these years, he thought Anne's lover was gone, but he was right next door." If Walt had stormed out of Zeke's Antiques and confronted Rusty about having an affair with Anne, who knows what might have happened. Something brutal, maybe.

Eli already had his phone out, calling his office. As he talked with the deputy, his eyebrows knit together. "Already? But it's only been a couple hours since—no, of course we want to be efficient. Thanks." He hung up and gave me a worried look. "They released him an hour ago. We should get back to your place. See if Rusty came over to finish your coop."

I hardly dared to put a voice to my fears. "You think Rusty might have killed Walt, too? I don't even want to think that he's capable of something like that."

His face was grim. "I don't want to think too hard about it. Rusty just has a few things to clear up. But this time, let me go first, OK?"

I nodded. For once, I wanted to drive as slowly as possible.

The farm was eerily empty when we arrived. Rusty's shiny black truck was parked by the Suburban, but he was nowhere to be seen.

"Wait in the car with the doors locked while I search the house," Eli ordered. I was tempted to talk back and tell him that locking the doors on a convertible wasn't going to be much protection in case of a surprise murderous rampage, but once he drew his sidearm, the words on the tip of my tongue vanished. I nodded mutely and watched as he cautiously approached the front door. He disappeared inside and I held my breath until he reappeared a minute later, shaking his head.

I started to get out of the car, but Eli shook his head and pointed to the barn.

"What?!" I practically leaped out of the car and barreled toward the barn, hollering all the way. "Rusty Chapman, you better not be laying a hand on my babies!"

"Darn it, Leona!" I heard Eli behind me, huffing and puffing. "Wait up—he's dangerous!" He caught up when I was slowed by the sticky barn door, and he gave me a glare so severe that I stopped with my back pressed against the door.

"It's my barn," I said stubbornly, tears pricking my eyes. "Just…don't shoot anything."

"No promises," he said, and added his strength to mine until the door squeaked open enough for him to squeeze through into the dark. "Stay outside."

I heard him click on his flashlight and then, taking a deep breath, I followed him inside. I reached to the right and used my elbow to flick on the light switch. The fluorescent tubes hanging from the rafters flickered for a moment and then buzzed to life, illuminating the dusty interior. The barn looked so empty without my Porsche parked in it.

"Thanks," Eli said without glancing back at me, sliding his flashlight back into its holster. Then, his voice brittle with annoyance, he added, "At least stay back by the door, please."

I ignored him and headed for the steep stairs to the loft. "I never understood why you law enforcement types like to run around in the dark. Rusty, are you up here?"

"Leona!" Eli cursed again. "What did I say?"

The loft was empty save for the rusty bed frame, so I backed down the stairs and rejoined Eli. "He's not in the loft."

Eli, who'd been checking under the workbench, stood and put away his gun. "He's not down here either, far as I can tell."

"If his truck's here but he's not here, then where is he?" I asked. Eli and I looked at each other for a single beat, and then

I knew exactly where Rusty was. We both started running as fast as our legs would carry us for the fence between the orchard and the Sutherlands' blueberry farm.

Eli held the barbed wire apart for me to climb through and then I did the same thing for him. Then we were off again, stumbling and panting over the rough ground between the blueberry rows. At first I kept up with Eli, but as the hill steepened and we drew closer to the farmhouse, I lost steam and he pulled ahead. A moment later he stopped so short I almost crashed into the back of him.

"He's been watching us," Eli said quietly, nodding toward the Sutherlands' porch that was visible at the end of the row. I peeked around him and saw a figure standing behind the telescope at the porch. The shock of hair above it confirmed it—Rusty had probably seen all of it, our return, Eli's armed search of the house and barn, my hundred-yard dash across the blueberry field. He'd been waiting and watching the whole time.

A chill ran up my spine, and I scooted closer to Eli's back, pinching his shirt between my fingers like I was following him through a haunted house. He drew his weapon again and held it down by his side as we slowly approached the house. Rusty gave a small wave as we neared. Eli lifted his gun and pointed it toward the house and I squeezed my eyes shut.

"Don't hurt him," I whispered, mostly to myself. Ruth would never forgive me if Eli killed her brother with me standing right there—even if he *was* a murderer.

"Where's Anne, Rusty?" Eli called. When Rusty didn't answer, I opened my eyes and saw he was motioning us closer. I automatically started to move toward the house, but right away I bumped into Eli, who had both feet planted firmly in the grass. Eli's voice deepened into a growl. "I mean it. Tell us where she is."

"She's inside," Rusty said calmly, nodding toward the door. He was strangely collected, standing there on the porch with a gun pointed right at him. It made me wonder whether Anne was dead or alive inside that house. Would he really hurt the woman he loved—the woman he'd apparently loved for twenty years?

"Can we talk to her?" I called up.

Rusty shook his head and idly picked up the hatchet leaning against the porch rail beside him, rolling the handle between his palms. "No. I don't want you telling her things about me that aren't true. I know you were at the pawn shop."

This darn county and its high-speed grapevine.

"We just need to know—" I broke off when Eli nudged me with his hip.

"I radioed for backup on the way back from Duma," he said quietly. "Just wait a few minutes and they'll be here."

"Anne could be hurt!" My voice came out high-pitched and insistent, the whine of a child. My own plaintive tone jarred me into action—I was my own woman and I didn't need Eli's permission. I raised my voice so Rusty could hear me. "I'm going to walk inside and check on her and make sure she's OK. Then I'll come right out."

"Just wait!" Eli hissed, grabbing for my arm to stop me, but I darted away from him, toward the porch.

Rusty shook his head sorrowfully as I approached, his grip firming on the hatchet's handle. "I don't want to have to hurt you, Leona."

I paused, one foot on the bottom step, weighing the distance between me and the door, and between the hatchet and my head. "Your sister is going to kill you if you lay a finger on me, so don't even think about it. I just want to make sure Anne doesn't need anything. Then I'll leave, I promise."

Rusty stood there for a minute, absentmindedly swinging the hatchet over his shoulder like a lumberjack playing baseball. I felt rather than saw Eli tense behind me, ready in case Rusty threw the hatchet. But Rusty just took a step away from the door, like he was making space for me to pass, nodding slowly. "OK. I trust you."

I started up the stairs but froze when Rusty aimed the hatchet at Eli behind me. "But not you! I don't trust you. Stay right there, Eli, or you'll feel the edge of this blade."

"Then you'll feel the point of this bullet," Eli said, his voice low and measured. I glanced over my shoulder at him and saw he had his game face on. So did Rusty; the two of them were staring each other down. Well, let them out-macho each other here on the porch—I was going inside.

The screen door banged shut behind me. Right away I saw Anne sitting at the table, shaking, tears streaming down her cheeks. The casserole I'd dropped off earlier was on the counter, still wrapped up and untouched, but a cutting board was out with an apple half-sliced, as though I'd interrupted her in the middle of cooking. Something about Anne's posture was strange, though, and I quickly realized that her hands were tied behind her back with baling twine. I grabbed a knife from the cutting board and used it to saw through the string.

Anne rubbed her wrists where the bindings had cut into them and then swiped her cheeks with the back of her hands. "Oh, I'm a mess, aren't I?"

"Don't worry about it," I said, glancing over my shoulder at the door. I didn't know how long Rusty would let me stay inside before he came in to check on Anne. "Are you OK? Did he hurt you?"

"Just a minute; I need to finish getting lunch ready." She took the knife from my hand and went to the counter and resumed slicing the fruit.

"There's no time," I said urgently. "We need to get out of here before Rusty comes back in. Who knows what he's got planned."

Anne paused mid-chop and looked back over her shoulder at me. "He won't hurt me."

"What are you talking about? Yes, he will! He tied you up and is holding you hostage! That never ends well."

She shook her head, a sad smile quirking the corner of her mouth. "No, he just tied me up so I'd hear him out. He's trying to convince me to marry him now that Walt's gone. I guess he saw his chance after all these years."

"Have you two been having an affair this whole time?" I asked, stunned.

The knife clattered down onto the cutting board and Anne turned to face me. "No! I broke it off with him twenty years ago—back when Walt chased Joe off with a knife, and then Joe disappeared. I didn't know for sure that Walt killed Joe, but I knew he would kill Rusty if he found out about us." She swallowed hard, fingering her silver locket. "I told Rusty we couldn't see each other anymore. We couldn't even talk. If he was going to do work around our place, he had to deal with Walt only. That's how it had to be."

I nodded sympathetically even as I scanned the door for any signs of movement. "I guess you couldn't claim to be doing housekeeping for Amos Chapman anymore once you had your necklace back, could you? Walt would have been looking for the money you were earning."

She nodded and turned back to the cutting board, slicing the apple into thin, even pieces. "That's what I told Rusty, too. The jig was up. No more sinning. He had to let me go."

"But he didn't let go...obviously. That's why we need to get out of here, Anne—please!"

"He still carries a torch, I guess," Anne said, her voice trancelike. "Maybe he's right. Maybe we should move off somewhere else and be together."

I could see she wasn't going to be any help. The past days' events had been too much for her fragile psyche. I moved over to the window by the door and, praying that Rusty was still facing Eli and had his back to the window, lifted the edge of the curtain a little so I could see what was going on outside on the porch. The two men were still in a standoff, their voices raised in argument.

"Just put down the weapon!" Eli's voice came faintly through the glass. "We can talk about this!"

The back of Rusty's head bowed. His voice was so low that I couldn't make out the words. But Eli seemed to have understood him.

"I'm not accusing you of anything. I just want to hear your side of the story." Eli held up his hands, pointing the gun away from Rusty, and then slowly put the gun back in the holster. "See? Now your turn."

Rusty didn't put the hatchet down right away. Instead, he half-turned toward the house as though deciding whether to do as Eli said or come in after Anne. I swiftly dropped the edge of the curtain before he could spot me through the glass.

"Anne!" I hissed. "Is there a back door to your place?"

"Yes—it's through the laundry room. Go on and let yourself

255

out." Anne scraped the apple slices into a bowl with the edge of her knife, then pointed the knife toward the other side of the kitchen, where a doorway opened to the dining and living rooms.

I grabbed her elbow and tugged her toward where she had pointed. "Come on—I think he's going to come inside."

She pulled her arm away and backed toward the sink, shaking her head. "I told you, don't worry. Rusty won't hurt me."

"Anne! He killed Walt! You had no idea what he's capable of! We have to go, *now!*" The voices on the porch were louder now.

Anne's smooth, pale forehead creased. "Why would he kill Walt? They were friends."

"Walt found out that Rusty was the one who stole his telescope," I said breathlessly, moving toward the dining room. "He went to the pawn shop and saw Zeke's records—saw that Rusty traded the telescope for your necklace. He figured out that you were having an affair with Rusty, not Joe. He probably confronted Rusty about it, they fought, and Rusty killed him in the blueberry shed. Come on, *please.*"

The voices were right outside the door now, and I could hear the heavy tread of feet pounding up the porch stairs.

Anne stood frozen, the knife in her hand, staring at the front door. "I didn't want him to do it."

I took a deep breath to calm my leaping stomach. "I know. It's not your fault. Just put down the knife and let's go. Actually, on second thought, bring the knife. We might need it."

Something clattered onto the porch outside, and Rusty's wail came through the door. "Oh God. Oh God. This is all my fault. I ruined everything."

Chapter 33

My heart stopped. My breath stopped. I think maybe the earth stopped spinning on its axis for a second. Had Rusty finally thrown his hatchet—had he killed Eli, too? I wobbled for a moment, dizzy from the lack of oxygen, and drew a deep breath just as Eli's soothing voice echoed from the porch. He wasn't dead. I sagged against the wall.

"We'll get this sorted out, man. If Walt made the first move—"

"Walt?" Rusty's voice through the door was fuzzy, confused.

"He found out about you and Anne. He confronted you about your affair. You argued, right? The day he died? What happened in the shed?"

Rusty sounded more agitated now, and his voice rose until he was shouting. "I don't know what you're talking about! Are you trying to trick me? I'm just here to protect Anne. Make sure nobody hurts her. Get back! Get—" He broke off and someone—or two someones, more likely—crashed against the door.

"We need to get out of this kitchen." I said grimly. I wanted to believe that Eli, with his Marines-made muscles and law enforcement training, was going to win this scuffle, but there were no guarantees in life. Someone was going to come through that door, and it might be Rusty with his hatchet. I couldn't depend on anyone to save me but myself.

"I didn't want him to do it," Anne repeated. "I told him it was worth it."

"What was?"

"Losing the necklace. I told Rusty it was worth being with him. I didn't care about it. But he didn't listen. He had to go and make a mess out of things that I had to clean up—that I'm still cleaning up."

She was still standing there with the stupid knife in her hand, gripping it so tightly her knuckles were white as her apron as she stared out the kitchen window at the blueberry shed. Her face was pale but her expression was unruffled, the same as it had been the night Walt was killed. The only difference was that then, her apron hadn't been white—it'd been streaked and spotted with red juice from the berries she'd been processing. Her gloves had been a mess, too.

What did Anne mean, *Rusty caused a mess that she was still cleaning up?*

What if…

What if it wasn't berry juice on Anne's apron the night Walt died? Whoever killed Walt would have been covered in blood. What if Rusty was telling the truth out there on the porch and didn't know anything about Walt's death. What if he wasn't the killer—and Anne was.

I looked at Anne again, and something in her bearing shifted. She knew that I knew with one look at my stupid face—the face that had given everything away on *America Today* was still showing its hand. She pointed the knife tip at me. "Sit in the chair with your hands behind your back."

259

I shook my head—no way was I going to let her tie me up and risk letting her and Rusty Bonnie-and-Clyde their way out of here. I edged away from her. "I don't think so. Why'd you do it, Anne? Why'd you kill Walt?" I asked, hoping the question would distract her as I weighed whether to dash for the front door or the other way out through the house.

Anne wasn't stupid. Brandishing the knife, she moved between me and the door to the dining room. My only option for escape was out the front door, and judging by the shouts, thumps, and grunts coming from that direction, it was no good option, either.

"I couldn't take another second of Walt's tirades," Anne said flatly. "He came home from Zeke's shop railing about something that happened twenty years ago—something I *buried* twenty years ago. I gave up everything that night, and it still wasn't good enough for him. So I just snapped."

I nodded and edged backward, hoping she wouldn't notice my movements. "It's understandable; he abused you for so long. I'm sure a jury will understand if you plead self-defense," I babbled. "I mean, Walt was a killer—nobody can fault you for fearing for your life! Come outside with me and tell Eli about how Walt chased Joe out of the house that night. Just put down the knife and we'll go outside together."

Anne's eyes flashed and she slashed the air in front of her, then pointed the blade at the chair she'd been tied up in earlier. "Sit down and shut up! I'm tired of people telling me what to do! You have no idea what you're talking about. Instead of making up lies, you need to listen. Just like you should have listened when I told you to *go home*."

I startled at her words. They sounded eerily familiar. And then I realized—that's what was scratched into the side of my Suburban. "It was you who called me a—" I left the word unsaid. "You ruined my paint job! But why?"

"You wouldn't leave it well alone. You kept asking questions around town about things that were none of your business! The forensics team was so busy in the blueberry shed that they didn't notice me walking over to your place." Anne's cheeks colored crimson as she glared at me, the few hairs that escaped her tight bun swirling wildly around her face. "You made me upset, Leona. Bad things happen to people who think they know what's best for me. Walt did it and look what it got him. Joe did it and look what it got him. I ended them, and don't think I won't end you, too."

"Wait...you killed Joe, too?" I blinked. "But why? I don't understand."

Her face hardened into a mask at my question. "It's simple. He tried to blackmail me. He knew Rusty took Walt's telescope and then blamed it on him. Joe said that if I didn't clear his name, he was going to expose the affair. I had to choose Joe or Rusty, and I chose Rusty."

My shoulders sagged as I realized the enormity of her deception. "Everything you told me was a lie. Joe didn't try and kiss you the night he confessed his feelings for you."

Anne gave a slight jerk of her head. "No. He knew I wasn't interested."

"And Walt didn't chase him with a knife. Did he even come home from poker?"

"No. I chased Joe. It was dark. He tripped and fell into the duck pond and hit his head on a rock, so I finished the job with the shovel that was there. Less messy that way than with a knife. Less cleanup." Anne looked lovingly at the blade of the kitchen knife in her hand.

"Less cleanup for *you*. You left it to Rusty," I blurted out, stepping backward and fumbling behind me for the doorknob. "You said you were cleaning up his mess by killing Joe, but really, he cleaned up *your* mess when he buried Joe's body, and he's been living with the guilt all these years. And you were going to let him take the fall for Joe's murder, and maybe Walt's too, weren't you? That's why you let him tie you up. You were never going to run away with him."

Anne's face darkened and she flew across the room at me, the knife poised to strike. I grabbed the only thing within reach—the pan full of Yelena's casserole that still rested on the counter. I swung it at her just in time to block her attack. The knife hit the cast iron with a clatter and the casserole fell out of the pan onto the floor, sending potatoes and eggs skittering across the linoleum. The knife flew out of Anne's hand into the sink and she screamed, clutching her wrist. From the strange angle of her hand and the contorted expression on her face, I could tell that the pan must have broken some bones.

Anne's breath hissed between her teeth. "You hit me!"

"I did, and I'm not sorry. I don't care if that makes me a terrible person." I said, echoing Anne's words the night that Walt was killed. Then, I'd thought she wasn't sad about Walt's death because of his abuse, but now I could see it was actually because she was the one who'd killed him. And I was the sucker who believed her—who stuck up for her. Anger rippled through me I gripped the pan's handle with both hands and brandished it at her, daring her to come at me again. She tensed, her eyes flicking between her injured wrist, the cast-iron skillet in my hands, and the two exits from the room.

"Eli!" I called before she could make a break for it. "I need a little help here!"

An instant later, Eli and Rusty both came bursting through the door. Apparently I didn't need to worry about what was going on outside—Rusty already wore handcuffs. Shock registered on his face when he saw Anne standing there, her hand limp and her face crazed.

"You hurt her!" he gasped, taking in my stance with the heavy skillet.

Tears seeped down Anne's cheeks at his words and her lower lip trembled. "She tried to kill me. I think she might have—might have—" She broke down, sobbing, then raised her face to look straight at me, her expression eerily cold as she said without a hint of emotion, "she might have murdered Walt."

"Don't be so desperate, Anne." I snorted a laugh and turned to Eli. "Listen, the only thing I murdered was Yelena's casserole. Anne's the killer—Walt's killer and Joe's killer, too. I'll fill you in on the details later, but basically she freaked out when I realized she'd committed both crimes and came at me with a knife. I knocked it out of her hand with the pan. It's in the sink—you can check."

Eli glanced in the sink to confirm my story and then looked back at me. "Wow. If I'd known you were this lethal with cookware, I might not have been so overprotective. You really can defend yourself!"

I grinned at him and flexed. "I told you—I really, *really* hate surprises."

Chapter 34

Three Weeks Later

The seat of my pants was getting toasty, so I rotated to face the bonfire, holding my hands up to warm in the roaring flames. I watched across the fire, contentment rising in my chest, as Eli and Mike Spence loaded the last barrel of freshly pressed cider onto the refrigerated truck. The first apple harvest was in, although not quite in the way I'd imagined it. Rusty had been right: I couldn't sell the imperfect apples for much, but I could definitely sell their juice for a premium—as long as I had a crew of enthusiastic cider-pressers at my disposal. Luckily, my friends were all willing to work for free.

I couldn't wait to show my progress to Andrea when she came for Christmas. When I called her and explained more about what had gone on in my marriage to her dad, she'd agreed to bring the twins to visit and stay for a few days. My heart glowed as I imagined them in snowsuits, chasing all the pullets around the yard.

Ruth nudged me with her elbow and then handed me a stoneware mug of hot mulled cider. I accepted it gratefully and breathed in the steam, fragrant with cinnamon sticks and orange zest and spices I couldn't identify. "This smells incredible."

"My special recipe," she said, taking a sip from her own cup. She tucked her wild curls behind her ear to keep them out of the way and pulled her rainbow cardigan closed against the damp, chilly evening. "I put cardamom and turmeric in it. That's what makes it taste so round and earthy. That, plus the cinnamon, makes it like a little fire in your belly, heating you from the inside."

"I'm definitely stealing that idea—if you don't mind," I said, enjoying the warmth from the cider spreading through my body, adding to the heat from the bonfire. "Maybe next year I'll sell mulled cider along with apples and eggs. I have to say, it's so satisfying to make a little money off the farm. I know it's not much, but it's a little promise of what's to come next year when my flock is laying."

"Speaking of, what're you going to call your farm? I mean, now that your chicken palace is finally complete?" Ruth nodded over at my recently completed coop, if it could be called that. Really, it was more like a second barn, albeit one that was designed to be impervious to predators of every kind—feathered, furred, or scaled. Inside the expansive run, the Magdas, Phyllis, Cher, Dr. Speckle, and Alarm Clock were milling about, scratching in the grass for bugs. I knew the grass wouldn't last long once I added the eighty-four chicks that were growing like weeds in the barn, but for now the lucky clucks were enjoying it.

"I'm not sure; I haven't thought much about it. You know how it is—people are going to refer to it as the old Chapman place forever."

"They will if you don't give it a new name," she said, nodding her head sagely. "Maybe it should be the Davis farm now."

I wrinkled my nose. "The world doesn't need another thing with my ex-husband's name, does it? It's bad enough that I'm stuck with it."

"The Landers Chicken Farm, then." Ruth smiled, but I thought there was something bittersweet underlying her expression. I knew that she'd be sad when her family wasn't attached to the property anymore, even as she pushed me to rename it. But maybe it was sadder to have the farm bear the Chapman name when it wasn't theirs anymore.

I shook my head. "No—not Landers, either. That will confuse everyone. They'll be like 'the old Landers place or the new one'? You know all my mail will end up at Dad's old farm. I'd rather name it something totally new, something that'll stick in people's minds, something that's more about the chickens than about the people. What do you think about Lucky Cluck Farm?"

Ruth giggled. "Honestly? I think that's perfect. You should have Tambra paint you a sign for the end of your driveway—her artistic talents aren't limited to manicures."

I grinned and admired my own fingernails, wrapped around the warm mug of cider. To celebrate the completion of the coop—and the end of the construction wear-and-tear on my nails—Tambra had treated me to a special manicure and painted each of nails to look like a feather. The two hours it'd taken? Totally worth it for the work of art I got to carry around with me all day.

"Are you talking about me behind my back?" Tambra asked behind us, a smile in her voice. Carrying her own mug between her pink-sparkly-gloved hands, she joined us next to the fire.

Ruth shook her head. "I was just saying Leona should have you paint a sign for the end of her driveway. She's going to call it Lucky Cluck Farm."

Tambra's eyes brightened. "Ooh! I'd love that! What a fun project! What do you think about it being chicken-shaped—or maybe egg-shaped?"

"I'll leave that decision up to you and Ruth—you're the ones with artistic taste." I grinned. "I'll pay you, of course, but it might have to be after I have some weekly egg customers. Things are going to be tight this winter until my girls start laying."

"No way. I won't take a dime from you. Not after all you've done for me." Tambra blinked away the tears that were welling in her eyes, fanning them with one hand.

"Me? What have I done?" All I'd done for Tambra lately was sit still while she painted my nails. It was her—and Ruth and Eli and Mike Spence—who'd been helping *me*. Tambra had touched up the paint on my Suburban so well that you could hardly tell where Anne had scratched it. Eli had worked shoulder-to-shoulder with me to build the coop, using every second of his days off to help me finish it in time. Ruth had organized the pressing party to get the apples processed before they rotted on the branch, and the Spences loaned me the cider press and gave me a family-and-friends deal on the refrigerated transport.

"You found Joe," she said simply. "And you figured out who killed him. Now I can finally sleep at night."

I swallowed hard, unable to keep from looking at Ruth as pain flashed across her face. I knew it was because she was thinking of her brother in jail. "I'm really sorry, Ruth. I never meant for Rusty to get in trouble—he's not a bad person; he just thought he was protecting your grandfather."

"It's OK," she said, reaching out her free hand to squeeze mine. "He should have known better than to cover up a murder, no matter who did it. Family loyalty, loyalty to Anne, whatever…he needs to be accountable for what he did."

"I guess so," I said, shifting uncomfortably and nursing my cider as Tambra nodded beside me. "How long is his sentence?"

"Eighteen months."

"That's not so long," Tambra said, her freckles glowing in the firelight like sparks from the bonfire. I noticed she'd been wearing less makeup lately, as though she'd come out of hiding along with her secret. She was still plenty glamorous, but somehow she looked more herself, too.

Ruth smiled sadly. "I hope it'll do him some good, actually. With Anne going to jail for a very long time, maybe he can stop putting his life on hold for her. I didn't know the reason why he was so stuck, but I think carrying twenty years of guilt for burying Joe—plus waiting around for Anne's heart—really paralyzed him. This could be a fresh start for Rusty. Maybe he'll get his life back on track."

I nodded as I clutched my mug and breathed in the calming scent. "He's a good person. He'll always have work here if he needs it. I understand if he doesn't want to, though—not after everything that's happened here."

"That's up to him, but I kind of hope he doesn't." Ruth leaned her head against my shoulder. "It's nothing against you, Leona. I just have high hopes he'll end up with a farm of his own someday. I know how empowering it feels to have my own businesses, and I want him to feel that way, too."

I totally knew what she meant—I finally felt like I was living the life I was meant to live now that my little farm was off the ground. But I couldn't help looking past my beautiful coop and up the hill at the rows of blueberry bushes and the white farmhouse beyond, its windows dark and empty. "Speaking of your businesses—do you have any word from the real estate circles on what's going to happen to the Sutherland U-pick now that Walt's dead and Anne's on trial?"

Ruth's face brightened. "I do, actually. I meant to tell you! Anne's family wants to sell to pay her legal expenses, and I got the listing!"

Tambra reached over and gave Ruth an impulsive hug. "That's fantastic!"

"It really is," I added, joining the hug. "Congrats, Ruth. I hope your commission when it sells is a little consolation for all the ugliness that this whole thing has dug up."

She made a face at my pun. "Well, if your new neighbors are terrible, you'll know who to blame!"

I threw my head back and laughed. "I don't think any neighbors could be as bad as a misogynist and a murderer—although I have to say I *am* going to miss Anne's pies!"

"Well"—Tambra's eyes danced in the flickering firelight—"I have a tiny little confession. I *may* have stolen Anne's recipe for fruit-of-the-forest pie. I snuck into her kitchen one bonfire night when I was a teenager and took it out of her recipe box."

Ruth's eyes went wide. "What?! Why?"

Tambra shrugged sheepishly. "Same reason I stole Joe's guitar—it was his favorite. He'd get the dreamiest expression on his face when he had a bite of her baking. Of course, back then I didn't know it was the baker he loved, not the pie. I thought maybe if I could bake as well as she could, he'd notice me. I never got the chance to try, though, and after Joe disappeared, I felt too guilty to even look at it. Anyway, if you want the recipe, Leona, you can have it."

I grinned, my mouth watering at the thought of another piece of that pie. "Cluck yes, I want it. Anne owes me at least one pie for coming at me with a knife, and there's no way I can collect on that while she's in jail."

"She'll spend the rest of her life there, if I have anything to do with it," Eli said. He and Mike and Bob had joined us on the other side of the fire and were warming their hands after the cold work of loading the refrigerated truck. "Speaking of the case, I just got some good news—the guys at the county office identified Hobo Joe. They went through all the missing persons reports from Toronto around that time and found one that was a match. His full name is Joseph Brag. His family was really thankful to learn what happened to him, and we're returning his personal effects to them. His guitar and original songs, too." Eli gave Tambra a sympathetic smile. "His mom wanted me to give you special thanks for keeping his instrument safe all these years."

Tambra put her hand to her mouth and nodded mutely. I could see tears shining in her eyes, and I hoped they were of relief knowing that Joe was remembered and loved by his family.

"You'll have to excuse me," she finally said, blinking and backing away from the fire, tripping over one of the logs we'd dragged over to sit on. Ruth darted to catch her arm so she wouldn't fall. "I appreciate you letting me know, Eli. I'm just having a lot of emotions, and I need some time to process. I really am grateful for the closure, though."

"Of course," he said gruffly, disarmed by her vulnerability. I was, too. It was a little uncanny seeing the typically beauty-queen-poised Tambra so undone, and I choked up a little.

"I'll come with you, honey," Ruth offered, and they walked together back toward the house. "I want to pay Boots a visit, anyway." My little crooked-toe, splay-legged chick was growing up just fine, but she preferred the house to the barn. When I'd moved her and her friends back out with the others, she was miserable, peeping and crying for me all day and night. So I let her back inside. Turns out, I'm a sucker for a house chicken.

Bob Spence cleared his throat. It seemed the emotions were too much for him, too. "We done here? I want to get this truck of cider down to Roseburg ASAP."

I nodded. "Thanks so much, both of you—for the loan of the cider press and the extra muscle. And for the trencher. I can't believe how much easier it was to dig the foundation than the way I was doing it before. I owe you eggs for life."

Mike waved his hand. "Come by the house any time. I want a progress report on how your chickabiddies are doing, anyway."

Bob pointed his finger at me. "I'm holding you to those eggs. I remember how good your dad's eggs were, and I expect yours will be a close second."

Six weeks ago, I might have balked at Bob and Mike's attitudes—they were telling me what to do, comparing me unfavorably to my father, demanding things from me. This was exactly the kind of paternalism I trying to avoid when I moved to Honeytree and hid out in the cottage to escape the grind of the gossip mill.

But after all we'd been through together, I wasn't mad. I knew now that they, like most everyone else in Honeytree and Duma put together, genuinely wanted my success and happiness. They might snicker over the viral video of my appearance on *America Today*, but they knew the whole story. They knew my father, my land, and my dreams. I wasn't just a clip, just something to poke fun at. I was part of their community.

"You got it," I chuckled. "You'll get the first dozen and you can let me know how they measure up. Thanks again for all your help."

Eli joined me on my side of the bonfire to watch the Spences' truck head down the driveway and turn toward Duma, where the highway met the freeway that led to Roseburg. He stood so close to me that I had to angle my head to look him in the eye.

"Thanks for your help, too," I said.

"It only took almost getting murdered to accept my help, but at least you got around to it eventually." He grinned at his own joke.

"Hey, you weren't there in the kitchen with Anne; a girl's gotta help herself sometimes."

His jaw dropped. "I *was* there. I clearly remember telling you not to go in that kitchen!"

"I know, but you were wrong," I said smugly. "If I hadn't gone in the kitchen, we never would have figured out that Anne was the killer."

He chuckled ruefully. "I'd never have figured out anything if it weren't for you. We'd probably never have found Joe's bones if it weren't for your ridiculous chicken palace plans."

"I'll ignore that rude comment on my coop."

"And Zeke never would have answered questions without your pretty face doing the asking." He reached out and brushed a smudge of something off my forehead with his thumb and then leaned back to admire his handiwork.

I made a face. "I wish you wouldn't say things like that."

"Like what?"

"That I'm pretty—it just isn't true anymore. That chick flew the coop a few decades ago. You said it yourself at the park. I look *different* than I used to. All the lipstick and blusher in the world won't change that. That's OK," I rushed to add, seeing his face fall. "I just wanted you to know you don't have to pretend. It makes me uncomfortable, even though I know you mean well."

He laughed out loud, looked at me, then laughed again. "I never lie, Leona. All I meant at the park was that I prefer you like this. You know, without all that glitter and paint."

I looked down at my well-worn overalls and grubby barn shoes. "Like this?"

"Like this." He pulled me closer. "Exactly like this. We make a good team."

I bit my lip to hold back my smile and stepped a little away. "That's not what you usually say. Usually you're telling me go home, stay put, and please don't run into the kitchen."

"OK, I take it back." He nudged me. "We make a good team—as long as you ignore me, apparently."

"Isn't that our deal? You advise, I ignore? I'm just holding up my end of the bargain," I said archly, peering up at him. Why was I batting my eyelashes at him? Motherclucker, was I flirting?! I quickly averted my eyes and stared at the bonfire as though I were trying to mine its depths for meaning. As if on cue, a log shifted and cracked, sending sparks up into the night.

"In that case," Eli said, sounding bemused, "If it's my job, I advise you to have breakfast with me tomorrow since I'll be sleeping over."

"Make it lunch," I said automatically. "You don't need to camp out in my driveway anymore now that the Flats are officially murderer-free."

"I wasn't planning on sleeping *outside*." He flashed me a wicked grin, and I thwacked him gently on the upper arm. He grabbed it in mock pain, staggering back a few steps.

I crossed my arms and scowled at him briefly, but I couldn't help breaking into a grin. "Eli Ramirez...I'm going to ignore that."

Killer Cast-Iron Casserole

T ry not to drop this on the floor when you're swinging the pan at a would-be murderer! It's too yummy to go to waste. It's easy to make and is a great way to use up eggs if you have too many in the fridge. Some ingredient amounts are given in ranges—use the smaller amount for 8-9" skillets and the larger one for 10-12" skillets.

Ingredients:

8-10 eggs
    4-6 cups shredded hashbrowns (fresh or thawed if frozen)
    1 lb chopped bacon or ground breakfast sausage
    1 yellow or white onion, diced
    1 cup cheddar or gruyere cheese, grated
    Salt and pepper
    Chopped parsley or chives to garnish

Directions:

Preheat oven to 350 degrees F.

In a large cast-iron skillet, sauté bacon or sausage over medium heat until fat melts, then add diced onions and sauté until the meat and onions are cooked through.

Drain excess fat, leaving 3-4 tablespoons in the pan. Over medium heat, add hashbrowns, stir to combine with meat and onions, then cook without stirring until hashbrowns are lightly crisped on the bottom (about 8-10 minutes).

Turn off the heat and flip over the potatoes. With a spoon or spatula, make evenly spaced "nests" in the hashbrowns and crack an egg into each one. Season each egg with salt and pepper and slide the whole skillet into the oven.

Bake for 12 minutes. Then, sprinkle the baked eggs with grated cheese and return to the oven for 2 minutes or until the cheese is melted. Garnish with chopped parsley or chives and serve for breakfast, lunch, or dinner.

Read More

Want to read more in the Clucks and Clues Cozy Mystery Series? Visit www.hillaryavis.com to see the full list of titles, download free ebooks, sign up for email updates, and more!

About the Author

Hillary Avis lurks and works in beautiful Eugene, Oregon, with her very patient husband and a menagerie of kids, cats, dogs, and chickens. When she's not thinking up amusing ways to murder people, she makes pottery, drinks coffee, and streams *The Great British Bake-Off*, but not all at the same time.

Hillary is the author of cozy mysteries about smart women who uncover truths about themselves, their communities, and of course any unsolved crimes they happen to stumble across. You can read more about her and her work at www.hillaryavis.com.